T0148501

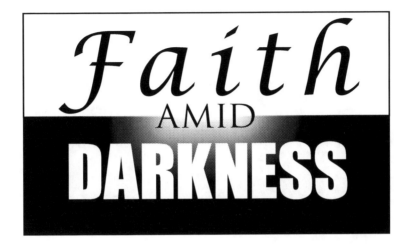

Danny Rittman

iUniverse LLC
Bloomington

FAITH AMID DARKNESS

iUniverse books may be ordered through booksellers or by contacting:

iUniverse LLC
1663 Liberty Drive
Bloomington, IN 47403
www.iuniverse.com
1-800-Authors (1-800-288-4677)

ISBN: 978-1-4917-1888-9 (sc)
ISBN: 978-1-4917-1889-6 (hc)
ISBN: 978-1-4917-1890-2 (e)

Library of Congress Control Number: 2013923011

Printed in the United States of America.

iUniverse rev. date: 12/17/2013

"Darkness, no matter how ominous and intimidating, is not a thing or force: it is merely the absence of light. So light need not combat and overpower darkness in order to displace it. Where light is, darkness is not."

The Rebbe

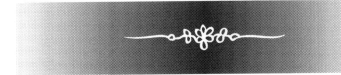

FOLSOM, CALIFORNIA, SPRING 1998

"You can smile any time now!"

The woman from personnel coaxed me into a pleasant expression as she took the photograph for my ID card at the Intel offices. It wasn't too hard as it was my first day and I was filled with optimism by the challenges that lay ahead. A quick flash and click later and I was up from the plastic-mold chair and off to the next part of orientation process.

About twenty of us were escorted down a long corridor illuminated by institutional lighting and lined with photographs of the rolling hills and open waters of the San Francisco area just to the west from which a few hearty employees commuted. Some knew each other from graduate school or previous employers in the volatile hi-tech businesses of Silicon Valley where teams coalesced, created great things, and after a few months went on to new outfits. Others recognized names on the still warm security badges by reputation or from articles in trade newsletters. A few years older than most of my new colleagues, I didn't find the orientation process as exciting as most others did, but designing new chips always attracted me and I knew the excitement of others would lead to hard work and creativity.

I jotted down a few notes as the spokesperson ran down corporate guidelines and handed out a slew of pamphlets. Mostly, however, I was enjoying the energy of the young people around me. I confess, I felt like I too was fresh out of college and exploring the world, at least for a few moments here and there.

My assignment was the R&D group and that was ideal for it meant working with remarkable new technologies and creating new ones. Pushing the envelope, as they say. In other sections, work entailed implementing accepted technologies, putting them into a family of chips. At R&D, I'd be looking for new manufacturing processes using nanotechnology. That, my friends, is creating microscopic machines to build microscopic circuits. At times, it feels like you're part of a science-fiction work instead of a business operation.

After the orientation lecture we enjoyed a light buffet of pineapple, sushi, and herbal tea. Yes, this was Northern California alright. Chatting, conviviating, and greeting old friends came with the food naturally enough. A man tapped me on the shoulder. "Danny! Danny Rittman! Welcome aboard. Let me show you to your office. I think we have one with a splendid view of the hills for you. We're still expanding the facilities here, so you'll be sharing an office for now."

"That'll be fine," I replied amicably. "I'm used to a cooperative environment and it's good to have a real person to chat with amid all the abstraction. Besides, we can help each other by increasing productivity and decrease the learning curve."

"Fair points, Danny." The manager clearly liked my outlook and flexibility.

We reached the open doorway inside of which an older man was looking intently into a large CRT monitor (this was the nineties, remember) where a circuit design was laid out for his scrutiny for flaws that could potential problems.

"Knock, knock!"

A short, rotund man in his late sixties with a balding pate slowly raised a hand to acknowledge our presence but continued with his work, occasionally muttering to himself and running a finger along a section of the circuit layout. Suddenly, he spun his chair to face us, slowly stood, and gestured for us to come in.

"Welcome! Welcome! You, young man, must be Danny Rittman. Your reputation precedes you—but I'm sure it doesn't exceed you."

Funny guy.

"Yes, Adrian, this is Danny. He will be with our team on the Tejas Project. Oh, and Danny, this is Adrian Nowak. He's been working in this field since . . . oh since computers were the size of those Sub Z refrigerators in everybody's kitchens out here. He's been a helpful consultant here at Folsom for the past year or so."

Adrian smiled with the compliment but it quickly receded. "Actually my experience only dates back to when the first 286 processor was taping out many years ago. My first design experience was here at Intel. Pleased to meet you, Danny." Adrian shook my hand firmly though with discernible kindness. I looked into his eyes and saw kindness there too, though a flash of tragedy seemed to appear before disappearing in an instant.

"The pleasure is all mine," I replied to him with simple pleasantness. I saw the kindness again and thought that I'd been mistaken about the hint of tragedy. I was new in the place and early impressions come and go, forgotten in a week or two. Usually.

"Adrian, can you please show Danny how to access the design software and the layouts? I'll show him the kitchen and other amenities. I'm afraid there aren't as many of those as we'd like, but with the new building coming online, we'll be up to industry standards. I see we've already cleared out the desk for him."

"I shall be delighted to do all those things and more. Come with me, young man. We'll start with the most important place—the kitchen. That's where the great breakthroughs happen anyway. Rumor has it that Hewlett ran into Packard during a coffee break. And that chance meeting turned out rather well, didn't it."

"Well then, here's to the founding of Nowak-Rittman!" I said, enjoying my wit almost as much as the others did.

"Nowak-Rittman, eh," the manager said warily. "Gentlemen, I hope you read those nondisclosure and intellectual property clauses in your contracts very carefully! All patents and any idea developed here belong to the Intel Corporation."

He was kidding, of course, but making a point as well.

The first day was going well. I liked Adrian. He was full of life and his eyes held the prospect of many life experiences I could learn from.

Over the next few weeks, Adrian and I got along swimmingly. He was much my senior so there was a certain amount of father-son affection but there was also that between an esteemed mentor and a grateful student. He taught me emerging techniques in integrated circuit layout design. He pointed out some faults with established methods and occasionally offered ideas how to fix them. It didn't matter if the issues were simple or complex; he had a sixth sense for finding innovations—especially in regard to a circuit's geometrical aspects. His intuition was almost always more useful than our colleagues' studied responses. His comments weren't just grumpy complaints; they conveyed profound understanding of a design's intricacies and truly thoughtful notions as to improving them. He was both insightful and concise. With each thought there was wit and soul. We thought one day we'd collaborate on bettering methods for the next project.

He laughed aloud at spontaneous wit, his or mine. He did the same when we came across an error, his or mine. In those first few weeks, I freely confess that the mistakes were mostly mine. But I was learning. Learning from Adrian. Father-son, mentor-student—and good friends. I felt fortunate to share an office with him.

The hi-tech world is well known as a place for young people. I say this as someone who looks around the office now in 2013 and sees that most coworkers are far younger than I am. Okay, I'll say it. I'm now old enough to be their father. Many of them anyway. Back then Adrian was old enough to be my father and I wondered why he hadn't put in for retirement. I don't think it was a money matter. I truly think he still loved to be out doing things and didn't want to sit around the house where, as he put it, he'd "just get into trouble."

Being from Israel, I'm not very adept at identifying the accents of Americans. Some will say a coworker's accent reveals he's from the Midwest or another's indicates she hails from *Boh-ston*. Go figure. In time, however, I asked Adrian about his accent and he replied more fully than I expected. He grew up in Poland and came to New York City long ago where he worked his way through night school at CCNY and earned a degree in electrical engineering. He met his wife-to-be in New York and they raised a son whom they cherished above everything else in life and who became "a good man."

"So where are you from, Danny? I think I detect a European accent," Adrian asked one day. "Germany maybe? Switzerland?" It was a working chat. Neither one of us took our eyes off our screens.

"Actually I'm from the country of Israel," I answered.

"Oh . . . Israel." Adrian stopped his work and turned to me with interest. "Friends and relatives talk so much of their homeland there in Israel, though for one reason or another I've not been for a visit. Were you born there?"

"Yes, in a city called Haifa. It's on the Mediterranean, about a hundred kilometers north of Tel Aviv." I pulled myself away from my screen and turned towards him. An unofficial break had begun.

"You know, Danny, I've known many people who've visited Israel but this is the first time that I've met someone who was from there. This is fascinating," he said nodding, "Truly fascinating."

That aspect of my life was nothing extraordinary to me or to people I knew back in Haifa or even in grad school in New Haven, but for Adrian the notion had an exotic quality. There was a pause—no, more of a hesitation. He was weighing whether to ask something, calculating whether it was appropriate. I opened my hand gently, signaling almost unconsciously that I was amenable to inquiries. There was more than hesitation now. I sensed he was now wondering whether his questions would lead to something hidden—hidden in him, something kept in the back of his mind or soul.

"Have you . . . Danny, have you ever met someone who went through the Holocaust?" His voice was quieter, his eyes soulful, almost aggrieved.

"Yes, I have. As a matter of fact, my father is a survivor." I nodded in acknowledgment. "The Holocaust is a very personal subject to me, even more so than for most Israelis, I would think."

I saw new light in his eyes. He was intrigued. "Astounding . . . your father went through that ordeal. Astounding."

"Yes, he spent some time in a few places whose names you might know. Dachau in Germany and then a few camps in Poland—Treblinka and Auschwitz." His eyes and a slight twitch indicated he knew the names. He knew them not from a book or a lecture or a documentary. He had known someone who had been to such places. Or perhaps he had an even more personal connection.

"My father," I continued, "was taken from his home in Hungary as a young man, barely in his teens, into the camp system. There he was judged fit for work teams which was the only way to avoid being put to death—gassed. Later, he was put in a boxcar and sent to Auschwitz where it was only a matter of time until he was sent to a gas chamber. Fortunately, the Russian army liberated the camp—in early 1945, I think it was."

"Yes, January of 1945. That is *fascinating*." Adrian trembled slightly and his voice quavered. "That is an absolutely remarkable story . . . ."

"Oh, there are many more even more remarkable accounts," I replied as a door was opening to the grim narratives my father would occasionally and reluctantly and very briefly recount. I waved my hand as though to suggest their extensiveness and enormity. "He could tell us very hard stories, events that he experienced in the camps and outside of them, but he rarely mentions what he calls 'those days'."

Adrian suddenly covered his face with his hands and shuddered. A soft gasp escaped his lips. Had I offended him? Had I dredged up something? "Are you alright, Adrian? Adrian, have I said something wrong?" He was elsewhere, in another place—a painful one whose location I could suspect. I wanted to clasp his shoulder but I held back and let the moment unfold.

"Oh yes. I'll be fine . . . I'll be fine. I apologize for that outburst of emotion. It's most unusual for me, I assure you." As he lowered his hands I could see tears welling in his eyes and a trickle coming from one of them. My cheerful coworker, quick of wit and mirth, was gone, replaced by a stricken, haunted man overwhelmed by dark memories.

He pulled a cotton handkerchief from the inside pocket of his sport coat and blew his nose into it loudly. Had the moment not been so puzzling and somber, I'd have chuckled. So would he, I'm quite sure.

Adrian looked out the window to the enclosed grassy area of the building. "Danny, my friend, tomorrow I'll tell you a story." No longer trembling, his voice no longer quavering, he repeated his promise. "I too experienced the Holocaust but in a different way from most." He turned to me, our eyes looking intently into each other's in a most sincere way. "Tomorrow, I'll tell you my story . . . ."

A thousand dark images raced through my mind from books and Yad Vashem, the Holocaust museum in Jerusalem. I wanted to hear his account then and there but I respected his judgment. It would take time to put together his words and to brace himself. "Of course, Adrian. I look forward to hearing your story—and to learning from you."

Adrian returned to his screen and finished his work. We didn't speak again that day. We nodded to each other as we left the office and headed down the corridor toward the exit. Young people were eager to meet up with friends at nearby watering holes and others headed home to their families.

I arose early the next morning, brewed my coffee, quartered a honey dew, and thought about what lay ahead. Adrian, I figured, was undoubtedly preparing himself too. I felt for him and respected him all the more for feeling the need to tell me. In fact, I felt honored. I still do.

I drove into the Intel lot and parked in the place allotted to me. The guard and I nodded as he looked at my badge and I walked down the corridor to the office. The door was open, the light on. Adrian had arrived even earlier than had I. That was hardly ever the case.

He looked at me as I entered, his eyes illuminated by thought and perhaps even by obsession. Perspiration beaded atop his balding pate, though the morning was cool and the air conditioning was on a low fan speed. I got the impression that he'd been there for quite some time and that he was eager to tell me his story.

I wanted to lighten things before he began. I wondered if it might make him think me glib rather than sensitive to his uneasiness, but I judged he'd think the latter. "An early riser this fine day, eh Adrian. Or perhaps a little argument with the wife? Did someone kick you out of bed this morning?"

No luck. Not even a polite smile. I sensed no ill will though.

"Danny, I have a question for you," he said, his eyes never looking toward me. "Do you know what a *Tefillin* is?"

I hadn't expected that question at all. "Yes, of course I do, Adrian," I replied haltingly. "It's a sacred object—two small black boxes, or phylacteries—used in prayer by those of the Jewish faith. Each box contains small parchment scrolls upon which verses from the Torah are written."

I'd gone through six weeks of instruction prior to my Bar Mitzvah on how to pray with Tefillin. Every Jewish boy goes through this rite of manhood. Well, maybe now with all the secularization in life not every boy does, but I think most do. The more observant of them pray with them everyday.

I sensed Adrian wanted to hear me say more.

"Though I am not Orthodox, I nonetheless uphold the tradition of praying over my phylacteries—every morning. The Tefillin has leather strips that secure the boxes with the holy scriptures to the arm and head. The Torah instructs that they are to be worn to remind us that God brought the children of Israel out of Egypt. I remember that the Rabbi I studied under warned me that if the boxes were to fall onto the floor, I'd have to fast a whole day. So, I treat them with great respect."

Adrian noted the reverence in my explanation and nodded.

"*Tefillin* . . . ." he murmured.

"How do you know of these matters, Adrian? Are you Jewish?" I sensed he knew a great deal about Tefillin and that it bore upon his story.

"Yes, I know about Tefillin. No, I am not Jewish," Adrian leaned back in his chair. His face lost the focus of just a moment ago. Sadness and pain were in its place. "Do you want to hear a story about Tefillin?" he asked gently. "Do you want to hear my story? I want you to be sure."

I became silent. It was as though he was offering a last chance out of an unpleasant ordeal. I found my words a moment later. "Yes, of course, Adrian. I very *much* want to hear your story."

He looked out into the court area for a few moments but soon turned his attention back to our office. I could see moisture in his eyes. He moved about to sit more comfortably, took a measured sip from his tea with a lemon wedge floating on top, and started to tell me his story. I think he'd wanted to tell these events to someone for many years. They'd been an immense burden on his soul and now he'd found someone to ease it, someone who'd understand his story.

I was there.

POLAND, 1939

I was born and grew up in a Polish town called Lodz, about a hundred kilometers southwest of Warsaw. Everyone knew each other and everyone's parents and grandparents knew each other. We looked out for one another's children and took pride in seeing them grow into adulthood and raise families of their own. We were a community, not like what we have now here in California and most of the United States. I lived in a relatively new neighborhood by the standards of early twentieth-century Poland—an apartment in a three-story building put up not long after the Great War of 1914. We lived on the bottom floor and just above us on the second floor lived Misha Coen and his family.

> He smiled widely as memories arose within him, especially on enunciating the boy's name.

Misha was a brother to me. We were both only children and we were always together—playing, reading, going to school, helping our parents. Maybe more playing than the other things. We went to the same kindergarten and grade school in Lodz. On weekends we slept at each other's home. Our parents were quite close as well. We all had dinner together several times a week, we picnicked in the hills and woods, and we helped each other during hard times or when someone was sick. I couldn't imagine life without him and his family. Our lives were intertwined and we thought they would be forever.

> He treasured every word at times and I could only try to imagine the emotions and images that passed through him.

My family was Catholic and Misha's Jewish, as I'm sure you know from the name. We all lived together and learned of each other's holy days, beliefs, and customs. We learned about their religion as they learned about ours. We celebrated high holy days together. Christmas would see Misha's family dining with us, and Hanukah dinner would be spent upstairs enjoying the Coens' hospitality. A Menorah and Christmas tree in each apartment, every December. I loved how they lighted the Menorah candles. They bought them from a shop in Warsaw, I believe. The light danced across the walls and ceilings, bringing joy and life to all of us.

Misha and I hiked out to the hills and chopped down a small fir that would become our Christmas tree. He helped me to decorate it with bulbs that had been my grandparents'. And under the tree, there would be a gift for our little friend upstairs. It was simple, it was enjoyable, and it was a beautiful part of life. Yes, those were good years.

But Danny, this respect for each other's religion was not shared by everyone in Lodz. There was a great deal of anti-Semitism in Lodz and in the rest of Poland as well. I don't mean snide jokes, I mean hatred. Many townspeople disliked the fact that we were friendly with the Coens. Some looked down upon us for it and refused to talk to us.

It was about this time that the Germans invaded. Yes, the fall of 1939. They overwhelmed the Polish army and we were occupied by the Wehrmacht, the German army. They patrolled the town, though only occasionally. There was a German police station too. They looked around the city and kept files. It worried our parents. Misha and I thought nothing of it. It was sure to go away soon, we thought.

> I nodded as I envisioned two children sharing so much and looking ahead to their lives. Yes, I'd read that anti-Semitism was strong in Eastern Europe. That of course was where this story was taking us.

One day, Misha's mother—Sara was her name—was shopping for groceries with Misha. It was a Thursday. I know because it was on that day that she prepared for the Shabbat the next day. Such breads and fruits she'd make! She always took Misha with her and sometimes I would come along as well, but not that day. I stayed home and rode my scooter. Misha's father, Moshe, had built it for me to go along with the one he made for Misha. If he made anything for his boy, he'd favor me with one much like it. Wood and metal . . . he could craft them into almost anything.

I came upon Misha's father outside our building. He was returning early from work, a package tucked under an arm. I greeted him and my boyish curiosity got the better of me. "What's in the box, Mr Coen?" I asked eagerly. He gave me a studied look to gauge my reliability. I somehow passed the test and he motioned for me to follow him upstairs to their apartment where he told me to sit on the sofa then looked around furtively. "Next month is Misha's Bar Mitzvah. Do you know what a Bar Mitzvah is, Adrian?" he asked as a gentle teacher might.

"Oh yes, Misha told me all about it. It is when a boy reaches the age of thirteen and he becomes responsible for his own actions. I already had my Confirmation two years ago. It is similar, I believe." I was proud of my knowledge and my detailed reply.

"That's correct! Very good, Adrian." He patted my head with affection. "That is *exactly* what our Bar Mitzvah means. And yes, it is in many ways and purposes similar to your Confirmation." Moshe's eyes sparkled and he beamed warmly, spreading his grey whiskers to the sides of his face reminding me of a gentle hare coming through the brush. "Until the age of thirteen, parents are responsible for a son's actions. When the young man reaches thirteen, he takes part in a Bar Mitzvah ceremony in which he says his own prayers and begins to perform his own deeds. Afterwards, he is on his own to conduct good actions and to be a good person in the world. He has to continue doing them for the rest of his life as a man. The young man receives his first Tefillin and recites their prayers for the first time."

Moshe Coen's voice fell to a near whisper, even though no one was nearby. "Tomorrow, Adrian, I shall give Misha his Tefillin."

I had learned of their sanctity and meaning for the Jewish people, so naturally, I was more than a little curious. "May I see them . . . please?" I asked hesitatingly.

"I was hoping you'd ask that! I truly was. Of course, Adrian."

He slowly opened the cardboard box, revealing a pouch of fine blue silken fabric with golden threads that formed a delicate pattern. Seeing it wasn't enough, not for a young boy whose thirst to learn all around him was unslakable. "May I . . . may I please put my hand on it?" I asked even more hesitantly.

Moshe nodded his approval and held the pouch out to me. I touched the delicate silk and thought it the most luxurious sensation there could be. "This pouch will always protect the Tefillin. As you can see, the threads form a Hebrew letter," Misha's father explained to me. "We have to handle them with great care."

I ran my hands across the exotic fabric with pleasure and fascination. What lay inside was all but calling out to me. I guess Moshe heard them too.

"Would you like to see the Tefillin, Adrian?"

"Oh yes! Very much so!" I felt like I myself was taking part in a sacred ceremony.

He slowly—no *lovingly*—opened the pouch and removed the objects. I had heard of the boxes, from Misha and older boys in the community, but I'd never seen them and they had a mysterious aura in my mind. There they were, the two small black boxes. Each a cube of about three centimeters—a little more than an inch, as you know. I recognized the lettering as Hebrew, as I'd seen Misha doing his homework. I didn't know their meaning, of course. That only added to their exotic nature and to my wonder as well! An immense impression had been formed inside me.

Moshe opened the boxes and inside were two smaller cubes, each with a leather strap attached to it. "These are made of hard leather," he explained. "And the strap is made of a softer leather—cowhide. Inside, there is scripture, written on a special paper by a person trained in the art of calligraphy. A Rabbi inspects them, looking for flaws, imperfections. It is a sacred process that he tends to with diligence and respect."

As a child I was fascinated by these details, especially when told with such earnestness and affection.

> Sitting in our Intel office, I was transfixed by the narrative, though I sensed that Adrian needed to pause. "Amazing," I all but exclaimed. "You seem to know more about the subject than I do!" Adrian nodded and paused for a few moments as he sipped a little tea, which must have been cool by then. The only sound was the slight buzzing of the lighting and occasional footfalls in the corridor. I hoped no one would stop in that morning and was pleased when I heard the footfalls pass by.

Misha's father gave me a full account. He was passing on his heritage to me, though I was not of his faith. He let me hold the Tefillin—feel them and even study them. They made a profound impression on me.

"In a few weeks, a Rabbi will instruct Misha in how to use them and how to say the prayers over them."

I wanted to learn more about them but I was afraid this would trespass upon Misha's special day, so I remained silent. Then Moshe carefully rewrapped them and put them back into the pouch. Sensing my insistent curiosity, Moshe patted my head once more. "One day, Misha or I will be happy to continue to teach you of our faith, young Adrian. You need only ask."

I was happy to hear that and I couldn't wait for the day, though I judged it would have to be after Misha's Bar Mitzvah. How could I have known just how I would learn more? How could I have known that I'd witness the sacred boxes' wonders.

We walked out to the front of our building, where my scooter was awaiting me. "This is my precious gift to my son Misha on the sacred occasion of his Bar Mitzvah. I'll present it to him tomorrow. Please do not tell him, Adrian. It should be a surprise." Moshe smiled to me as though to assure my silence. It did and I nodded. "Thank you for keeping the secret. You shall ever have my trust," he said as he tousled my hair. "You are a good neighbor and friend, Adrian Nowak. You know, Misha loves you like a brother. He considers you his best friend, a member of our family. And you know what, Adrian? I love you as a member of the family too."

I stepped onto my scooter and said, "He is my best friend too. And you, Moshe, are like a second father to me!" Moshe was moved by this, more than a young boy could have expected, more than a young boy could have comprehended. "Ah . . . that is wonderful to hear, my son. Wonderful to hear. I shall see you soon, I am sure."

But that was almost the last time I would see Moshe for a long time . . . . The next day, the SS came to Lodz and took the Jews away. They took Misha and his family away.

> Perspiration had beaded up on Adrian's brow. It was all quite taxing on the old guy and we needed to do some work. Intel had not hired us to tell each other stories, powerful though they may be.
>
> "How about if we continue tomorrow?" I suggested. "I'd love to hear more but we both have obligations to meet."
>
> "Yes, yes, you are right. Tomorrow . . . there will be more tomorrow." Adrian stared at his screen for many moments before he could put the past behind him, if only incompletely, and concentrate on the matter of designing a new semiconductor. As fascinating an

endeavor as that was, its place in my mind was not what it had been the day before.

I thought of what Adrian had related to me on the way home, while making a pasta and spinach meal and as I sat down to listen to music with a glass of Napa Valley sherry. It was intriguing to speak with someone who'd lived through those horrible days of the Second World War and the attendant killing of so many people. It would help me better understand not only the period but also what my people endured—and what my father had endured. What my family could see etched on my father's worn face and hear in his brief, infrequent recollections of those years, I could now hear in Adrian's memories.

Just before nine, the phone rang. It was Adrian. He suggested we show up to work early the next morning in order to have more time for his story.

I agreed without any hesitation.

SPRING 1940, THE SS COME TO LODZ

It was a dreadful day. It began with the sounds of shouting and screaming. I ran to the living room window and saw soldiers with helmets that sloped down behind the ear. I could see some men barking out orders to the others who complied immediately. I recognized their language as German.

"Juden raus!" they shouted. "Juden raus!"

We heard the German tongue often enough in Lodz even before the war. There were Germans in most of Eastern Europe since who knows when. Hundreds of years. And we'd all heard Yiddish, a German dialect spoken freely in much of Europe. The Third Reich had defeated Poland a few months earlier but it didn't mean much to young boys. Some had older brothers or fathers who were prisoners of war, though no one I knew. Well, that morning we were going to learn what the German occupation held for us.

"What's happening out there?" I worriedly asked my father as he and my mother stood behind me. He knew town affairs well but even he had no idea what to expect that day. We could only watch as groups of armed soldiers walked purposefully down the streets, some pointing to buildings and barking out orders. After a few minutes, as the process continued inexorably, we gasped as we saw the soldiers, their weapons drawn, herding people to the road leading to the town center.

"Juden raus!" they shouted. "Juden raus!"

"Mama, why are those ordering the Jews out?" I asked.

"I don't know, Adrian, I truly don't." My mother had tears in her eyes and she covered her mouth to stifle sobs and an urge to scream in horror.

My father was beginning to comprehend what was transpiring. "I've read about the rise of National Socialism—the Nazis. They are here . . . they are here in our town and it will never be the same. Bad times are upon us. Bad times . . . ."

"The stories of hatred and savagery are all true," Mama whispered.

In my youthful innocence I could only wonder how anyone—soldiers or civilians—could be so cruel. The soldiers prodded people with the muzzles of their rifles, clubbed them with the butts, and kicked them pitilessly if they fell. Young children, women, and old people were not spared. Some in confusion, others in shock, the people moved along down the road, clutching a few belongings, wondering what they'd done and what lay ahead.

To my dismay, a detachment of soldiers came to our building and I shrank into my mother's arms. We heard the heavy boots clomping up the steps then loud raps on the doors then more shouts and confusion. We heard boots and lighter footfalls of people coming down the stairs and then from our window we saw Misha and his parents shoved out into the street and joining the terrified group of people being led away. I remember one tall soldier roughly shoving and kicking little Misha—a mere boy of thirteen.

Instinctively, without thinking about any consequences, I broke away from my mother's side. She tried to stop me but I ran into the street and tried to reach my friend. I was so confused and angry that I couldn't consider anything else in the world than my only friend. I ran to Misha amid the throng and hugged him.

"Come, Misha, let's go home," I said. "You and your family should get out of this line of people and come stay with my family!"

A powerful hand grabbed my collar and tossed me backward as though I were a small toy, sending me to the hard ground. I looked up to see a large helmeted soldier. As I tried to stand, he punched me in the face. My ears hummed and my eyes saw bright dots flying around. I touched my swelling nose and saw blood on my fingers.

"You! Boy! Get away from them," he shouted. Anger and sweat were on his reddened face. His small eyes sunken into a plump face made me think of a farm animal.

My father ran to me and held me. "Come, Adrian, let's go back home now." He pressed a handkerchief to my nose to stanch the flow of blood.

"I could take the kid along with the Jews, you know!" the towering fat soldier sneered. A doltish leer came across his face.

"That will not be necessary, sergeant. I'll take him home with me straight away," my father said, trying to calm the oaf.

The soldier glared at my father. He seemed to enjoy a father's fear for his boy whose fate he held in his hand. "As a matter of fact, I can take your entire family with them. Anyone who helps the Jews is no better than them—and goes *with* them!"

"No, please. Just let us go on our way back home. No harm has been done." My father was negotiating for his beloved son's life. He grabbed me with all his strength and took me back home. The ominous roundup went on behind us.

"But dad," I cried, "they're taking Misha and his family. Where are they taking them?"

"I'm sure they'll be back . . . I'm sure."

My mother, tears in her eyes, hugged me when we reached the doorway. I didn't think she'd ever let me go again.

We watched in silence as the soldiers pushed the despairing group of people down the street to Lodz's train station. Most people didn't speak, either out of confusion or fear. Misha silently offered his little hands in my direction, as though pleading to be with me. My heart filled with sadness. I wanted to protect him from these brutes . . . but I couldn't. Pain, remorse, helplessness—they all stabbed my being like the soldiers' bayonets. Oh, the sad sight! Those poor people pushed along down the street of their own town until they disappeared, leaving only a haze from the dust and dirt they'd kicked up. That was all that was left of them, it seemed.

> Adrian nodded as though acknowledging each pathetic detail. Then he raised his eyes to me and said that he did see Misha and his father later on. That cheered me as I entertained the prospect of a happy ending. But Adrian's words trailed off. At first, I thought he was simply gathering his thoughts, then I sensed he was debating whether or not to go on. My curiosity nagged me with considerable urgency. I wanted to know more, right then. After a few moments I asked where he saw Misha and his father again. Adrian looked at me for a while in distant gloom.

In Auschwitz. In Auschwitz I, to be precise.

THE RUMORS OF THE CAMPS

Auschwitz . . . . It's very name still conveys horror and evil two generations after the end of the war. And may it continue to do so for many more generations. My father was there. Adrian's story could help me understand him a little better. Furthermore, I felt an urge to know more about the place. Not everyone was put to death. How did those allowed to work get by on a daily basis? How did they go through that experience? How did they survive?

I decided to read about the Holocaust so I ordered a few books online. Tomorrow, there would be more of Adrian's recollections. We met before work as we did before and after a few pleasantries, he began.

The Nazis occupied Poland and embarked on their effort to rid Europe of the Jewish people. We learned of it. We were given lectures and pamphlets stating why the Jews were evil and why they needed to be eliminated. I must admit that many Poles already hated the Jews and the Nazi propaganda teams had a ready audience. Not so in my family. We knew Jews. Not just Misha's family, others too. The lectures and speeches were to us just lies of an unwelcome power we hoped to be rid of soon.

My parents were fearful that word of our respect for Jewish people would get out and we would become objects of interest to the SS. A file might be opened on us, inquiries made among our neighbors. Rumors and allegations would become facts in a dossier and worse things might befall us. "The Nazis will kill anyone who helps Jews or even voices fondness of them," my father admonished us. So we kept our thoughts to ourselves and went about our lives, as best we could.

Stories came of dreadful camps—one in southern Poland, not far from Lodz—which the Nazis had initially built for Polish political prisoners. After the invasion of the Soviet Union in June 1941, the camp was used for Russian prisoners. Later, it was used for others, mostly Jews but also Gypsies. Yes, there were Gypsies. Don't let me forget that. In time, they became death camps . . . extermination camps. In German, *Vernichtungslager.*

A boy barely in my teens, I couldn't comprehend the meaning of those words, let alone what lurked behind them. They've become common enough in our day. I was very sad that my best friend on earth had been taken away from me. Jews, the older people came to understand, were imprisoned in these camps. At first, we refused to credit the stories. "It can't be," cried my mother after one of our neighbors told us of what a relative had said after delivering supplies to a camp near the village of Oswiecim. "Such things are inhumane. The world could not allow them to take place. After all, we have the Red Cross and other international organizations. I simply don't believe it. I cannot believe it."

All that mattered to me then was that my best friend, my brother, was not with me anymore and this made me very sad. A few months later the SS came once again to Lodz. They took a groups of us away for an unimaginable purpose—working in their camp system.

> He reached for my hand and held it. I felt him tremble, as though pleading for something from me. As much as I thought I was prepared to hear almost anything, and as much as I thought I could handle whatever Adrian would tell me, these words stunned me. I continued to hold his hand, pressing it slightly to offer strength.
>
> Adrian needed to pause a moment. I too needed time to clear my mind and process what I'd just heard and brace myself for what would follow. The camps . . .

Treblinka . . . Auschwitz. Those images from documentaries and museums flashed before my eyes again—dark, foreboding, powerful. I walked down the hall to the water cooler and filled two paper cups. We silently partook, almost like soldiers between battles silently refreshing themselves.

I thought there'd be more that day. I think we both did. However, after a few minutes of silence, Adrian shrugged his shoulders and said, "Enough . . . enough this day." So we left the office as dusk came and went to our separate homes.

I realized that it was Friday. Sundown brought the beginning of Shabbat. I might have thought more of its meaning that night than I had for many years.

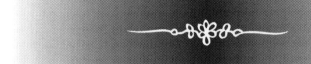

THE RESTAURANT

It was the weekend, no work for a couple of days. Adrian and I agreed to meet at a restaurant. He knew the area better so I asked him to choose a place, preferably a small quiet place. I don't think either one of us cared for larger establishments. He suggested Mimi's Cafe, a place he'd dined at many times. I said that was fine.

Images on the walls depicted the Loire Valley and its quaint villages. Cobblestone-like flooring and a gaslit streetlamp or two added to the ambience. The hostess and waiter smiled and greeted Adrian, though not especially warmly. I don't think they knew him very well.

We didn't return to the story that night. I thought we would and I think Adrian did as well. The transition from a good meal to talk of concentration camps isn't an easy one, I can assure you. In any case, we needed a break from the narration. Our meals were excellent and the servers gracious. As much as I wanted to talk about something at work or in the news, the conversation would have been artificial. So I steered the conversation to the more general context of the period in which he grew up, hoping that might be more pleasant and perhaps place the more dismal events in somewhat of a context.

"It is both amazing and rewarding to meet someone who lived through World War Two," I said as our after-dinner coffees were served.

"The years certainly raced by, especially after the war," Adrian nodded. "I was thrown into a maelstrom without my consent and had to struggle through it. I've only told my wife the general contours. The rest . . . the details . . . I've told no one. I'm beginning to tell you and I think that will suffice. Yes, I think it will suffice."

"Oh my . . . ." My eyes probably bulged a bit in astonishment. "It must be very onerous to go back through it all."

"Yes, yes. It is onerous. But I am glad that I've met you. Now I can tell you everything." His eyes looked out past me, far off into the distance. "You once said that your father was in the camps, so this subject must be more than an idle discussion of events long past, no?"

"Not an idle discussion at all. Most of my father's time in the German camps was at the Auschwitz complex. He only rarely speaks of those times and when he does, it's only a few sentences. There is a gap in our family's understanding of his life. We'd like to know more but there are boundaries which one cannot easily or politely cross."

"Do you write, Danny?"

The question surprised then puzzled me.

"I enjoy writing. I would love to write stories, maybe one day." I fidgeted in my chair as though something had been activated in me. In our field, we might say a circuit had been opened, though not one that led to clear thinking and speaking. "I don't have the time for it just now, but one day. Yes, one day."

"Well, maybe one day you'll write this story down, even if it is many years from now," he murmured. "I'd be pleased if people were to read this story, this all too true story. Danny . . . will you write my story? One day?"

My mind raced through what this would involve. Not simply the time, but also the attentiveness and, well, the devotion. Prior to meeting Adrian, I'd read many books, in part for pleasure, in part to learn to notice things in life and to understand them and to write them down so as to understand the life experiences of other people and pass them on. People like Adrian Nowak. Though I made no meaningful assessment that evening and I couldn't possibly have known what it would entail, I nonetheless gave a reply—and made a commitment. "Yes, I'd love to write down your story, Adrian. In fact, I'm honored that you would want me to be your biographer of sorts." He was elated. "Do I have your permission to write your story?"

"It would be *my* honor, young friend, for you to be my biographer—of sorts." Adrian extended his hand to mine and we shook on it, good-naturedly, even joyfully.

I think now that I had only a vague notion of what it would mean to write his story. I didn't know the full story at all. Even though I'd made a commitment, there was a "well, someday" aspect to it. The notion stuck with me for many years and I honed my skills with other writing projects. One might say I was preparing of the main event. As Adrian observed, the years certainly race by.

FROM LODZ TO TREBLINKA

Adrian continued his story Monday morning, with no prompting from me. A little coffee and a pause in our quotidian chat was enough for him to pick up his narration.

The Nazis had been rounding up hundreds of thousands of Jews, Gypsies, and other "undesirables" from all over Europe, especially in Poland. So burdened were they, that they lacked the personnel to run all the camps they'd built.

To ease this shortage, the Nazis began to conscript local men—and boys. I say "conscript" but it was a cruder system than the word suggests. In November of 1940, a truck with a squad of German soldiers came into a Lodz and ordered all the older boys and young men to assemble in the town square. There was nothing terribly systematic about the procedure. It was simply, "You, you, you, and you." We were unceremoniously ordered into the backs of trucks and driven away. No time to gather belongings or say goodbye to the family. The war was on and the Reich needed able bodies—German or Slavic. It didn't matter anymore.

They brought us in from all over Poland to a reeducation center, with no leave or assurance of our eventual return. We were taught the history of Germany, the Reich's racial ideas, and the plans for a new Europe. Man or boy, we were all young and impressionable—easy to rework into pliant workers for the Reich. We could be shorn of our former beliefs from our families and churches then taught new things, things the Reich believed, things the Reich was built on. Or so they thought. Most of us simply did what we were told.

What we once accepted, we were expected to reject. Where we were once open, we were expected to close shut. Where we once loved, we were expected to hate. Yes, there was much hate in the reeducation centers. But there was even more in the camps.

Danny, you must know what a *Kapo* was?

> I knew the term from my father's occasional mention but more from the books I'd been reading. I replied that a Kapo was a trustee, a prisoner selected to act as cadre and enforcer. They were given a few minor privileges—better food and shelter. And of course they were allowed to live, at least for a while.

Yes, some Kapos were Jews. Others were political prisoners, criminals, and sheer psychopaths. They could all be of service to the Reich. Well, those of us conscripted into the Nazi camp system were essentially Kapos, though our privileges were better and we needn't fear inevitable death at an extermination camp. I was sent along with several other Polish boys to northern Poland, a place called Treblinka.

> My breathing stopped at the mention of that name, second only to Auschwitz in notoriety and horror.

We traveled to Treblinka by train—a long line of cattle cars packed with Jews. The SS guards who commanded us explained our work to us.

"You will travel with your prisoners and you will learn to hate them. You will smell them, you will rub up against them, and you will see that they are not human beings. This will help you to hate them as we do and to perform your duty all the better."

They issued us blue triangular patches to sew on our tunics which identified us as conscript laborers. We also had the letter *P* on our patches to apprise the SS that we were Poles and able to translate the language. Oh, we all spoke some German. Most everyone in Poland did.

The worst of the Kapos wore green triangles. These were hardened criminals—murderers, rapists, and other loathsome people. They had been locked up for their crimes but the needs of the camp system granted them release. Their special attributes, shall we say, were put to use in the camps. Cruel people given absolute power . . . these men of the green triangle enjoyed doling out abuse—humiliating and even killing. They could kill on mere whim, without fear of consequences. The Nazis gave them a free hand to do whatever they wanted and they became the horror of the camps.

Then we were shoved into cattle cars, along with the Jews, for shipment north. The experience was excruciating and horrifying. The interior was packed with people. There was no room for anyone to sit let alone lie down. Everyone had to stand. And the stench! The cars had been used to transport animals—cows, pigs, I don't know what else. But the cars had never been cleaned.

Thirst! Everyone became thirsty. The only water was from the rain that dripped down from the cracked and broken planks of the roof. Yes, the stench got worse. Much worse. Children then old people then everyone had to relieve themselves where they stood. Crying and gasping and gagging . . . .

The train ride lasted the better part of a day and the next morning we disembarked. Between the planks on the side of the car I could see a sign along the tracks that read "Treblinka." Here our experiences would only become more horrifying.

The cattle car's doors made loud creaking noises as soldiers pulled them open. More memorable, however, were the gasps and screams as the opening door revealed immense piles of corpses in front of us. These, we learned, were the people who had not survived their transportation the previous day. They were simply stacked as high as shed along the railroad tracks like . . . like *cordwood*. No time to dispose of them yet. Another train was coming, and that was us. That was our first encounter with Treblinka. You never forget such things, as much as you might wish.

Adrian exhaled as he relived that sight. *I could only try, though one's mind imposes limits.*

This was Treblinka I—a labor camp, not a death camp. The SS cadre assigned us to a barracks for conscripted labor and the next day gave us another round of training. We learned how to treat prisoners—the Jews. I still remember the commandant who gave us an orientation speech. A wiry man with the appearance of a dishonest clerk.

"You are Poles. That's very good fortune for you. If you were Jews, your position would be much worse. Though you are not German, we nonetheless expect you to hate the Jews as much as we do. You are designated 'preferred prisoners,' not destined for elimination. At least not of a high priority."

He smiled to us, proudly and happily, as though a teacher using levity to enthrall new pupils. Then he continued.

"You will help us guard the inmates. You will watch them and see that they conduct all work that we assign them. Remember, German soldiers are your superiors and their orders will be obeyed without question. Your dedication and perseverance will be rewarded with good food, clothing, housing, and treatment. Do not let these generous privileges slip away from you.

The work here at Treblinka I is of great importance to the Reich. We have schedules and they will be met. Inmates in reasonable health will give us a full day's work. Those who are unable to do so, for any reason whatsoever, will be immediately sent to extermination. *Klar? Ist das klar?*"

We crisply replied that his words indeed were clear to us. I for one was aghast and terrified. As the orientation continued, we were given an outline of Treblinka's purpose in the scheme of things. On any given day, there were a thousand or two prisoners at the camp. They worked in gravel pits for roads supporting the army, or at Malkinia station loading railcars, or on irrigation systems of the North Polish farmlands, or in the crop fields. Farm work was mainly for the women.

There were workshops inside the camp that repaired buildings and pipes and the like. These camps, Danny, were like small towns with workplaces and fields and dwellings.

An atmosphere of intimidation and fear pervaded the camp, cultivated as part of the effort to keep to schedules. We were instructed how to maintain the atmosphere of intimidation and fear. Each aspect of our instructions introduced with, "It is recommended." So it was recommended that we shout loudly. It was recommended that we hit and kick prisoners. It was recommended that we make examples of people.

It was very hard for me to hear of such policies to be imposed on people I knew to be good and innocent of the terrible things the SS claimed they'd been part of. Though still in my teens, I had enough sense to know lies when I heard them. I detested the Reich for taking away my best friend that day and seeing the Treblinka I camp made me detest the Reich even more.

I could not comprehend their hatred of minorities. I wondered whether it was random or one person's prejudice or an elaborate story was behind it all. I pondered this question day and night. What could be behind such enormity? No answer ever came to me, not then and not since.

THE GRAVEL PIT AT TREBLINKA I

Some conscripted Kapos fervently believed what we'd been taught. Others learned to feign acceptance. The latter group became adept at displays of hatred for inmates. We had to, for fear of our own lives. I've mentioned the Kapos with the green triangular patch already—the beastly convicts. They did not feign acceptance of the SS worldview. They did not feign hatred and cruelty toward inmates. Believe it or not, I asked some of them why they went about their work so diligently. I did this of course without revealing my true thoughts. They were unable to articulate any reason at all. I don't think those Kapos needed any orders or rationales to be cruel. It came to them naturally enough. Their prewar resentment and sadism easily blended with the Reich's ideology.

There were many shocking scenes in the course of our training. I'll never forget one young Kapo—no more than fourteen. An SS guard ordered him to kill a Jew. No reason; just to maintain fear and confusion. It was quite hot and an old man who'd just marched back from the gravel pit was too exhausted to go on. He fell to the ground—a common enough scene in summer months. Inmates were never given enough water and many of them became badly dehydrated. The SS guard barked out an order for the young Kapo to beat the old man to death with a wooden cudgel. The boy looked down at the old man writhing on the ground, pleading for water, but the boy could not respond to the order. I don't know if the boy felt pity or just couldn't bring himself to commit murder. The guard repeated his order and the boy just continued to look at the man. The guard suddenly drew his pistol from a side holster and shot the boy in the temple then fired three shots into the old man's chest. We were all stunned by this lesson. We learned that refusing an order or even delay would lead to our deaths.

> Adrian's drank from a water glass, the ice nearly gone, then looked at it almost in disgust, There was nothing I could say then that would not have sounded trivial, insipid, even disrespectful.

We learned to do things that we never imagined we'll have to do . . . such as killing people.

> I hoped he'd not broach that subject but it was too late. I listened carefully and with more than a little trepidation. Adrian looked at me desperately and I could see the agony and despair in his eyes.

We had no choice. If we would not obey, the Nazis would kill *us*. See, for the crazy Kapos it was a game, a sport. They enjoyed killing people, but for many of us it was a nightmare.

> I told him that I understood and that there was no other choice before him. I tried to reassure him but he did not seem to be convinced by my words and he abruptly continued.

I had to kill a prisoner once. Yes, I say I *had* to do it. I've thought about it over the many years and I remain convinced that I am not trying to absolve myself by seeking refuge in lies. I *had* to shoot that poor man.

Two of us were instructed to supervise a group of inmates—a *kommando*, as a work groups was called—while they were toiling in a gravel pit whose output built roads. The Germans had invaded Russia in 1941 and logistics were critical. It was a very hot day. July 1941, I think it was, but we had no calendars in our barracks. Flies and mosquitoes flitted around us constantly and we were trying to escape their landing paths, though without much success. Inmates shoveled stones and dirt into wheelbarrows and others hauled the heavy loads up to waiting trucks. Grueling physical work in the summer heat, with no breaks. They were all hungry and thirsty but the orders said no food or water until evening. Whether inmates lived or died was of little interest to the SS. If some died from exhaustion, more would come to replace them soon enough. My heart felt for the poor fellows, even as I looked down at the canteen on my belt.

I heard a faint call for help. "Water . . . please . . . water!" Another Kapo and I went down to the pit and found a gaunt man writhing on the ground, pleading for help. I looked at the poor guy and closed my eyes for a moment. I didn't want to look at him. I didn't want to contemplate how to handle the matter. His ribs and shoulder bones stuck out in grotesque ways from his emaciated body. He couldn't have weighed more than ninety-five pounds—what a young boy would weigh. His facial skin pressed taut against the bone with bristles of grimy gray hair covering his jaw and chin. It was like seeing a skull with patches of white tissue paper stretched across it.

He looked like a cadaver but his eyes held a flame—a flame of vitality, a flame of life. Despite his surroundings and plight, there was a delicacy to the flicker of life inside him, as though he had been a thoughtful, loving person before all this and somehow kept a good deal it. I was transfixed by that delicateness. It was puzzling, it was paradoxical, it was well out of the ordinary. But it was there before me . . . in a gravel pit, near a concentration camp in northeastern Poland.

"Water, please . . . . I can't go on without . . . ."

I looked around for SS guards and saw none. The other Kapo understood my dilemma and what it might portend. He was concerned and increasingly alarmed. "You know we can't give him any water, Adrian. They'll kill *us!*"

I didn't answer. I looked around again for SS guards and again saw none. I pulled my canteen from my belt and poured a little water into the attached cup.

"Drink . . . and *quickly*," I urged.

The other inmates stopped working and looked at the sight. I'd just risked my life for an inmate. No one spoke. A Kapo with some decency left in him. A Kapo who still had some humanity, if only a cupful. The man gulped down the water in a second or two and handed me the cup. I quickly secured my canteen back on my belt.

"Get back to work! No one said you could stop!" barked my colleague. The inmates complied, of course. The old man managed to pick himself up but before he returned to his toil, he smiled weakly at me. His thin lips were too atrophied for anything more than a weak smile. Still, I saw it—and felt it too. A smile of gratitude from a doomed man, a man whose death had been delayed—no more than delayed— by a fellow human being. I felt good about myself. In an instant, however, he was shoveling gravel and I was supervising a team of living dead.

"If an SS guard had seen you giving him water, you'd be dead now!" My fellow Kapo almost spat those words at me. "You must never do that again, you know. Think of yourself! Think of *me*!"

"Yes, I know," I replied somberly.

> Adrian had saved a life back at Treblinka. He saw the warmth in my reaction but he did not respond to it. He looked at me as though I were naive. There was more, I sensed.

But my water did not buy him much time. The inmate was sick, too weak to go on much more. A few drops of water had brought him a few hours of life, no more. He again fell to the ground. This time an SS guard was nearby. I pursed my lips in helplessness and fear as I saw the soldier approach the old man sprawled out on the ground.

"Stand up! *Auf*! Back to work!" He kicked the poor man in the ribs and I was surprised I didn't hear a frail bone break into pieces.

I don't know what happened to me but I found myself running to the scene. Maybe it was the dim life in the man's eyes or his smile of thankfulness or something else I cannot even after these many years identify. The SS soldier was surprised by my sudden presence and he looked at me as though demanding to know why I was there. I stumbled for words and asked if he needed any help. He said he did not and turned back to the inmate.

"*Auf*! Back to work now, you filthy Jew!"

I found myself saying that the kommando was doing well and there was no need for such actions. He gave me a thorough look and I looked into him. He was maybe nineteen or twenty, only a few years older than I. A boy, but one filled with hate. Sensing why I'd come, he became angry.

"I didn't ask you anything about the kommando nor did I ask for any help from you," he shouted in contempt. Each word became louder and more venomous. I wanted to get away but he stopped me. Something terrible was about to happen though I didn't know just what. Then he handed me his pistol—a Walther P-38—and pointed to the old man.

"Shoot him," he ordered. His words were crisp and forceful. They did not invite rebuttal or call for explanation.

I held the pistol like it was a terrible and foreign object—something I could not understand and had never expected to hold in my hand. It felt cold, heavy, and repulsive. Everything in the gravel pit seemed to be collapsing on me. I took breaths in desperate gulps as my heartbeat rose to what seemed dangerous levels. I'd been ordered to kill another human being. It was something I'd only thought of in the abstract. But the pistol in my hand was not abstract and neither was the pitiful old man in front of me.

"Now?" I stupidly asked, my face filled with torment and fear.

"Yes, now. On my authority." He enjoyed my suffering. "What's the matter, Kapo? Can't you kill this filthy Jew?" A sickening grin spread across his face. "Shoot him! Shoot him right now, I say! On my authority!"

My heart raced alarmingly fast and my mouth was dry as cotton. I tried to moisten my lips but to no avail. The SS guard took on the appearance of pure evil. This monster was treasuring every moment, every bead of my sweat, every look of dismay.

I looked at the old man lying before me, expecting to see hatred or betrayal on his face, but there was something else there entirely— compassion. He felt my agony . . . . Then he smiled to me, as he had a few hours earlier, in different circumstances. He was reassuring me that he understood. I blinked to clear my senses of this illusion but his reassuring look was still there. He slumped on the ground and nodded, giving his assent.

"It is alright, my son. Do what you've been ordered to do. It is alright."

Had I heard those words or was part of my soul tricking my conscience? The work kommando halted, captivated by what was transpiring in the pit.

"I am very sick, my days are few . . . ."

Even the SS guard was stunned into silence. The old man turned his gentle gaze to him. "You also are just a child who is told what to think and how to act. A day will come and you'll see that all this is wrong, very wrong . . . . But for now, you just obey orders."

I looked at the SS guard and the old man's words seemed to have ably encapsulated his being. There before me stood a boy, wearing the uniform of a system and obeying its orders—horrid and mad though they were. The SS guard returned from his moment of reflection, the meaning of which had eluded him. I suspect it would haunt him, perhaps the rest of his days. I hope so.

"Shoot him now!" he shouted. "Shoot him now or I'll shoot you both!"

His face was red and contorted hideously as his ire rose to new levels. I had no doubt that he'd shoot me. I was seconds away from death. Strangely, I wasn't afraid. I wanted it to happen. I wanted him to kill me and end my nightmarish existence. It didn't seem a bad prospect just then, early though it was in my career.

It was the old man who saved me. Yes, *he* saved *me* this time. "Do as he says," he said with almost fatherly affection. "You will help me too. Better to die in a gravel pit than in what they're building in the other camps."

I aimed the pistol at his head. He closed his eyes, and I closed mine. But I wanted the man's death to be swift; I owed him that. So I opened my eyes to ensure proper aim. A squeeze of the trigger, a loud report, my eyes flinched closed. A flock of crows flew startled from the trees around the gravel pit, shrieking hideously as though trying to escape the evil in that pit. I couldn't look to the ground but I knew I had not flinched too much and my shot must have crashed into the man's forehead.

I handed the pistol back to the SS guard and returned to my duties. My *other* duties. I was filled with one thought: I had just killed a good man. This thought has never left me, and it never will.

> Two men, of different generations and upbringings, sat quietly in a semiconductor company, both moved, if not devastated, by the retelling of events from long ago.

> "What a burden on your soul," I whispered. I couldn't say anything else that day.

> We focused on our work and went on as though nothing extraordinary had happened but our hearts felt pain that would not soon ebb away.

My sleep that night was fitful. Adrian continued his story the next day.

TREBLINKA II

I was transferred from the work camp of Treblinka I to a sister camp. The new camp was called Treblinka II and it was an extermination camp.

> Adrian trembled as he began to talk of Treblinka II, the notorious death camp of northeastern Poland. He had to pause and collect himself before continuing. Each moment made me more concerned.

I'd developed the idea in my head that Treblinka I was the apex of horror and that nothing could approach it, let along exceed it. A few hours in Treblinka II, however, disabused me of this misconception. No dream or hallucination could approach the place—or so I thought at the time. We assisted SS guards in mass exterminations using carefully planned and executed procedures which their creators prided themselves on. The procedures were, after all, innovative and efficient. What factories did for tanks and planes, the death camps did to Jews and others.

Treblinka II operated around the clock. Some people were simply shot. Gas chambers were being planned. Later, the immense number of corpses were hurled into pits or incinerated, producing a dreadful stench discernible to eyes and noses miles away. It was as carefully planned and operated as any factory. And I was a foreman, of sorts. Yes, I was a foreman in the operation.

I saw train after train of poor human beings brought in, stripped of their belongings and dignity then herded to their destruction. I could not believe I was part of this and I told myself that it was all imagined, that I was not there. I was being shown these things by mysterious outside forces. Walking through the days in feigned remoteness was, oddly enough, the only way I could hold on to my sanity. Had I not, my mental and physical health would have deteriorated quite swiftly. It happened to some Kapos. And the camp knew what to do with them.

For the first few weeks I worked on a team of guards and Kapos who handled the newly arrived trains. That is to say, the newly arrived inmates and victims. There was a process there. Many upon arrival were simply designated for execution.

There were many Ukrainian guards at Treblinka. Some had fled to Poland after the Bolsheviks took power in 1917. Later, after the war with the Soviet Union began in June 1941, the camps had many Ukrainians who'd been drafted into the Soviet army and taken prisoner by the German army. The Ukrainians hated the Russians and the Jews equally so they willingly served in SS units, either in the camps or in the combat units known as the Waffen SS. They had their own barracks. I had nothing to do with them outside of supervising work kommandos with them.

Danny, would you believe there was a zoo near the Ukrainian barracks?

> That astonished and puzzled me. A zoo? My quizzical
> look spurred Adrian to explain.

Yes, a small zoo. I was never there but I saw it in the distance and heard guards talk of it. Not many animals. There was a fox and a few other creatures. It was a way for the SS to think of their lives as having a semblance of normality and decency. A walk through the zoo might restore their illusions about themselves after a day of herding people to their deaths.

I recall seeing one of the Ukrainian guards on one occasion and only that once. He was said to be especially cruel. A fellow Kapo said he was known by many inmates as "Ivan the Terrible."

I knew that name, of course. I mentioned to Adrian that in the 1980s everyone in Israel watched the trial of an ethnically Ukrainian man extradited from the United States and put on trial. He was accused of being this Ivan the Terrible of Treblinka.

Yes, I followed it too, It was on the news every night and in the more prominent newspapers. He was convicted, but a higher court ruled that he was *not* Ivan the Terrible, though he was convicted of other crimes. Danny, I was sure that the man on trial was indeed Ivan the Terrible. He looked so much like the man I saw at Treblinka. Oh, but years change our faces—and perhaps our memories too. Or at least parts of them.

Death was a daily companion. It was all around us, day and night. My fellow Kapos adopted the required cruelty. Perhaps the dark spirit of the camps crept into their souls or perhaps they simply wanted to curry favor with the SS. I thought about confronting a few of them about this but soon thought better of it. I'd be risking my life for no great purpose. They'd become part of the dark spirit, and I had not. They had become, in some sense, the enemy, and I had no ally.

I tried to help inmates when I could—allowing extra water or sneaking a little food from the mess hall—though I could not risk getting caught by the SS or other Kapos. They tended to be everywhere, as mistrust was encouraged in the staff. As with any institution or setting, however, there are cracks, weaknesses, lapses, and miscues. I looked for them to exhibit my humanity, especially to myself.

Sleep was marred by images of cruelty and horror and death. They do not leave you at the close of the day. They come back at night, jarring you awake, demanding attention. A summary execution would be especially difficult to rid oneself of and a recollection might startle you in your sleep. It wasn't just me. Nights in the Kapo barracks were interrupted by people calling out or screaming from ghastly dreams.

Many times I wondered how the world could go on while these things were happening every day—at Treblinka, Auschwitz, Dachau,

Buchenwald, and many other camps across Europe. Yet I knew that ordinary life was going on. People were going to dinners, picnics, nightclubs, and other routine places. All the while, a train was being loaded or unloaded, a work kommando was toiling itself into oblivion, and men, women, and children were sent to their deaths.

Why isn't the world doing something, I asked myself. There must be some people who have witnessed what was going on here and hastened to get word out. My common sense told me that. Why is nothing being done? Where is the world?

My illusion that I was not truly there came to bear on this matter. It explained the world's indifference. The world was doing nothing because those horrid things weren't really happening. It was just a vivid illusion. That gave me hope that I would wake up from this. I'd be back home with my family, back home in Lodz. It was was only an intermittent escape. Daily experience hit me with unmistakable reality. Then I'd look forward to the end of the war which would bring the end to my work. Or I'd look forward to some sort of miracle that would end all this. Many of the inmates believed that their Messiah would come. I hoped more for a foreign army, even if it were the Russians whom most Poles mistrusted.

A few months later, in the spring of 1941, I was reassigned once again. The system was expanding. Camps were getting larger and building satellite camps around them. The war in the east was much larger and longer than planned and resources were allocated to the war and to the extermination program too. I thought my transfer was welcome news. However, I was heading for another camp complex with work camps and an extermination camp. This complex was for southern Poland what the Treblinka complex was for northeastern Poland. The name came a local village called Oswiecim. The name was Aryanized into Auschwitz.

ARBEIT MACHT FREI

When I arrived at Auschwitz I feared the same madness and savagery of its twin to the north, though on a larger scale. The SS soldiers we talked with about the place all agreed it was a much more robust than the Treblinka complex. I shuddered . . . and braced myself.

To my surprise and great relief, another group of young Polish Kapos and I were initially assigned to Auschwitz I, a sprawling camp of over a square mile where inmates worked on labor teams. Initially, Auschwitz I seemed less harsh than anything at Treblinka. I was actually taken by the sign at the entrance, "Arbeit macht frei," which translates as "Work is liberating." I thought to myself, this place must not be too bad. It is just a work camp. Yes, I admit it. Our hopes influence us too much.

We were assigned our quarters and the prisoner barracks, or "blocks," we would supervise. We started our duty the next day. After breakfast we led groups of Jews to work at private businesses on camp grounds that produced chemicals and munitions. I was relieved that on this first day I saw no killings. We marched the inmates back to their barracks to prepare for the next day. I lay in my bunk that night and thanked the heavens I hadn't witnessed any deaths that day.

The camp was expanding rapidly and there was a great deal of construction work, especially in building inmate blocks and laying additional railroad tracks. A new camp would soon be built just to the west, which would be known as Auschwitz II, or Birkenau.

Things were in a flux. Movement was all about. Go here, go there. Shortly later, I was assigned to supervise inmates working in farm fields and on camp maintenance. The relief I felt in my bunk was not to last. So many Kapos. Polish ones, Jewish ones, criminal ones. I've mentioned already the nature of the Kapos with the green triangle patches. They were criminals and inmates feared them the most. One of them gave a speech to each new group of inmates that had the misfortune of being assigned to him.

"Are you a doctor? A musician? Or perhaps a professor? Do you know the meaning of this green triangle? This means that *I* am in charge here. Furthermore, this means that I am a convicted murderer. I myself have been convicted of killing ten people, so death and torture are for me a way of having fun. This club I am wielding is my best friend and I suggest that you carefully listen to every word I say. Otherwise, I'll have to turn to my best friend here and ask him to assist me in reaching you."

After this speech he would beat an inmate at random with his best friend. He had no mercy. He broke teeth, noses, arms, and legs, leaving behind him horrified inmates who would blindly obey any and all his commands from that moment on. Witnessing the sadistic Kapo's handiwork that day, I murmured to myself, "Welcome back, madness." And the madness went on day after day, month after month.

Over the months, as the new camp was built and its distinct purpose was revealed, I discovered that Auschwitz I was similar to Treblinka I. It was a place for inmates to work as long as they were still fit for labor. I was introduced to a new procedure—"selection." I will tell you of the first time that I was assigned to assist with one. The inmates were divided into those capable of working and those who were not, with the latter being sent to their deaths across the tracks in Auschwitz II—Birkenau. The appearance of a minimal amount of health, or the lack of it, was the determining factor. We aligned the inmates in rows and had them stand naked in front of German medical officers. The healthy were sent to the right and admitted into the camp, the others were sent to the left—to Birkenau, with its gas chambers and crematoria, or "Kremas."

An orchestra composed of inmates with musical talents played as new inmates came from the trains and walked toward the procedure. The group selected to die—about three-quarters of the total—included almost all children, women with children, the elderly, and all those who appeared on brief inspection not to be fit. I witnessed this process almost every day for several months. Sometimes with people fresh from trains, sometimes with the inmate population which had to be culled of its weak.

Though as a Polish Kapo I was able to walk about the camp somewhat freely and eat better food, with every morning I felt I couldn't handle the circumstances that lay ahead. I pondered ending my life, by my own hand. I considered rising against the Germans, killing a few of them before I was killed—swiftly out of rage or slowly out of a need to make an example. I even thought about organizing an uprising. But fear held me back. The SS had ways of dealing with uprisings, as we shall see . . . as we shall see. Once again I took refuge in thinking my surroundings were mere illusion and I would one day be awakened.

Life is a long mystery. Just before I gave up, something took place. The event changed my life and saved me. An event inside the Auschwitz complex gave me a hold on reality and a measure of hope.

AN OLD FRIEND

It happened in late 1942 at one of the morning selections. It was gray with morning clouds and mists, and everyone, including the Kapos, felt the cold. It penetrated our uniforms and coats and we waved our arms and stamped our feet to improve circulation. The SS officers did not approve of such unsoldierly behavior, as we were supposed to be models of discipline and superiority and not mere mortals affected by the weather. Even many SS personnel could not maintain their impassive teutonic demeanors. The poor prisoners had it much worse. Their work clothes were thin and tattered and offered little protection from the elements.

We assembled the prisoners for the selection. Classical music played, this time from horn-shaped speakers atop tall posts made from pine trees hewn from adjacent woodlands, probably by an earlier inmate crew now long gone. The pleasant and delicate music accompanying the process of sending people to gas chambers was as paradoxical and revolting as anything life can cast one's way. It horrified me. I used to cup my hands around my ears or hum to myself to block the musical insult. Would you believe that to this day I cannot abide classical music? Truly, I cannot. Especially Wagner.

We received a large shipment of Jews during the night—several more cattle cars than usual—and about a thousand people had to be separated into men in one group and women and children in the other. Then they were led to the field between blocks and the path to Birkenau and arranged in rows and files to learn their fate. I'd seen the process before many times and knew the faces and cries and groaning to expect. I'd become immune to it. Yes, I admit it, I had become immune to suffering and death. Anyone's suffering and death.

As I was leading the inmates to their location, I approached a young man, standing with his eyes to the ground and looking lifeless. Such people had lost their will to live and I couldn't blame them for that. "Let's go," I barked and he started to trudge forward toward the field. I was marching behind the group, alert for stragglers, when I noticed something on his back—a scar or birthmark, I couldn't tell. I moved closer and realized it was a birthmark, one distantly familiar, resembling a fishhook. It wasn't easy to recall memories from my life before conscription. It was only about two years since I was taken from Lodz, but the abrupt and dreadful break with my childhood—that's what it was, my childhood—made it difficult to make connections between my two lives, my present and my past. I stared at the fishhook and images and thoughts gradually assembled in my mind and suddenly came together with a powerful jolt. My heart raced and shivers unrelated to the weather rocked me.

Misha had such a birthmark.

I studied the youth's head and as much of his face as I could see from my position. There was no longer any doubt. It was Misha. My dearest friend Misha Coen was walking not three meters in front of me. I thought back of us walking together to play in a park or swim in a creek. The memories were appealing, even entrancing. I thought if I held on to them Misha and I would magically fly back to Lodz on the wings of memory. I wondered if I could talk to him and be a child again.

But we suddenly arrived at the selection field and I found myself trying to calculate my friend's chances. He was about sixteen, a little taller than when I'd seen him last, so he wasn't a little boy who'd unquestionably go off to a gas chamber in Birkenau. But he looked terribly dispirited. I wondered where his father and mother were. Then I realized he probably wondered the same thing.

The inmates were shoved and cowed into rows and columns. I purposefully took up a position to the left of the inspection stands so I could have a clear view of the inmates as they presented themselves. My heart pounded so hard I was afraid that it was audible. I tried to relax, to pretend that nothing was bothering me, but I was watching every inmate. Row after row, men and women and children, hundreds and hundreds. They came before the SS doctors, received a cursory inspection, and went off to the assigned group. The group designated to die that morning was quite large, perhaps because there were more old people than usual, perhaps because this group had been more gravely weakened by their ordeal than usual.

An hour after the process began, a light rain began to fall on the poor souls in the selection yard. They lowered their heads, making my search for Misha more difficult. More and more people came up the stand and went off one way or the other. After another half hour, I again spotted Misha. He was standing frailly, shivering, awaiting his turn before the stand. I could see him more clearly now. He was gaunt and pale, except for red welts which I took as the results of beatings. I could see his ribs and clavicle all but protruding from his spare flesh and thought back to the man in the gravel pit. Strangely, despite the circumstances, I felt a glimmer of joy in seeing him and I took it as a sign that there was something of my boyhood and humanity left in me. Misha didn't notice me.

He was still downcast, broken, dispirited. Had he given up? Didn't he know the doctors looked for this appearance? It was part of the screening process. Such people, the SS calculated, would not perform labor in a productive way and had thus lost any utility to the Reich. Feeding and housing them in even the most minimal way was a misallocation of resources. Everyone familiar with selection process knew that. Misha must have given up.

I had to think of a way to save him. There couldn't have been more than a handful of inmates between Misha and judgment.

My mind raced for a way to help—another heartening sign. I was not so foolish as to think I could heroically whisk him away to freedom. Nor could I try to persuade the doctor that my judgment as to a boy's health was superior to his. That would have raised suspicion and led the two of us to one of the chimneyed buildings across the tracks. I reasoned, however, that a less despairing face on an otherwise reasonably healthy boy might greatly improve his chance for assignment to a work detail—and life.

I looked around and spied a pile of mud near a garden maintained by inmates, with vegetables, flowers, and pots. Odd sights amid the bleakness of a death camp, I know. So there was both a garden and classical music that day. The rain was making the ground beneath me quite slick and memories of our boyhood raced before me until one fixed in my mind, announcing its relevance for this desperate moment, sending a small amount of hope and even humor through me.

I surreptitiously stepped back from the inspection platform and headed toward the mud pile, which my keen sense of smell soon determined was composed not only of mud but also of another substance used in gardening. I nonetheless quickened my pace as I turned to see Misha's turn rapidly approaching, and with a loud cry of feigned surprise, I hurled myself headfirst into the foul muck. In an instant I was a mess, a sickening but I hoped comical mess. I exclaimed some Polish words that would awkwardly translate into "Oh boy, oh boy, oh boy," as though I were loudly lamenting my clumsiness. I looked at my audience with a doltish expression. My pratfall and exclamations were so theatrically delivered that the finest circus clown in Warsaw would have commended me and maybe even imitated me in a later performance.

The selection process came to a halt. The grim process gave way to an unexpected moment of levity. Several SS guards and even a few doctors laughed aloud at this clumsy, muck-covered Polish boy. I looked to Misha. He had seen my act and heard my words, though I was too far away for him to recognize my face, obscured as it was just then. He did, however, look in my direction and a faint recollection stirred inside his forlorn mind.

You see, Danny, many years ago, a similar incident befell Misha as we played in a pasture not far from home. And when his mother saw her little boy covered with muck on the doorstep, she could only say those Polish words of "Oh boy, oh boy, oh boy," which caused Misha to laugh uncontrollably that day. And as I saw a glimmer of hope fire inside my friend there on the gray selection field, I exclaimed those words once more, "Oh boy, oh boy, oh boy," but this time adding, "I guess we won't be playing in the muddy field anymore," as he had replied to his mother on the doorstep. He smiled charmingly to his mother that day long ago, eliciting a look of maternal affection for her hapless child.

Misha smiled! He truly did. I saw it. Even there, in the selection yard, naked and shivering, he smiled, as he had on our building's doorstep. His smile showed life and vigor and a will to live. It was a wonderful smile!

A hulking SS guard pointed to me and barked, "You clumsy fool! Go clean yourself up! Immediately! You're a disgrace!" I readily walked off to the Kapo barracks where running water awaited, if only a cold trickle. Looking back to the platform, I saw Misha standing in front of a doctor. He ordered him through the routine of lifting his arms to the sides, coughing, and opening his mouth for inspection. The doctor then looked at his ears and listened to his chest. Misha, a trace of a smile still discernible, was sent to stand in the group slated for labor. Misha would live.

For the first time in many long months, I felt good.

OLD FRIENDS

I was eager to find my old friend, difficult and risk-laden though that would be. After dinner at a dining facility where the guards, administrative workers, and some Kapos ate, I searched Auschwitz I for Misha. My position as a conscripted Kapo allowed me some freedom of movement so I went through the rows of blocks, large wooden buildings, a hundred feet in length, each holding about five hundred men and boys, though some held the same number of women and girls. There were probably over a hundred such blocks in Auschwitz I and the same over in Auschwitz II otherwise known as Birkenau. The latter was the newly constructed death camp equipped with four gas chambers and crematoria and scores of inmate blocks—perhaps as many as Auschwitz I.

Luck wasn't with me. I began to worry. What if he was the victim of an arbitrary execution in the course of the day? What if he had been sent across the railroad tracks to Birkenau after all? As my search went on fruitlessly, I began to despair. I began to think my brief feeling of hope and joy had been pointless. Perhaps it had even been an illusion my soul had created either to torment me or give me hope.

I entered one of the last blocks in the inmate sections, and there, lying on his front on one of the long wooden shelves lined with fetid straw and a few old mattresses from when the camp was a Polish army barracks, probably in the same position that he was in as a young child, was Misha. I remember it well. He was resting his head on his two hands, looking forward—probably dreaming. As I entered the building and walked to his place on the shelf, he looked directly at me. After all, I was in uniform and the sudden entrance of a Kapo was unsettling to say the least. He had been elsewhere before coming to

Auschwitz so he knew the sounds and sights of SS tyranny. Our eyes came upon each other. Misha tried to place me, but that took a few moments as there'd been such a jarring departure from our old lives in Lodz. Suddenly, a look of recognition then joy spread across his gaunt face.

"Adrian!"

"Misha!"

We ran to each other and embraced like children returning from long absences from home. The others in the work barracks were too tired or dispirited to comprehend our elation. Many were probably too puzzled by the sight of a Kapo and an inmate hugging each other.

"I'm truly sorry for the stench. It's from the mud pile that . . . ."

"Who cares, Adrian, who cares! As though I smell any better. We've all passed beyond the stage of such small concerns. Bodily odors are the very least of our worries."

He put a hand on my shoulder as we sat on the long shelf, the thin slats creaking under our weight, slight though that was. "It's so good to see you, Adrian." His voice cracked and tears welled in his eyes, as they did in mine. I pressed him to my heart again and my tears streamed down into his hair. It was wonderful yet distressing to see him in those circumstances but I pushed all that aside and just relished the companionship of a boyhood friend.

"Look at you! Oh my, but you are so thin," I stammered.

"And you also, Adrian. We will both get better now, I know it. But what are you doing here?" He knew I wasn't Jewish and was hardly someone deemed a political risk by the SS. He briefly regarded my triangular patch with the letter "P" on it—signifying Polish conscript, as you know. "Are you working for them? How could that be?" Misha asked out of concern, not out of accusation. He was concerned with my plight. I recounted for him the bewildering events that took me from my home and brought me to Auschwitz, by way of an indoctrination center and Treblinka.

"So you are a Kapo?" he asked with surprise and curiosity and perhaps a little sympathy which I very much appreciated.

"Yes, sort of a Kapo. We are privileged prisoners, really. They trust us more and give us a little more authority than inmate Kapos." It was difficult to look him in the eye. "But we have no choice. We fear beatings and death too. And sometimes we get them. We all see the horrors and madness—unbelievable. Some Kapos are truly on the Nazis' side. Crazy ones, with the green patch. You must beware of them . . . ah, but you probably know this already."

Misha nodded and clasped a hand on my shoulder. For a brief moment I was lifted out of my shame and despair. We were children back in Lodz again, innocent of the knowledge of what humans could do to other humans. The world was play and adventure and family. The future was limitless and death an abstraction or something only for very old people. I wanted that moment of innocence to stay with us. We both did. But my eyes opened and I saw the rows of bunks and the desperate, emaciated, dying people. The fence wire came down around us.

"What are going to do about this, Misha?" I asked with open concern and hidden fear. "I know that you are safe for a while. They're expanding the railroad tracks, so you'll be on this project for a few months at least. It's high on the camp's priority so you'll get better food."

He simply smiled, as though accepting the few weeks, after which . . . who knew. I, however, could not be so accepting. I could not share his acceptance of what might or might not happen in a few weeks. "Yes, but what comes after that? Misha, across those tracks is an *extermination* camp—the final station. The other camps lead here. The trains go back empty. No one leaves here. You've seen the smoke from the chimneys."

"Yes, Adrian, I know. We've all heard of what goes on here." I'd taken away his momentary joy. We sat there quietly for a few minutes, each with his thoughts, each searching for a plan. Two boys in Auschwitz, trying to think things through and find a way out.

"Well," I at length said, "I just got my best friend back and I should not spoil this moment with gloom and foreboding and talk of what might lie ahead. You are safe for now."

"We are not in the most pleasant place on earth, my old friend," Misha said almost mischievously, his eyes aglow with youth and vigor. "We'll worry later—and we'll both think."

Together we walked out of the barracks into the surrounding blocks and fields, a few hundred meters from the garden and the pile of muck. We felt once more that adventures lay before us.

LIFE IN THE CAMP

The most pressing objective of the SS then was the construction of railroad spurs into the camps themselves, both Auschwitz I and Auschwitz II. The railroad spurs would speed up the process of disembarkation, separation from belongings, and selection. Efficiency. That was paramount.

In the mornings, Misha, along with several hundred inmates, toiled on the expansion of the railroad tracks into Auschwitz I and II. I helped choose the kommandos and asked to oversee the railroad work. The SS officer's look suggested he wanted to know why I wanted that task, so I replied, with as much sincerity as I could feign and with a dash of starch in my posture, that it made me feel like I was contributing more to the Reich. As we would say today, he "bought it" and I'm sure my face showed contentment. The SS officer and I had differing understandings of the meaning of my pleased look. I would be with Misha and I could look out for him, within limits. My alternative was to oversee the selection process for the new arrivals.

Months went by on the railroad projects. Summer 1943 had come and with it came heat, greater thirst, and flies. We marched out in the morning to the railroad sites and trudged back in the evening. The distance was less than a kilometer from the block but the march back was often very difficult for many of the men. The fear of beatings and the prospects of a little soup kept them going.

As a Kapo, I couldn't show any signs of friendship or sympathy. I had to snarl and shout at the laborers who were hefting shovels and immense cross ties. Mornings were cool and brisk but by mid-afternoon the temperatures reached uncomfortable levels, which took a toll. At noon they were given only a half-liter of water and a bowl of thin potato soup. Watching Misha suffer was painful. I was unable to sneak him more water or soup out on a worksite. Proximity to my friend only underscored the limits to helping him. I was a mere boy in an immense bureaucracy.

As for Misha, it was enough for him to look over to me every once in a while and see an encouraging look. I watched over him constantly, giving him hope and cheer. In the evenings we got together in his block. I brought him part of my dinners, which improved his outlook and health and chances.

One day, while out on the railroad line, a bit removed from the main work teams, an idea came to me. I approached the two SS guards with an obliging look on my face, which I'd learned to adopt. "Hey guys, take a little extra time on your break. Have another cold drink. No sense all of us standing around out here in the hot sun. Don't worry, I've made sure that they fear me." And to demonstrate my mastery, I approached an inmate and kicked him—hard. "Put some back into it!" I shouted. The startled man picked up his pace. The SS soldiers enjoyed my display of power.

"An ambitious lad," one guard said. He was a bit portly and he was clearly mulling over my offer. A little more time back at the mess hall struck them as appealing. And who knows, perhaps a little snack from a cook friend?

"Why not? It's a small kommando and they've been cowed well enough. The kids can handle them. Let's go." The other guard was of the same mind. "Watch the prisoners closely—very closely. And if there's any trouble, call out for us immediately."

The chubby one grinned as a teacher would to a promising pupil and patted me on the back. I replied with a chipper smile and off they went to the enlisted mess hall no more than a few hundred meters away.

There was only one other Kapo that day and he was Jewish, so I felt safe. I told him to fill the two buckets we had with water from the

Sola River not far from where we worked. He looked at me with incomprehension.

"The water's for the prisoners. Now get going," I told him quietly. "And if you tell anyone, I'll kill you with my bare hands." I accented my order with a stern, maybe even angry, expression. It had good effect. He ran off toward the river bank, buckets rolling back and forth with his strides.

"Water's on the way. We can all take a ten-minute break," I announced to the kommando.

They all lifted their tired eyes to me with incredulity. This was unprecedented and I think many of them wondered if it were one of the cruel tricks that guards and Kapos enjoyed playing on them to prove their mastery and pound in hopelessness. I needed a way to convey my sincerity, but how? After a moment's thought, I simply nodded and assumed a pleasant look on my face, briefly replacing my tough-Kapo pose. They looked at each other and saw growing acceptance. Their incredulity faded. One by one, they put their shovels and cross ties down and rested on the ground.

"You are a clever fellow, Adrian—and a great one too!" Misha commended.

"I should have come up with this long ago," I said, disappointed in my belatedness. "But let's enjoy the break, late though it is."

The Kapo was returning with the now heavy buckets, walking slowly to minimize spillage. "The water's here," he panted as he placed the containers on the ground. The kommando—perhaps a dozen or so—regarded the water eagerly and in conjunction with the absence of repressive force, I wondered if chaos might break out. And a noisy chaos at that which would bring hell down on all of us. I had to exert authority.

"One by one," I ordered. "You may come up to the buckets for a drink, one by one." I spoke quietly but sternly, my eyes moving from one prisoner to another. "I do not want to see pushing or shoving or running. Everyone will drink today." I think I was talking like a schoolteacher! The group formed a line and each partook of two cups of water—an unheard of occasion. The effect was immediate and apparent. They were all refreshed and more fit. They enjoyed the break from routine but soon enough, curiosity set in.

"Why do you help us?" one man asked.

I took in the man as I pondered my reply. He was gaunt with grey stubble and sunken eyes. Hardly distinguishing characteristics in the ocean of sad humanity. But there was something distinct about him. His eyes had retained life and vigor and his spirit radiated kindness and light from his emaciated form. I shook my head trying to find words to explain myself to bridge the yawning chasm between inmate and Kapo.

"This is all an immense insanity," I sputtered, unable to maintain eye contact with my jurors. "I want you to know that I was taken from my home and forced to work here. I didn't come here on my own."

They looked at me with astonishment. There before them was a Kapo, explaining himself to them.

"Misha and I grew up together. We were neighbors—in Lodz. Best friends, practically brothers. One day, the Nazis took him and his family away. Not much later, I was conscripted into a forced labor unit. The Nazis needed guards and Kapos. Manpower shortage from the war." I looked at the men around me. Human beings, no better or worse than I. "I wish I could help you everyday . . . I wish I could save you all." I regretted those last words as it made them remember their chances of leaving Auschwitz.

I looked to the man who'd posed the question. I was uncertain of his response and I would not have been surprised had he judged my words trivial and self-serving then gone on to condemn me. Instead, he looked at me with almost paternal fondness—a young man who stood before them so humbly and so self-reprovingly. His fondness warmed and illuminated the entire area.

"You are a good young man," he said in a voice soft with both kindness and weariness. "One day, all of this will be over. You'll find yourself a free man again and your soul will be clean. You will be able to look yourself in the mirror every day without shame or guilt." He paused and released a long sigh. "Not so of all of them here. No, not so of all here. Most of the guards and Kapos . . . their souls will be forever stained. They will have to face far more than human justice. They will have to answer in a higher court. And there, for the first time, they will have to answer to themselves. In a way, though only in a small way, I pity them. Many of them are simple children who obey orders, as though the words had come from their father. Orders that inflict incalculable harm."

Everyone there listened in rapt silence. He spoke well, with clarity of expression and moral vision.

"I was a teacher in a high school. World geography and history were my fields. Now all I can think about is how will history be taught after this?" His hand motioned around him, though his eyes remained on me. "We live in the darkest hour human beings have known." He coughed uncontrollably for a few moments and I saw blood mixed in with his spittle. "I do not believe that I will live to tell the world about the horrors in the camps, but many will. This will end one day. An army—Russian or American or British—will come here." The work kommando became even more focused on his words. "The liberators will find all the bodies and learn of all the atrocities." He shook his head and the fire of humanity flared in his sunken eyes. "I feel pity for the souls of the soldiers that find us. I feel sorry for them for what they are going to see. Their souls will see all this and shall never be the same."

His words penetrated my being and I thought about them for many days. I recall them to this day. He was right. Liberators did come and found the crematoriums, the gas chambers, and the masses of human remains. Those days of Treblinka and Auschwitz and the other camps were indeed the darkest points in human history and I'm glad that I lived to see soldiers liberate Auschwitz and mete out rough justice.

"Adrian! The guards are coming back!" warned the other Kapo.

"Everyone, back to work—quickly!" I said with urgency and more than a little fear. The two guards walked uncertainly back to our kommando, their eyes bleary and their faces bloated. I suspected they'd imbibed more than cold drinks on their break.

"Any trouble here, Kapo?" the portly one asked with a noticeable slur in his speech. The smell of cheap brandy reached me ten feet away.

"No trouble at all," I responded quickly and proudly. He seemed satisfied.

"What are you looking at? Back to work, dogs!" he shouted to the prisoners.

And with that, everyone returned to their toil, their pace improved by the break. The guards were pleased. They probably thought the prisoners' performance stemmed from their stern oversight.

That night when I visited Misha, he hugged me. "Thank you, Adrian. You gave us all a break from the toil." He had happiness in his eyes but I saw something that I didn't see in him since I saw him at the selection at the other day.

I saw hope.

MORNING PRAYER IN A BLOCK

The next morning, when I entered Misha's barracks, there before me was a remarkable sight. Scores of inmates were performing morning prayers, some in groups, others alone, all with heads bowed. Misha sat on the side of his bunk, eyes closed fervently, lips moving slowly along with an ancient prayer. I quietly and respectfully moved closer and to my delight, I saw that he had been able to retain something of great meaning to both of us, though more to him, of course. He managed to get them past the surrender of personal belongings when he came into Auschwitz and kept it secreted away in the obscure places only prisoners know about. There before him, lying on his bunk, were his Tefillin—the sacred tokens of his faith his father had given him shortly before he and his family were taken away from Lodz.

Acknowledging my presence, Misha motioned, if only with a friend's eyes, for me to join him. I stood near him and listened as he said the prayers that I'd heard him say so long ago—prayers I'd learned a few words of and tried to say with him. It warmed my heart. It gave me a feeling of escape and of home. And it did the same for Misha and for the others there in Auschwitz. From that morning on, as often as I could given my position and duties, I came to Misha's block to pray with him. At first, they all kept my presence a secret. Such information could have been traded to the SS for a favor or a little food or a few more weeks. In time though, we came to trust one another.

One of those mornings, Misha recounted his separation from his family. The question of their fate occurred to me the moment I saw him that morning as he marched to the selection yard. I didn't, however, inquire. I had my fears and I knew that Misha would tell me when he felt the moment was right. As he looked up from his prayers, he wistfully spoke of how for many weeks after they were taken from Lodz, he and his mother and father had prayed over the Tefillin. It helped to keep them together and give them hope. One day, a group was taken away, his mother and father with them. Misha did not know where they were taken or what befell them. His inquiries at each of his new destinations turned up nothing. I knew, or at least suspected, the worst for his parents, but of course never expressed that.

Misha was an intelligent young man and he'd seen much since Lodz, but he always held on to the belief that his parents had not been put to death and were alive someplace, where they were holding out for their son and managing to survive day by day. Prayer gave him that hope.

There was an intricate, centuries-old ritual. Misha would wrap the Tefillin seven times around his left arm first, place the part on his forehead, and recite the prayer before tightening the remainder of the hand set on the middle finger of his left hand. He was in a different spirit. He concluded with general prayers for the day, which he'd known by heart for many years.

I must confess that watching and taking part in prayer amid those bleak conditions often struck me as incongruous, even absurd. I have to think that, at least at times, even Misha felt the same. But when he placed the Tefillin on his arm and head, the surroundings and incongruities and absurdities fell away. His eyes and soul became reinvigorated. Life and hope returned. He forgot what he would face later that day. He forgot his hunger and thirst and frailty.

"The Tefillin," he said, "reminds me that we must have hope—a hope of life. It offers the power to continue. I know there is good in the world . . . and it will prevail one day."

Such is the power of prayer. It kept him persevering, and it did the same for me.

PHILOSOPHY IN AUSCHWITZ

Misha and I used to have what adults would call philosophical discussions. Life amid the world war and the Holocaust pressed young minds to address larger issues than they'd ever consider in ordinary times. Such matters were for college students and older boys speaking with clergymen and professors. But in Auschwitz, our minds and souls searched for answers. We pondered good and evil, human nature, and what would come from this.

Misha was deeply depressed one day. I patted his back and tried to cheer him. "Soon the war will be over and all this will fade away as though it never happened." I instantly regretted the last few words. Sometimes our efforts to help are clumsy.

"I miss my parents . . . ." He started to sob. "I don't even know where they are."

I sat next to him. "I'm sure that they are doing well. They're probably in other camps. Auschwitz is a huge system of many camps. There's an arms plant a few hundred meters from where we are. And beyond that, in Monowitz, an artificial rubber factory and a place where they make drugs. They could be at any of those places. And I hear the food is better there too." My suspicion, however, based on my understanding of the system, was that it was likely they had been worked to death or sent to the gas chamber, perhaps one not so far from us at that moment. Worse lies have been uttered in this world. Of that I have no doubt.

Misha raised his eyes toward me. "How can they do this, Adrian? How can they separate families, mothers, and children? How can they kill so many people, day after day?"

I could never offer an answer, only comfort. "I don't know, Misha, I really don't." Hearing hopelessness in the voice of a dear friend and seeing it on his face as well is very trying, especially if that friend has been your source of strength.

"Where are the good people? I know they are there somewhere," he continued. "Maybe we just need to talk with the German guards—individually, beginning with just one. Maybe we can explain to him, and then to others, that we didn't do anything wrong. They've been misled, that's all. Some of them will understand." Tears poured out from his eyes, as his words didn't buoy him at all, optimistic and youthful though they were.

I just nodded.

"I mean, all of these soldiers were children once, just like us. They will understand. There must be someone with a good heart who will understand," he stuck to his forlorn plan.

"I wish I could believe that," I said quietly. "But I don't think so, Misha. You saw yourself how they treat Jews. They think you are not truly human beings, only a much lower order. Something happened to them. I can't explain it. Something just happened to them . . . an awful period in the thirties followed by a leader claiming he had all the answers."

Misha's boyish eyes were red and swollen. He felt that I was right. "Then we are going to die . . . . like all the others. Like all the thousands of others they are killing here. Tens of thousands—more. We are all going to die." He raised his eyes back to me. "It's just a matter of time . . . ."

My eyes welled up but I didn't want Misha to see. I stood quickly, breathed in, and tried to sound confident and reassuring. "No, no, don't talk like this. We will survive. We are young and strong. They keep the young and strong ones for work details. You've seen it yourself in the selections. And besides . . . ." I paused as I tried to conjure up a plausible scenario for our survival. "I've heard talk about the end of the war. It's coming soon." Having found something, I continued. "This madness cannot go on forever. It will burn itself out one day. The Russians will liberate the camps, even the ones around Auschwitz. I heard it from some soldiers. The Russians are already close to the Polish border." I saw hope in Misha. I'd put it there. "The end of this is coming and it is coming soon. Then all of us will be free again. You will be reunited with your family—your mom and your dad. We'll all go home."

Misha wiped his tears and looked at me. Much of his despair was gone. I smiled as much as I could.

"You really think the war will end soon?"

"Yes, I do. The Third Reich's days are numbered."

"And I'll see my father and mother again? And we'll be able to go back to our home in Lodz?"

"Yes, Misha. These things will all happen soon."

He breathed deeply and looked about, taking on what he saw and what I'd said, weighing each with the judgment of a boy and an inmate.

"But until then, we have to continue to survive," I stated determinedly. "We have to care for each other and help each other stay alive."

He nodded quietly. "I still think that we can find some good German soldiers who will help us."

"Well, even if there are some good soldiers, we can't risk talking to them. There is no way to know who is good and who is bad. Addressing the wrong soldiers can lead to deep trouble. The soldier might get angry at such words. He may even shoot you."

It was painful for him to realize that his simple plan of reaching out to the decency he thought lived in all of us was of no use in places like Auschwitz and Treblinka. He needed to see some goodness in people—the goodness he saw in neighbors and friends from our boyhoods.

"I can't believe that all Germans are the same," Misha told me one night, just before he'd nod off and I'd return to the Kapo barracks. He refused to believe that evil existed on such a huge scale, even in the Third Reich. Even in Nazi Germany, amid all that darkness, he believed there were good people—an abundance of them. In time, we found a few cases in Auschwitz.

THE SOLDIER-INMATE DIALOG

"Good times are here!" Adrian exclaimed unexpectedly as he arrived at our office. He'd brought some pecan danishes and mineral water. We partook almost jovially for a half hour or so. Then we returned to his story. I think he needed good cheer to prepare the two of us for this passage. So we nibbled on the danishes and talked of lighter matters. I think if we hadn't done that from time to time, we'd both have become clinically depressed or he might have called the whole narration off and we'd sit quietly in the office and do nothing but talk shop—with a dark cloud over us.

After a short pause in discussing the parks along the lake just to the north of Folsom, Adrian suddenly returned to the events of long ago. That was his way.

Misha's group was on the railroad expansion detail every morning, sometimes into Auschwitz I, other times through the gaping brick maw leading into the Birkenau death camp. Many afternoons I'd offer the two guards assigned to our kommando the opportunity to head back to their barracks or the mess hall for an unscheduled break. Then the other Kapo and I would also take a break with the inmates. A little water and rest restored their energy and spirits.

Adrian smiled softly recalling his acts of kindness, which of course entailed considerable risk for himself and the other Kapo. More swiftly than it appeared, his smile faded into sadness.

Ohh . . . . I knew it was all temporary, if not illusory. I knew it the whole time and so did everyone there. They were all marked for death, one way or another. Worked to death, beaten death, shot to death, or sent to a Krema to be gassed. I'd seen the system long enough. I could give them a little rest and a little water . . . I could try to keep them from the crueler of the SS and Kapos. But for how long?

One day, our kommando was away from the track spur where other kommandos were laboring. We were hauling water from the Sola River for the others. The SS guards returned from their break more drunk than usual. They usually had a beer or two, a round of schnapps, perhaps a little brandy that a guard's family had sent, but this time . . . this time they were *stinking* drunk. Angry and belligerent too. One guard shouted at the workers for no reason—not that they needed one. One of the privileges of being an SS guard was having tremendous power over inmates. His shouts became mixed with laughter—a common enough occurrence as cruelty can be enjoyable to some people. Then he aimed his rifle, an old Mauser K98, at the inmates, alternately pointing directly at an inmate then moving on to another—again, enjoying the sense of mastery. That sense too was temporary and illusory, based only on the duration of the Third Reich, which gave great power to people with little talent and no decency at all. I'd seen enough of such episodes to know that he might shoot someone at any moment.

The soldier fixed his aim on the bearded man who had thanked me for the water break a few days earlier. I could see that the Mauser was aimed directly at the man's head and I saw a murderous momentum building inside the guard. He couldn't have been more than a few years older than I was.

"I'm going to shoot you . . . and you can't do anything about it," he said in a surprisingly slow and unemotional way. Everyone froze, including me.

"No!" came the anguished cry of a young worker. He was a teenager, usually a very quiet boy.

The drunken soldier turned his head to the boy, without moving his rifle from its target. "You, be quiet! Otherwise I'll shoot you first and then I'll deal with this one here the same way!"

It was clear that the young man had a connection to the older one. His father, perhaps. Or maybe an older man who assumed a fatherly relationship to a young man who might have reminded him of his son whom he'd been separated from. I knew too well that shooting someone in front of his loved one was not uncommon. I think it added to the cruel sport. Fathers and sons, mothers and daughters . . . only the devil could think of and perform such things.

There was nothing I could do. My rekindled humanity could offer no service here. I stayed silent. The bearded inmate began to speak. I expected to hear him plead for his life or for the boy's life. That was not the case.

"I want to ask you a question, please." The man spoke calmly and quietly, without a trace of fear on his face, though a rifle was aimed right at it. He looked directly at the guard, as though making a routine inquiry at an office or store.

The SS guard was certainly not expecting this and I think he became confused. "Go ahead, ask your question," he replied gruffly but haltingly.

"What will killing me give you?"

The soldier grinned uneasily at the unusual question. He looked about at the other workers and then at his fellow guard, who was enjoying the improvised entertainment.

"What will killing you give me? I'll be eliminating a Jew! I'll be making a contribution to the world. It is my part in your people's elimination from Europe and the world."

The old man let his shovel fall to the ground and took a few steps toward the SS soldier. His steps were slow, though more from deliberateness than from fear. His emaciated form was no threat to the soldier, so he held his fire. The man stood not ten feet from him.

"What do you want, old man?" the soldier cackled. "Do you have something to say to me?"

"Yes," he nodded. "I want you to look carefully at us."

The soldier looked at his fellow soldier and nodded his head toward the old man. "This one's gone crazy!" It was common enough but it wasn't the case here.

"I am looking at you and I see a young boy," the old man said. "How old are you? Nineteen? Maybe twenty?"

"Yes, nineteen. I am nineteen years old," the soldier replied matter-of-factly. He looked into the old man's eyes and became riveted for a brief moment, as though captivated by his words and humanity. Startled back to old form, he shouted, "Stop talking nonsense! Are you trying to confuse me with Jew tricks?" He aimed his rifle more determinedly at the old man's head.

But the old man stood fast. He continued in a warm voice, like that of an uncle.

"What is your name?"

"Kurt," he answered, "Kurt Lessing."

"Kurt, when you dreamed about being in the army, as all boys do, what did you dream about?"

"I dreamed about being a good soldier," he said in drunken confusion, taken aback by a man his father's age using his first name. "I dreamed about being a hero, fighting the enemy, and saving my country."

"Exactly." The old man let Kurt's own words sink in. "You wanted to be a good soldier. This is good, Kurt." The old man was complimenting him, encouraging him to continue a train of thought. "But where are you now, Kurt?"

"I am . . . I am in Auschwitz." Kurt was confused.

"And what are you and your friends in the SS doing here at Auschwitz, Kurt?"

"We are . . . we are eliminating the Jews . . . we kill Jews . . . I told you!" Kurt returned to his sense of mission and crisply added, "We kill your kind!" He spat the last words.

The old man paused then posed another question.

"Why do you kill us, Kurt? Have we done anything wrong to you? Or to your family or to your friends?"

Kurt drifted back into confusion. "Well . . . no . . . not to me personally, or to people I know. But they told us that you are . . . *enemies* . . . you are poison, you are subhuman!"

"Why, Kurt? What makes us subhuman?"

"I don't really know. I just know it."

Everyone on the labor detail, inmate and guard alike, watched in astonishment as this dialog played out before them.

"We don't do any harm to anyone, Kurt. All we do is follow our religion and beliefs, which preach good and purity. They tell us to help others and support the weak and elderly. We never harmed anyone, Kurt. Not our men, not our women, and certainly not our children."

Kurt was frozen, partly from alcohol, partly from playing a part in a surreal drama.

"Your head has been filled with nonsense. You know that killing babies can never be justified. And the children and the elderly? Did they harm anyone? Could they do harm, even if they somehow wanted to? Kurt, you know such people are incapable of harmful acts. You *do* know that."

Kurt seemed in shock, as though these words had torn into his soul.

"You and your military are killing—no, *murdering*—hundreds of innocent people here every day. Men, women, children, even babies. For nothing. It's a massacre, an insane horror. And it is wrong, Kurt. Very wrong."

Both guards stood wordlessly.

"I am already dead, I can feel it." The man's voice fell off into a lament. "I have a lung disease—tuberculosis or something of that sort. Lack of food and water, beatings, endless work . . . they take a toll. But what of you, Kurt? What about your friend here?" he pointed towards the second guard. "What of your souls amid all this—*after* all this." His hand motioned toward the watchtowers and barbed wire of the camp. "One day, when the war ends, how will you explain to the world what you have done here? But worse, what will you explain to yourself?"

Kurt looked at the old man as though seeing him for the first time. Then he looked at all of the workers there that day. He saw their emaciation and ragged striped clothing. The hideousness leapt out ferociously at him. Kurt saw what his duty was doing. He opened his mouth, I think in horror, but no sound was able to escape. His rifle fell from his hands.

"Kurt! Kurt! Are you not well?" The second soldier rushed to him but Kurt pushed him aside and gasped, "The old man is *right* . . . he's *right!*" He turned to the other soldier and muttered, "Did *you* ever think about what we do here?"

The other soldier could form no reply.

"We are butchering children . . . others too. We put them in those putrid barracks, starve them, work them to exhaustion, and when death comes to them, we hurl their corpses into mass graves. Or we send them to the *showers*." He mulled over that euphemism. "Yesterday, I shot a seven-year-old boy. Or was it two days ago?"

"Kurt!" the other soldier answered firmly, trying to pull him back to his duty. "Pick up your rifle. He was a Jew. He deserved to die." The tired rationales were no longer working on him.

"Seven years old . . . and he harmed us? He harmed the German nation?" Kurt shook his head and laughed bitterly. "Don't you see?" he asked his friend in slurred speech. "What are we doing?"

The realization was powerful. Kurt turned back to the old man. "You are right, old man. This is not war, this is madness. This is the truth I realize only now in my present state."

Only silence ensued. No one dared speak. They simply looked at the two young SS guards now paralyzed by doubt. I looked for Misha and saw a glimmer of happiness flash across his face. He too was reluctant to speak and I was glad he didn't. I was ready to intervene had anything flared between my friend and either of the guards. But Misha simply stood there smiling as Kurt's humanity reasserted itself, albeit in a drunken stupor.

The other guard was puzzled by Misha's smile. Clearly, it wasn't from mockery. I think he realized what Misha saw. He looked at his machine pistol and dropped it to the ground. "What have we done?" he mumbled as he looked at the stickmen around him and trembled.

The old man, seeing Kurt's dismay, approached him and went so far as to clasp a thin hand on the epaulette of Kurt's SS tunic. "It is not your fault, young man. You are a soldier who believes in his authority and obeys its orders."

I was transfixed by that scene. It was other worldly. A Jewish inmate was comforting a member of the SS. Kurt began to weep then he burst into tears like an ashamed child. "Can you forgive me?" he sobbed as he looked at the boys and men of the work detail.

After a few moments, Kurt stopped crying and exclaimed, "I don't deserve to live. After all that I've done, I don't deserve to live." He reached for his rifle on the ground.

"Kurt!" the other soldier shouted as Kurt placed his head to the muzzle and flicked off the safety.

"I am very sorry for what I've done to all of you and your families," he said placidly. "I am very sorry." With that, he pulled the trigger and the round tore a hole through the back of his skull, sending pieces of skull, blood, and brain tissue high into the air.

"No!" the other SS soldier screamed futilely. He then glared at all of us and I was afraid that he'd kill every one there. He grabbed the old man and aimed his machine pistol to his head. "You did this! You did this to him! I am going to kill you right now!"

But he didn't. He, like Kurt, was disoriented. He needed something to grab hold of to help him comprehend what had happened and killing a Jew seemed to fit at that moment, though only for an instant.

The old man stared back. "No, I didn't do that to him." He looked down to Kurt's crumpled body, a pool of blood building near his grotesquely opened skull. "The poor fellow realized what he was involved in. My heart is with this poor man. A youth who wanted to be a hero, probably as do you. It is your government, it is your leaders that killed him. His soul was already dead, like many of yours. As I said, I'm already dead. Everyone who has seen this camp, its horrors and madness, is dead—forever. Even should we somehow emerge from it someday . . . ." He looked at the remaining soldier and smiled.

"You may kill me now if you want."

The soldier looked at his dead friend then lowered his machine pistol and stood there in silence. The situation and his position called for action. "You!" he looked to me. "Watch them. I'll . . . I'll go for help." He then ran back to the camp.

Misha wept silently.

"A casualty of war," said the old man. "A casualty of war."

Unbelievable, I know. But I saw this. I saw this with my own eyes on a railroad leading into the death camp of Birkenau. I don't know what became of the other guard or how he explained Kurt Lessing's death. But we never saw the other guard again. His name was Arnold Kuhn, I believe. Maybe Kuhn was sent to another camp or perhaps he was transferred to the Waffen SS and sent to fight the Russians.

THE SEARCH

"You see, Adrian? I knew that there truly *are* good men among them," Misha said that evening in the inmate block as we tried to make sense of Kurt Lessing's suicide. Misha was slowly nibbling on the bread with a small dab of butter that I'd brought him from my mess hall. Our fare was only slightly better than that given to inmates, but there was a little more of it and I was glad to secret a little to my friend. I even brought tea in a canteen I'd stolen from a dozing guard and hidden under my striped Kapo shirt.

"Yes, there are some . . . but you saw what happened to him," I answered. "I am glad that you kept quiet during the whole thing. You have to remember, Misha, even if some of them have regrets, most do not. And they will kill you in an instant without regrets. Kurt was the exception and there's one less of his exceptional kind now. Do not call attention to yourself. Not under any circumstances."

Misha nodded as he took in my advice. "Your bread was excellent and most welcome, Adrian. Thank you very much. Now for our evening tea!"

I tousled his hair playfully. "No need to thank me. I ate at your home on many occasions. Your mother made such wonderful meals, remember?"

Fond memories of home meals arose within him. "Yes, I miss her food . . . ."

"And I didn't even say thank you then," I added. "I just devoured everything within reach."

"You didn't need to say thank you, Adrian," he laughed. "You are part of my family. You are a brother."

"I remember the pastry that your mother made for your New Year—Rosh Hashanah." I think my mouth watered at the thought. "Honey, crushed almonds, cinnamon . . . ."

"And the same for Hanukkah." He licked his lips for fun. "I could eat quite a few right now. We all could!"

"Yes, I remember them very well. We once snuck into the kitchen and made off with a half dozen of them."

"Oh yes," Misha recalled. "And my mother asked us about the incident minutes later."

"I think the powdered sugar on our faces left little doubt who the culprits were," I added.

"She didn't get mad, she just made another batch," Misha noted fondly. I knew where these memories would lead but there was no way to prevent it. "A wonderful mother . . . . Oh, I miss her so much." He released a long sigh and lay back on his bunk.

I missed my mother too, though the circumstances of our separation were less horrifying. I shared an idea. "Tomorrow, after we come back from the railroad work, we can ask about your parents in the other blocks. And we'll ask the people to ask around the other blocks. I'm sure there's a lot of such questions here. Maybe someone will know about them."

I was of course trying to push aside any thought of discovering something dreadful. We'd all seen the selections and we all knew what awaited those judged too weak to perform labor. The sadness spreading across Misha's face told me these thoughts were occurring to him.

"Yes, we can try that. But Adrian, you must know that they may be dead already. There's so much death here . . . so very much.

Thousands . . . tens of thousand. Many people's parents, maybe my own. Why *not* my own?"

"We should not lose hope," I interjected. "They may be at one of the nearby camps like Monowitz. Unusual things happen here, some of them good."

He thought about my words, rolling his head back forth. "Yes, you're right. There is a chance. Always. Tomorrow we shall begin the search."

I saw hope come across his face, and with it came strength which I knew served inmates well. At the same time, I didn't want his hopes to get too high only to be cruelly dashed upon discovering that his parents had been worked to death or shot for sport or marched over to the gas chamber. Still, I shared his hope that night. It was difficult not to feel the hopefulness and cheer of a boy as wonderful as Misha.

Each day after work, we went down the rows of dark blocks arranged across Auschwitz I. A Polish conscript and a Jewish inmate might have caught the attention of SS personnel, but if so, they simply thought I was taking him to do some work in another part of the camp. Though boys we were, we had to avoid any signs of friendship. We also had to avoid any appearance of purposefulness. That would surely have aroused suspicion.

We went about our investigation quite systematically for boys our age. We'd enter the first block in a row and look for someone who appeared to have been there a long time. Tattered striped pajamas were a sign. Then we'd search for someone who was new to the camp and had been brought in from another part of the Auschwitz complex. We would ask about the parents by name and describe their appearance and how they spoke. We'd ask if there was anyone in the barracks from Lodz in the expectation that people from the same town might be more likely to know the whereabouts of former neighbors. We started with the men's blocks and in the course of a few weeks we worked our way to the women's sections.

Everyone was very understanding but none could offer any help, though they promised to make inquiries and we came back to hear if there'd been word. That process was a common enough part of life at Auschwitz, trying to find out what happened to friends and family members. There couldn't have been very many pleasant discoveries. At least not many that lasted more than a short time. But the project gave them hope and as I said, it brought strength too.

We'd been through scores of blocks in the camp and returned to hear if there'd been any results from the inmates' investigations. Nothing. There were always new people brought in, put through the selection process, and either put to death or put to work. But Misha's family had been put in the system many months ago. There were rows of blocks over in Auschwitz II and Monowitz but we had no way to go there. We could only ask others who'd been there.

One morning, I was ordered to assemble a cleaning kommando. I picked Misha and a few others and we took two horse-drawn wagons to collect material near the electrified fences along the camp's long perimeter. It was a common enough work detail as papers, rags, an odd shoe, and the like accumulated there. And so did the corpses of inmates who were electrified, either as they tried to escape or as they put an end to their ordeals by their own will.

Grabbing hold of the thick wire for an awful moment must have seemed preferable to another day of beatings and horrors, which would likely end in death anyway. Better, they thought, to have some say in one's end—a final moment of personal will and autonomy. The powerful surge of electricity contorted the bodies into grotesque positions. Some lay on the ground, others were still grasping the wire, either from sheer determination or from the tightening of muscles and ligaments caused by high voltage. Often we had to shut off the power and pry the gnarled, burned fingers from the wires. I turned my head away on many occasions, I can tell you.

Picking up the bodies wasn't as physically demanding as, say, laying railroad track or shoveling gravel. Once the bodies were collected, we turned to the less ghastly work of picking up the paper and rags that had blown against the fences. This work was comparatively easy, physically and emotionally.

It was October of 1943, I believe, late fall and chilly, the skies were gray and unpromising. As our grim work proceeded, a light rain fell, making the poor workers shiver all the more. Heavy mists hung over the camp. A block only a hundred meters away was heavily shrouded in a white haze. Not seeing those dreadful buildings was almost a relief.

We finished the electrified outer fence and turned to the regular inner fence and I could see a group of men and boys standing outside a block shivering in the damp cold, a few guards and dogs around them. The inmates looked especially emaciated and frail—too far gone to be on labor kommandos. Oh, I suddenly realized. They had been through the morning selection and were about to be herded across the tracks to a Krema in Birkenau. They were all about to die and they knew it.

One of the men walked in our direction. He started to look familiar and I thought he must have been on a kommando I'd worked with last week or the week before or the one before that. People came and went. Misha ran from the work detail and pressed against the inner fence, shouting, "Father! Father!"

The glimmer of recognition I had for the man was quite dim compared to that of his son. Yes, it was Moshe Coen—Misha's father, the gentle maker of toys for the children of Lodz. He was shockingly thin; his bones stuck out from his taut pale skin. Life flashed into his sullen eyes as he heard his son's voice and he limped as best he could to the fence and clutched his son's hands. Everyone on both sides of the fence put together what was going on and they all stopped to witness a moment of familial love, some for the last time.

"Misha, how are you, my dear son?" he asked anxiously. It was a simple enough question, one heard a dozen times a week, but here, at this moment, it meant "Thank God, you're alive! And thank God, I've lived to this moment so that I could see you one more time."

"I am doing well, father. Really, I am!" Misha could only fall back on familiar words as he searched for more meaningful one. "And this is Adrian, our neighbor. He is of great help to us."

Misha's father was very puzzled. Adrian? A Kapo? How can that be?"

"They came and took me too. I hate who I am . . . but at least I can watch over Misha."

A million words could not have adequately explained my place there that day along the fence. Had I tried I'm sure it would have become a tearful plea for forgiveness. I thought briefly of Kurt Lessing and his exit from this world. Moshe Coen looked at me and at my clothing with the triangle signifying Polish conscript, studying my being, it seemed. He had much to ponder and so little time to do it. He'd seen much of the process and was able to see my small and unfortunate place in it. His gentleness spoke of understanding for me. It was a look which I shall neither forget nor stop cherishing. I felt relief and forgiveness.

"This is wonderful news, Misha—and thank you ever so much, Adrian." Moshe, even in this excruciating moment, was happy. "This is the Lord's way to help both of you. You are together, you will survive. I am very happy to know that Adrian is watching over you, Misha. Adrian is your family. He always was and always will be . . . ."

Seeing Misha and his father together made me think of my family and a reunion we too might have someday—one far from here, I hoped. My throat tightened, my eyes welled up. I forgot my position entirely. "I am trying to do my best for Misha," I whispered amid sobs.

Misha suddenly saw his father's wretched condition. "Father . . . you are not well. So . . . thin and weak."

"Do not worry about me, Misha," he lovingly chided. "You have to take care of yourself now. I am old. It is you who has all your life in front of you. It is you who must find a way to survive."

Misha wept aloud. I looked around us to make sure that there were no SS guards to find a way to take perverse pleasure in what was taking place.

"Misha, listen to me. You and Adrian need to survive. You have to do it together." He turned to me. "You both need to live through this madness and tell the world what you've seen so that nothing like this can ever happen again."

"Where is mama? Is she here with you?" Misha asked with little hope in his voice as he looked at the silent men and boys behind them, many of whom were watching the scene along the fence—their last moment of decency and love.

His father shook his head. "No, Misha, I am sorry but I do not know. They separated us early on. I haven't seen her in over two years. We must hope and pray she is well somewhere."

The three of us shared a concern for her and I silently prayed that if she'd met her end, it was less horrid than many I'd seen.

"I still have the Tefillin you gave me for my Bar Mitzvah," Misha said almost brightly. "I recite prayers every morning."

"This too is welcome news, Misha. Exceptionally welcome. This makes me so happy. You have to continue to pray over your Tefillin every morning. It will give you and Adrian the power to continue. In the Tefillin there is power, there is wisdom, and there is hope."

Misha nodded, as did I, though the father's eyes were understandably not on me.

"Of course, father. Adrian is with me in everything I do."

Soldiers shouted from the block behind Moshe. The mass of people were being ordered to form up. I knew what it meant but I spoke not a word. Moshe held his son's hand through the fence and looked into his eyes as though trying to embed it into his memory for his final moments that would come within the hour. Yes, I'm sure that's what he was doing.

"Listen to me, Misha. You know that I love you with all my heart. There is so little time and I have to tell you the truth. I've never lied to you or hidden anything from you, not even bad news. All of us here," he motioned behind him without his eyes leaving his son, "we are the weak ones from the morning selection. They are going to take us to a Krema now."

Misha sobbed silently. Tears ran down his face in streams but no sound came from his throat.

"I wish I had better words to deliver to you but I am afraid that this is what lies ahead. Look at me, Misha."

Misha raised his reddened eyes to his father's.

"I love you, son. You are the most precious jewel in my life and in your mother's as well. You have to be strong, never lose your faith, never lose your soul, and most important of all, never lose your hope. Do not mourn too long for me. Seeing you, I will die more happily. This moment is a precious gift to me . . . and there is nothing I could want more than this last moment with you."

The shouting of the guards became louder and more insistent and the dogs were prodded to snap and growl.

Moshe turned to me. "Adrian, you are my second son. I love you and I want you to stay safe. Protect both Misha and yourself as best you can. Adrian . . . I thank you."

I wept. I wept openly and profusely and without any of the shame an older boy might have felt.

The father kissed his son's hands and walked slowly toward the block—more firmly now, I thought. I placed my hand on Misha's shoulder and we watched as his father took his place in the group and walked away from the block, into the chill morning mists, across the railroad tracks, and toward the building with the tall chimneys where death awaited.

Misha and I returned to our work along the fence.

AN INTERRUPTION

The next day, Adrian was in no mood to continue. He explained—half-heartedly, I judged—that he was getting behind in his work and that he had to be more attentive to chip design than to "old stories." Naturally, I did not press the matter. I sensed he needed a break and he would continue when he felt up to it.

The following morning, however, he complained again of being behind and I wondered if his narrations hadn't become too burdensome. He was neither young nor old, but he was clearly weighed down by memories and recounting them to me. As much as we like to think that talking about dark things in our past is helpful, I'm not sure it's always true. The memory of seeing a beloved neighbor walk away to his death is unlike most things that our psychologists come across, as is Adrian's experience with the old man in the gravel pit of Treblinka. Or what he'd later tell me about walking to Birkenau in the middle of the night.

After a few more days of silence, I was afraid that Adrian no longer wanted any more of this and that he'd never revisit those days, not with me or anyone else. We'd greet each other in the morning, share lunch, and discuss news of the day, then bid each other farewell at the end of the workday. The continuity of our meetings had been broken. I had to accept that. My father, after all, almost never speaks of his experiences at Dachau and Auschwitz, and I learned to accept that long ago.

One evening, as we were about to head home, Adrian said, "Would you like to continue hearing my story tomorrow? Or have you heard enough of an old man's ramblings?" His face reflected his warm nature—something I'd seen little of in recent weeks. Seeing it gladdened me and I replied, "Of course, Adrian. Whenever you are ready, I'll be pleased to listen."

I can't say why he wanted to continue. Maybe he felt he'd piqued my curiosity too much and could not leave me hanging. Maybe there was a pleasant story he wanted me to know, or perhaps a still darker one he felt obliged to divulge. Maybe after several days reflection, he truly did find it helpful to let things out. I hope so. In any case, I looked forward to the next day.

READING THE KADISH

Every morning, Misha recited his prayer over his Tefillin. As often as possible, I stood beside him. Many of the men and boys in the block thought this a sign we were losing our minds. They had lost faith completely. They looked around Auschwitz and Birkenau, saw trains coming in every day, smelled the smoke belching from the Kremas, then looked into the skies. They concluded there was no higher power watching over them. Nothing would save them or punish the men who were doing this. They accepted the machinery grinding away and awaited their deaths without expectation of a better day. Such people, most of them, eventually fell into a daze and left us.

Yes, we like to say that trying times strengthen faith, but I tell you it was not the rule there. Hopelessness and descent into madness were far more common and that's how many of them made their final walk across the tracks. An exception was that seventeen-year-old boy praying over his Tefillin.

One morning, Misha was upset. Not from sadness, more from anxiety. He hadn't spoken a word but I could see something was wrong. Straw had been pulled from his mattress and lay strewn across the floor. "It's gone, Adrian! My Tefillin is gone!" He reached again into the straw mattress where he'd hidden the leather pouch but again there was nothing. Misha looked at me with a now frantic look. "I can't find it anywhere."

The Tefillin had been a precious gift from his father whom he'd just seen sent off to a gas chamber. They were a symbol of tradition and sacredness and continuity from his past to the present. They gave hope in the face of whatever lay ahead.

Misha was thinking things through. It wasn't a matter of losing it in an SS inspection. There hadn't been one in the last few days and guards didn't like to poke around the fetid mattresses and straw. And there was no question of his misplacing it or leaving it out. Anger flashed across in face. "Someone stole it. Someone in this block. Someone here right now."

He scanned about the dark room and saw inmate after inmate looking at us, as though Misha's plight were just some sort of brief distraction from daily routine. The event was merely a trivial drama of no consequence or meaning as everyone knew death would take them.

Amid the room of blank faces there was an exception. A man with a measure of sympathy left in him saw Misha's anxiety and silently motioned toward an old man standing by his bunk with a look of feigned disinterest on his face. Yitzhak Lieberman was his name. Misha's ire flared once more and he ran to the old man and grabbed his arms.

"Where is my Tefillin! You have it, old man, I know you do!"

I'd never seen such anger in my little friend. His eyes squinted into menacing slits, furrows rose in the sparse skin of his forehead, and his right hand became a fist not two feet from Yitzhak's face. The old man, too weak to stand up to him, stepped back unsteadily in fear. He held his hands out for protection and to suggest surrender. Misha let him speak.

"I am sorry . . . ." Yitzhak meekly answered. "I am very sorry. I'll give you your Tefillin back." He reached down to his bunk and, under his torn, grimy blanket, lay Misha's prized belonging. The old man, his hands trembling from alarm and frailty, handed the Tefillin back to the boy. Misha's anger subsided but his glare stayed fixed on the man, as though demanding an explanation.

"Today," Yitzhak said without further prompting, "it is thirty days since they murdered my son. He was here in this wretched place with me for a long time. I thought that it would be me who died first." He smiled bitterly at his assumption in a place where so many had proved meritless. "After all, I am much older . . . but then he got sick. I think it was pneumonia or another respiratory disease. He was coughing blood for several days and his strength was leaving him. I gave him my rations of food and water and covered him with my blanket at night. I begged for help from the guards, but . . . nothing. He continued to fade from me. One month ago, at the morning selection, he was judged to be incapable of further work and sent to the condemned group. I watched him walk over to that group and stand with them before walking off to that place." He motioned awkwardly with a scrawny hand toward the worn pathway to Birkenau.

Misha listened intently to the man. His story, after all, had similarity to his own recent experience. Misha was still uncertain why he stole the Tefillin. The old man went on.

"I wanted to recite the Tefillin prayer this morning and to say the Kadish for him. I hoped to put them back into your mattress before you noticed. Truly, I did."

Misha's face swiftly took on compassion. Who could not have done the same? The other men looked on with compassion as well. The old man's story and the Tefillin there before them in Misha's hands had sent breath across a fading ember inside many there.

"You could have simply asked me," Misha said in a conciliatory way before turning to the others. "Any of you, if you wish to borrow my Tefillin, simply ask."

Misha handed the Tefillin back to the old man. The youth's compassion was intact if not strengthened. "Please, recite your prayer." The man placed the material around his arm and head and prayed the Kadish, the Jewish prayer for the dead, which he knew by heart. We stood around him as he thanked God for the life he'd given him.

After that, many of the men borrowed Misha's Tefillin. A measure of hope returned to those who did. Maybe to others in the block too. They did not pray every morning and there was no sudden restoration of faith. You must remember that these men were sick and undernourished and many of them could never rise from their despair.

Misha and I continued to pray every morning. It was not part of my faith. I'm not sure what my faith was back then. But seeing Misha's spirit rise had the same effect on mine. Deep in prayer, his face was almost illuminated, as though an unseen sun was sending its warming light. The beauty of his words, though in a language I barely understood, lifted us both from our circumstances for another day.

> *The Tefillin held a special significance in Adrian's story,*
> *even though he was not of the Jewish faith. I don't think*
> *he was of any faith at all. Yet when he mentioned them,*
> *a warmth came to his voice and face. And over the weeks,*
> *as his story unfolded, he mentioned them more and more.*

SOLOMON OF WARSAW

One day a man was almost beaten to death. It was a common enough occurrence but this one had an added element. It was fall, probably 1943, and we were marched out in a rough formation to work on a road outside the camp which led to a new bridge across the Sola River. Along with another Kapo and me, were two SS guards, both of them notoriously sadistic, even by camp standards such as they were. Yes, there was a range of cruelty in the guards and this pair was among the worst. They eagerly took part in torture and murder. They found it fun.

One was named Otto. Short and plump, he would beat inmates for no reason. They worked hard and did not speak out. Nonetheless Otto would single one out and begin to shout angrily at him then beat him. Sometimes it would just be for a few minutes, other times it would go on and on until blood flowed and teeth were kicked loose. I saw him beat more than one poor fellow to death. As the beating continued, Otto became frenzied, his eyes wild as though possessed. There was nothing we Kapos could do about it. When we went out in the mornings with Otto, we wondered who among the inmates would be killed that day. Undoubtedly, the inmates had the same dread as soon as they saw themselves assigned to Otto's detail. It was like a malevolent lottery that someone was doomed to lose.

As I oversaw the work detail, I took cautious looks at Otto. He stood about idly, occasionally sitting down to roll a cigarette. Would you believe there was a brand called "*Ostfront*"? It means "Eastern Front." As he sat on the ground he began to mutter and spit, perhaps as he recalled a minor offense taken in his youth before he donned the imposing uniform of the SS. All who saw this shuddered. It was a sure sign that evil was swelling within, from brooding to anger to action, and it would soon enough demand release. His finished his smoke and stood, scanning the group of workers for likely prey. His eyes seemed to bulge. I'm sure I saw more of the whites than only a minute earlier. His gaze fell on a man named Solomon.

Let me think. We had two Solomons in that group. It's a common enough name, drawn as it is from the Biblical king. They were quite different from one another. The one from Lvov was talkative and thought highly of his opinions, though not many others did, I can tell you. The other one was from Warsaw, quite tall and generally not given to a great deal of talking. Otto's attention fell on Solomon of Warsaw. He never saw what was coming.

Warsaw Solomon was struggling to push aside a large tree branch. It must have weighed a hundred pounds. His back was to the enraged SS soldier. He kicked Solomon to the ground and began to club the poor man with his Mauser. Over and over the wooden butt came down hard on the helpless man. He could only hold out his arms to soften the blows and deflect them from his head. Most of us turned away as we'd seen it all transpire many times before. We felt sorry for poor quiet Solomon, whom we were sure was about to be killed.

We heard Otto's curses and the sickening noise of the blows finding their mark. When we heard no more cries from Solomon, we thought he'd been bludgeoned into unconsciousness or worse. Feeling the need to know his fate, I stole a look. Otto was sitting atop Solomon and delivering measured blows with his stout closed fists, yet I could see that Solomon was still fending off punches in complete silence, even though blood was flowing copiously from his nose and mouth. Enraged by a strange silence that detracted from his pleasure, Otto determined to hit all the harder until, at length, he was too exhausted to continue.

Otto looked around at us, gasping for air, alternately closing and opening his now swollen fists. "If any of you here think that I am crazy," he bellowed, "raise your hand in the air." Otto glared at us and we all returned to our work. No one spoke and of course no one raised a hand. Turning to his victim, Otto roared, "If you are not capable of working, I'll shoot you right now." He then chambered a bullet into his Mauser, switched off the safety, and pointed the muzzle at Solomon.

No one could get up after that beating. No one. The human body can only take a certain amount of hunger and abuse. Solomon was surely about to be shot. A bullet would do what Otto's rifle butt and fists could not. Solomon writhed on the ground, moaned softly, then slowly stood up. Blood covered his shirt front and sleeves. He spoke not a word, he simply went back to pushing aside that immense branch as though nothing had happened. Even Otto was astonished. He didn't shoot or even beat anyone for the rest of the day.

At the evening we all gathered around Warsaw Solomon as he lay on the bunk, too weak to eat with us at the mess hall. Someone secreted a few morsels of bread but Solomon only took a bite or two. As determined as he'd been that day, he was unlikely to live out the night. I'd seen many cases like his and I'd acquired a macabre ability to judge mortal wounds. Solomon was a pleasant man all right, but it was his time. People like him came and went, I'm sad to report. I wanted to leave him to die his own way, without an outsider standing over him. Many others in that block had the same thought.

Not so Misha. I'm not sure why. Maybe Misha thought of quiet Solomon as a gentle uncle.

"Solomon . . . Solomon? You can't give up on life," Misha said standing aside the poor fellow's bunk. "You were very brave today. We all saw how brave you were. Even Otto. He beat your body but not your spirit." Misha looked at the bloodstained shirt and blanket for a moment. "You have to eat and get stronger, Solomon. Otherwise, you'll die on us."

Solomon looked at Misha as the boy spoke to him but offered no reply. Misha presented a crust to him, but he wouldn't take it. He had no interest in food or anything else this world had to offer. I wondered if the beating had finally taken its toll and if Solomon was able to form any response at all.

"Come, Misha. There's nothing more to be done." I whispered as I tugged lightly on his shirt.

But Misha would not give up. "Solomon, you are the Lord's creation. You have to protect your life. You have to watch over yourself. This is the Lord's wish." Solomon continued to look toward Misha, his eyes never fixing on him though.

"Too many blows to the head," someone whispered. "Too much swelling." Several people silently stepped back from where Solomon lay. Misha and I stayed.

"He hears your voice, Misha, but I don't think he comprehends your words," I suggested, tugging once more on his shirt.

"I believe he comprehends me . . . he simply no longer sees meaning in life. We need to show him there is meaning." Misha scrambled to his bunk and returned, the Tefillin in hand.

"Inside these boxes, Solomon, there is sacred scripture. They are meant to remind us that there is a greater power than us which gives meaning to our lives and that every one of us is important in the world. There is a purpose for every one of us, even if we don't know what it is. Your soul is important and has its purpose. If not today, then another time. You have to hold on to your life, my old friend."

Solomon's eyes saw the Tefillin and he stared at them intently. Recognition showed on his face for the first time in hours.

"You have a purpose in this life. You have to keep your faith. You have to obey the Ten Commandments. One of them tells us, Thou shalt not kill. When you refuse to eat, you are disobeying the Lord. Only the Lord has the right to take you back to him. You must try with all your might to stay alive."

Misha paused and gauged the old man's response. He did not speak but he did continue to stare at Misha's Tefillin for well over a minute. I thought this would be the last act of the old guy on earth, so I looked away. I heard a soft "oh" come from Misha and turned back to see Solomon reaching out weakly to the Tefillin.

"Do you know how to say the prayer, Solomon?" Misha asked gently.

Solomon nodded and slowly took the Tefillin from Misha.

"Would you like me to help you pray?" Misha offered. Solomon found the strength to shake his head. The breath of life flared inside the beaten man. More light was in his eyes, more motion in his face and hands. To our astonishment, and to the astonishment of many others who were now coming back to the scene, Solomon slowly stood up and began to pray and wrap the Tefillin straps around his arm and head. Each of us wanted to help him but we stood fast in awe. He recited the prayer from memory, pausing only occasionally to breathe in or to fight off a sharp pain that pierced him. His voice became clearer and louder with each sentence. He concluded with a bow of his head before returning the Tefillin to Misha. He then sat back down and ate the rest of the bread, thanking God for it.

Prayer for an SS Guard's Mother

Adrian and I sat in the cafeteria after lunch and talked about things unrelated to his story. However, enjoying a pleasant meal, with the opportunity for seconds and thirds, and an array of beverages concocted from exotic fruits, and . . . well, the chasm between that time and the present was too immense to grasp. When the conversation entailed talk of the future, it was difficult not to think about his past, my father's past, and the pasts of all those others whose futures had been taken away. Then there were the others whose present was made empty and joyless by ever-present images of the past which flashed before them at unexpected moments.

Our conversation trailed off for a moment and neither Adrian nor I wanted to restart it with something trivial just to avoid a silence. We were good enough friends by then not to be uncomfortable with a silent moment. I was about to suggest heading back to the office when something suddenly fired within him. He put down his orange juice and brushed a few strands of hair from his balding top away from his brow. "Oh . . . I'll never forget that day," he said almost enthusiastically, as though there was an aspect that had just come to mind.

One of the oddest events was the morning Misha missed a selection. I don't mean that he failed the examination; I mean he failed to show up for it. Those things were not, shall we say, optional. The temperature was well below freezing and the ground hard as sheetrock. Even the SS personnel felt the cold, despite their woolen coats. They cursed and muttered and stamped their feet as though their lot in life were difficult and unfair. The irony struck me and it probably did others too.

The inmates stood, naked, huddled into small groups to gather a little warmth and shield each other from the biting wind. I calculated from beneath my tunic and coat that many of the reasonably healthy men undoubtedly became weak and feverish from exposure. The calculation was irrelevant to the SS. There would be another train soon enough.

I scanned the long lines and huddled groups for my friend. Where is he? Where is Misha?

We'd been rushed out of the block that morning and I was not able to come out with him. I wondered if he'd somehow failed to wake up despite the shouts and curses of the SS and Kapos. I continued searching the hundreds of people in the field but without finding him. A headcount had been finished and the guards were looking at their notes, probably because someone was missing.

I stealthily took my leave from the field and headed for Misha's block, my pace increasing along with my concern. Missing a selection would bring fearful consequences. As I neared the block, an SS corporal walked in front of me from the right and I slowed down to keep my distance. I was horrified to see that he was headed for Misha's barracks but there was no opportunity to race ahead of him without inviting suspicion. Maybe Misha was at the selection after all and I'd just been unable to see him in the crowds. My gut told me, though, that Misha was near his bunk reciting his prayers. I was horrified to see the SS corporal enter Misha's block.

I paced outside the barracks, half expecting to hear a harsh beating or a pistol shot. Only after a few minutes of anguished silence did I summon the courage to go in. I had no idea what to expect or what I might do in the worst case. I immediately saw the corporal standing twenty feet ahead, his back to me. Standing before his bunk, arm and head wrapped in his Tefillin, was Misha. He was praying as fervently and obliviously as though in his parents' home or in temple.

This, I was sure, would be Misha's end. A Jew to the SS was a horrible thing, a Jew in prayer was far worse. The ire must have been building in this guard as it did in Otto.

As much as I tried to think of an excuse or a diversion or a plea, nothing came to me. The soldier continued to watch this Jewish boy pray. I could not see the guard's face but I imagined a smirking sneer or a building rage. Misha raised his eyes and a look of surprise came and went in an instant as he saw the man and accepted whatever would follow. He lowered his head and returned to his prayer. Again, I thought Misha's end was imminent but again I was wrong. The soldier stood and watched him finish his prayer, after which he looked up to see the soldier draw his P-38 pistol and aim it at Misha.

Again, my mind raced to find a way out of this. I was too small to tackle the soldier, besides he was armed and I was not. Misha looked at the man with complete calm, accepting his death, accepting an exit from this place. Hearing my breathing or perhaps my heartbeat, the soldier turned around. His face showed surprise but then sadness, melancholy, maybe even grief. He lowered his pistol.

"One of my best friends from school," he murmured, "was Alexander Adler. Back in Berlin, before the war and all this. We were friends, during school, after school . . . . He prayed over those things too."

"Tefillin," Misha replied softly.

"Yes, I remember now. They are given to boys on their thirteenth birthday. Something to do with the Bible."

"Each box contains a page of scripture."

"I had to hide the fact that he was my friend," the soldier continued in somber voice. "They took him one day. A soldier pulled him out by the hair, in mid-afternoon, as we sat in class. Geography, it was. We were shocked . . . and frightened. The soldier noticed our response and explained matters to us. 'This is a Jew,' he said in the manner of a teacher. 'A Jew is not a human. A Jew is a plague on this earth. We have to treat them like we treat roaches or a disease.'

"Alexander's face was twisted in pain and terror, yet the soldier concluded his lecture and returned to the task at hand. Alexander was a popular lad. By God, he was kind and witty. So one of the classmates protested that Alex was our friend. The soldier stuck his face in front of the boy's and shouted, 'Don't you ever say that a Jew is your friend. It could cost you your life. *Versteh*? Understand?' The boy nodded in terror. 'Anyone else want to declare this Jew a friend?' No one dared respond.

"I really wanted to speak up . . . . I looked at the fear in Alex's eyes . . . . Here was my friend, I wanted to help. But no one said or did anything. Satisfied with our timidity, the soldier smiled smugly. 'Good. You have all passed your first lesson in National Socialism.' He turned to our teacher who stood there, very pale. 'My apology, ma'am. We are collecting Jews in this district—orders. They will be taken to a better place. Please continue with your lesson.' He left our classroom, dragging poor Alex behind."

The soldier there before us in the Auschwitz inmate block had grief plainly written across his face. Misha and I stayed silent. I was uncertain where these recollections were going, though I felt the danger had passed.

"I saw Alex later that day. His body lay in the street not far from school. My best friend . . . dead . . . his blood around him. I ran home and cried. My father tried to explain that he was only a Jew, but I wouldn't listen. My mother said the men who did that were beasts and one day, they'd be defeated. I was later recruited into the SS, and here I stand."

He looked at the front and arms of his tunic as though they were completely foreign to him—and they were for that moment. Misha spoke to him, with sympathy. *Amazing* sympathy. *Incomprehensible* sympathy.

"I am sorry you lost your friend," Misha said.

"My mother is very sick," the man whispered. "The doctor says Mutti will not live long."

Life confronts us with many baffling things. Things it should prepare us for but does not. One of those things I've faced in my many years was feeling sympathy for an SS guard holding a gun as he stood over my best friend. I don't know, Danny, I really don't. Life is so baffling at times.

"We have a special prayer," Misha offered. The soldier's eyes showed interest. "In this prayer we ask the Lord to help cure sick loved ones, the people dearest to us, like our mothers."

"Would you . . . ." he found himself saying, confounded by the paradoxical turn of events.

"Yes, I will say the prayer for your mother."

Misha clasped his hand on the man's shoulder as though he were a friend. I wish that a picture had been taken so that people could see this and not count on my limited powers of expression.

"What is your name?" Misha asked.

"Müller, Bruno Müller."

"I am Misha Coen. I'll say the prayer of the sick for your mother now." His voice, though soft, reverberated in the empty wooden barracks. The wind occasionally rushed by, causing the building to creak. Misha continued his fervent prayer, right hand on Bruno's shoulder, left hand holding a small leather-bound book of prayer. Bruno seemed to recognize the sound and rhythm of Hebrew and felt drawn in by them. Misha completed his prayer and closed his book.

"I sincerely hope your mother gets better, Bruno."

For a moment I saw the face of a small boy. The helmet seemed out of place, as though he'd taken it from another boy's father, tried it on, but determined it was not for him.

We can be captivated by such moments and time and events can overtake us. Someone had to step in. "We have to bring Misha to the selection," I said.

"By God, you're right," Bruno said as though suddenly awakened. "I have to bring you outside."

"I have to hide my Tefillin and prayer book first," Misha said as he scurried over to his straw mattress. He and Bruno regarded each other awkwardly as each recognized that the spiritual interlude was over and an uncertain future lay ahead.

As we headed for the door, I realized something. "Wait," I said, "we can't just go back there. Misha, I have to do this." As soon as he turned, I punched him as hard as I could on the nose. Well, maybe it wasn't as hard as I could but he fell to the ground, his nose bleeding profusely. He looked at me in puzzlement.

Bruno was angry. "What the hell . . . ." he grabbed my hand and was about to punch me right back when it dawned on him, as it soon did on Misha, that absence from morning formation had to be punished. And if he wasn't punished by my punch, it might have been by a guard's bullet. A swollen nose would most likely put an end to the matter, without affecting his chances at the selection.

Bruno's face softened, a sign of fondness for Misha, which gladdened me. "Ready?" Bruno asked. The three of us collected ourselves, prepared to assume the roles in which fate had cast us, and walked out of the barracks bound for the yard. In the distance we heard shouts and cries. Some people stood before a platform, performed the motions ordered by the medical personnel, and were sent off to one group or the other.

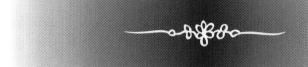

"Big Joe"

Saturdays gave Adrian and me time for longer meetings. It was also an opportunity to get out of the office. The atmosphere in a park or restaurant was more open and it might have made the narration less trying. It felt that way for me and I hope it did for him as well. Our talks were taking a toll on him. He looked older, more worried, and less disposed to joy and wit than before. I wondered if it were taking a few years off his life.

Out in a park along Granite Bay, just north of Folsom, we continued. A half mile away to the east were the rolling hills along Lake Tahoe. We sat at a picnic table and enjoyed the fruit salad I'd brought from a grocery store. Something light. The conversation began with the news of the day—politics and hi-tech stocks. I didn't prod. We walked over to a coffee shop not far away and had lattés and pound cake. We sat down. Again, I didn't prod in the least. He looked off into the skies to the east.

There was one man, about forty, cheerful, and powerfully built. We had a name for him. In English, it might go something like "Big Joe." You could see his once strong frame even after many months in the camps. Broad shoulders, residual muscle tissue in his chest and arms. Despite all he'd been through, he remained optimistic and pleasant. It was infectious. Even the SS guards joked with him from time to time. Very strange, I know. But there are glimmers of light even in the darkest of places and Big Joe offered a few glimmers to all.

"What are you so happy about?" the guys in the blocks would sometimes ask, either because they were looking for a light moment or because they were genuinely perplexed. "You have no food, no clothes, fleas dine on you, and you may be sent to your death any day. What are you so happy about?"

"It could be worse, fellows, it could be worse," he always answered. "As long as I'm . . . well, at least somewhat healthy and I can eat, breath and work," he breathed in and inflated his chest comically, "I am happy. What is out of my hands is out of my hands. I shall be happy in life, no matter what I have to face."

Some of us thought he was just an especially jovial chap. Others thought the poor guy had lost his mind, snapped, and become lost on a blissful island that his mind had created and fled to. Misha and I didn't think he'd snapped. We liked him and enjoyed talking with him. His spirit encouraged us and I like to think that we took in his happiness and passed it on to the rest of the men in the block and out on our kommandos. It was like having a little nourishment and sharing it with others.

The SS guards did not understand him and didn't care to for that matter. Happy or crazy, Big Joe amused them. And that probably helped him on more than one occasion.

One day, one very hot day, we were on a detail in a quarry, hauling large rocks up to the road. Bored and enjoying his mastery, one soldier looked at an especially large rock and came up with an idea to make his day more enjoyable. He would order an inmate to pick up the rock and if he could not, he would shoot him. On announcing the rules of the game, the prisoners froze in fear and wondered who among them was to die, but the fellow guards found it a splendid idea. They laughed and hooted as though in a barroom about to deal the cards and enjoy a round of beer.

The guard picked one of the shortest and thinnest prisoners and ordered him to begin the event. The reason for his choice was obvious. Poor man. He frantically looked at the guard. He knew he'd never be able to lift the immense stone. Nevertheless, he tried with everything he had. Everything he had *left*. He approached the rock, stooped to put his leg muscles into it, and grabbed hold. His face became beet red and he groaned pitifully, but nothing came of it. He tried once more but failed again. The SS guards laughed at the sight and looked forward to what all knew would come.

"Here goes the first one." The guard aimed his Mauser at the poor man and shot him in the chest. The bullet exited his back, splattering blood behind him on the ground. "Who's next?" the soldier inquired, as though an obliging clerk in a crowded store. The guards chuckled and looked into the work team.

Everyone stood in terror, knowing that the rock was simply too big. I too was scared. I paced about, hoping Misha would not be chosen. He was far too little. The next selectee was even frailer than the first. Unwilling to give them sport, he simply said, "I can't lift that damn thing. You might as well shoot me right now!"

"Your proposal is accepted," he replied. And without discussion or demurral, he shot that poor man to death also. Two men dead in this display of entertainment.

Everyone wondered how many more he'd shoot. He couldn't shoot them all as that would interfere with the work schedule, but the limit was unknown. Someone was about to be chosen when Big Joe stepped forward in large strides like a circus performer. "May I give it a try, cap'n?"

The guards laughed all the louder. They whistled and clapped as though to encourage him onto the stage for a performance. Big Joe stood smartly at attention then marched to the rock as though on a parade ground. Appreciative of the parody of army life, they cheered him on even more. He approached the rock and pretended to slowly raise it, grimacing and groaning for the audience, a corpse on either side of him. Big Joe feigned that the imaginary object was too heavy and looked to the guard, shaking his head. The guard grinned and tapped the bolt of his rifle, indicating that the preliminaries were all very entertaining but the show had to go on to the next act.

Big Joe addressed the rock once more, this time in earnest. He bent down, grabbed hold as best he could to the craggy surface, and lifted with all his might. Everyone cheered, inmate and soldier alike. There was a moment of incomprehensible unity as though we were all watching a favorite player in a critical football match. With authentic grimaces and groans, he strained and pulled, though the object was only barely budging from the ground that it was partially embedded in. At length, it was just slightly off the ground and we all cheered and encouraged him to new levels of strength.

Big Joe looked once more to the soldier who then moved the muzzle of his rifle in small circles in the direction of Joe's chest and head. There was something comical in the soldier's motions but we knew he was eminently capable of pulling the trigger at any moment. The other guards laughed heartily and I thought of people in the Coliseum of ancient Rome gloating as the gladiators fought to the death before them. I also thought of the sort of children who abused a small animal for play. The ability to feel sorrow for another's pain is not universal, I'm afraid.

Big Joe made growling sounds—I'm not sure if it was for amusement or motivation. Veins and ligaments stuck out from his arms and neck and he shook under the strain. With a loud cry, he lifted the rock to his knees and looked at us reassuringly before emitting another cry and hoisting the rock to his chest and then higher and higher until it was above his head. He desperately moved a foot about for balance and indeed was able to maintain his stance. He stood like a mighty Olympic athlete, enjoying himself immensely, before tossing the rock forward and letting it hit the ground with a powerful thump.

I thought of Samson and wished that this immense rock would bring down the Temple of Death the SS had built, even though it would come crashing down on me as well.

Big Joe relished the effusive applause and cheers from his audience and bowed to them, hands folded behind his back. The SS guard slung his rifle, walked up to Joe, and patted him on the back. "Very impressive, big man, very impressive." There was almost respect in his voice—something I'd not have thought possible from him or one of his ilk.

Shortly thereafter, the show was over, the moment of unity gone. We returned to our dreary work. How many others would have been shot while trying to lift that rock? We all knew that through his skillful display of strength and humor, Big Joe had saved a few lives that day.

Not long after that day, I asked Big Joe again how he could keep his humor and wit amid so much bleakness. Joe was lying on his bunk, hands clasped behind his head.

"Each of us has his day written above," he observed in a matter-of-fact way. "I am not going to worry about it. If my destiny is to die tomorrow, I die tomorrow. If not, I live another day. For that, I am grateful. It is all in a greater power's hands."

Hearing Big Joe speak of his faith was to me at first out of place. After thinking about it over the next few days, my response changed to amazement. I began to wonder just how he managed to raise that rock. Danny, I don't think the two of us could do it right now.

I smiled and imagined Adrian and me trying to get a purchase on one of the flint boulders adorning the front of the Intel building where we worked. Adrian laughed bitterly, though obviously not for the same reason. He said he asked Big Joe other questions, more perplexing ones, perhaps unanswerable ones.

"Why doesn't this greater power do something? Why does all this go on?" I asked one night while Joe and I sat in the block. There was no need to specify what "this" was, though I might have motioned about with my hand. Most of the men were lying on the wooden shelves and straw, eyes closed or staring above at another shelf or at the creaky ceiling. I'm sure the same question had occurred to everyone there. Many had given up on finding an answer and fallen into despair. Others found no answer but asking the question brought solace and restored hope, at least a little, at least for a while. They thought of themselves like the biblical figure Job.

Joe looked at me with an uncharacteristic seriousness. I wondered if I, a gentile, had crossed some boundary and gone into the territory of someone else's faith or at least a highly personal matter. I soon felt embarrassed and was about to apologize and withdraw the question from his consideration. But Joe's face relaxed as he formed a thoughtful reply.

"Everything has a purpose, everything has meaning—even if we don't see it. I have complete faith that even *this* has a reason."

My response was less than gracious but it reflected my frame of mind. "Including all these beatings and shootings? There's a reason for those things? How can you explain this madness and inhumanity that goes on and on and on?" I had gone on too disrespectfully. Joe was my elder and an esteemed one. He manifested no complaint.

"I cannot. I cannot explain the reasons for these things." He spoke calmly and with strength—of course. "We humans can see with only our eyes. We cannot begin to comprehend the world and all that goes on in it. Nonetheless, for everything there is a reason."

"Even for those buildings across the tracks?" I pointed in the direction of the darkest part of Auschwitz-Birkenau. It was the darkest part of the world.

"Even for those brick-chimneyed buildings," he said, pointing in the same direction I just had.

I understood his position, though I must confess it never became my own. I always admired his faith and I think of him when the matter of faith amid horror surfaced. It still does.

There was a sawmill in the camp, which cut freshly hewn timber into cross ties for the railroad spurs into the camps. The purpose of those tracks you will know by now. More and more, every day, from all parts of Europe. I think Hungary was a common place of origin by 1944. The railroad had a high priority and so the work that contributed to its better functioning had a high priority too. Workers in the sawmill and on the tracks were given better food and water rations. Someone had done a few calculations and determined that it would increase productivity. Maybe someone was promoted for that. He might have received a medal too.

There were beatings and shootings and exterminations, but there were also accidents to contend with. And the sawmill with its massive tree trunks, whirring blades, and flying chips was a dangerous place to work. One of the tasks entailed hauling tree trunks from flatcars into the mill. That was a job that called for strength—Big Joe. Yes, my good-natured friend was on one of those kommandos.

I heard a shout of alarm and looked over to a flatcar piled high with stout trunks. One of the top ones was about to slide down at any moment. The guards barked out orders to lash it down before it came crashing down. I'm sure they were worried about keeping to their schedule. But the trunk continued to teeter, then to slide. Workers ran away, fearing for their lives. Big Joe grabbed hold of the lashings from the other side of the flatcar and pulled down as hard as he could. His muscle and sinew once again bulged from his frame. But other logs creaked and separated, sending the unstable top log tumbling over to Joe's side. We called out a warning as it came thundering down. Joe instinctively used his hands to fend it off but it struck him across the torso.

An SS guard was first on the scene for some reason or another, possibly because Joe's strength was important to the schedule. "Are you hurt badly?" he asked kneeling beside him.

"Oh no, I'm not hurt. I'm as good as ever, Herr kommandant. Kind of you to ask." His humor was intact—a positive sign.

"Then back to work now!" the guard shouted.

So much for the compassion of the SS. The rest of us were worried. Joe had taken a dreadful blow and it must have done considerable damage. Nonetheless, he got up, wiped his hands on his work pants, and flashed a grin to us. "Well, what are we standing around for? Let's get these logs into the mill!"

The SS guards laughed at the sight. One said, "That guy is strong as Hercules. Shame he's a Jew."

That evening, Joseph collapsed onto his bunk. He had been injured but how badly we couldn't know until the swelling and bruises appeared. Had he not gotten up after the accident, he'd have been shot on the spot or sent to a hospital where he'd be used for ghastly experiments.

"So you took quite a blow today," I said to coax a description of his injury.

"Yes . . . quite a blow." His voice was low, his cheerfulness gone. Each breath brought pain. "My chest . . . maybe a broken rib. Don't worry about me. I'll be fine in the morning . . . a little rest, that's all."

Misha, a few others, and I sat around him. We wondered if he'd be healthy enough for the next selection. Had there been one right then, his fate would have been sealed. Surrounded by glum faces, Joe thought chiefly of us.

"I would tell you gents a few jokes to rid you of those sad faces and cheer you up, but it's better I rest a while." A weak smile came, despite his pain and prospects.

"Joseph, you are such a clown," Misha said lovingly, taking his hand.

"Yes, a clown . . . ." Joseph's smile took on a bitter look that we'd not seen before. "You know what they say about clowns, don't you? They make everyone laugh—"

"But they themselves are sad," Misha finished. "You don't seem sad to me, Joe."

"Well, this clown needs to rest before his next show." He turned to his side and groaned until he found a position that was at least a little less painful. He fell asleep quickly and had a good night's sleep.

Big Joe got up the next morning and went off to the sawmill with the rest of us. His chest was swollen and discoloration was appearing on his rib cage. The others took the more arduous tasks and worked all the harder to keep up production. At night, we looked at his chest and saw the discoloration spreading and darkening and I wondered if the higher power had chosen Joe's day. Yes, we all had a day marked for us, every inmate and every conscript.

Misha asked the older men if there were a doctor in one of the nearby blocks.

"Did you see Joseph's condition?" I asked Misha few nights later. There was probably anxiousness in my voice— a sign of surviving humanity. He was speaking with an older man whose appearance suggested he was a new arrival.

"Oh yes. Of course, I did," Misha replied forlornly. "His chest is black and blue."

"He has broken two ribs," the older man said with unexpected certainty. "The bruises are from internal bleeding and this has brought infection and fever. I am Leon Rosen. I was a physician in Lublin and though I do not have access to any of my equipment, I am reasonably sure of my diagnosis. I'm afraid he is in need of more proper medical attention . . . ."

Although Dr Rosen spoke calmly and professionally, his words chilled us. There was no medical attention for any of us and even Dr Rosen had no way of treating Joe. We slept only fitfully that night. In the morning the swelling was worse as a great deal of pus had accumulated in his chest cavity.

A young man looked on and said, "Maybe he should be taken to the hospital."

We looked at him in disbelief. Was he making a joke amid this? Had he lost his mind and latched onto some quaint phrase from a foggy past, a past in a sane place where there was reason and civility and hospitals. On looking at his reasonably intact work shirt, we realized that he was new here and had not completely understood what Auschwitz was or what any of the other camps in Germany and Poland were.

Big Joe recognized the man's naiveté and spoke up, though haltingly and in obvious discomfort.

"One less soul will make their camp more manageable," he said with a partial chuckle. "My young friend, we are in a labor camp that is attached to a death camp. There is no hospital for us, though there are other buildings here to serve us when our health fails."

Misha put his hand on Joe's forehead and could not refrain from a slight gasp. "You're burning with fever, Joe!"

"Am I?"

We moistened a ragged shirt and placed it on his forehead. He appreciated it but soon developed tremors. Though we were only in our teens, Misha and I had seen dozens of such cases. In those dank and unhygienic quarters packed with ill-fed men, infections were common. You could sense the presence of germs and fungi with every breath. Fevers built and led to the inevitable. Tremors were a sign of irreversible decline. Such people died in a day or two, their corpses placed outside the barracks where a work crew would toss them into an immense pit or haul them to the crematorium.

"He'll not make it past the next selection," Dr Rosen grimly noted. "This may be his last night in this wretched place. I envy him."

We all remained silent, wondering if this was reason for sorrow or relief—relief that Joe was free of *tsoris*. Misha and I stood outside the barracks, as we could until the guards shouted us inside and locked the doorways.

"There's nothing more to be done for our friend," I lamented.

"Maybe . . . ." Misha's mind was churning way—pointlessly, I thought.

We didn't find anything to talk about that night. We looked out into the skies, which seemed uninterested in the plight of two boys— or in anything at all.

Misha woke me shortly before dawn.

"Come, I have an idea," he whispered.

I knew where we were going, of course. The night had not been kind to Big Joe. His brow was beaded with sweat. The strength we'd known to dwell in his face and body was ebbing. Had he not been so strong, he'd have been left outside a couple of mornings ago.

Joe's eyes blinked open.

"What are you boys doing here so early?"

"I'm sorry . . . we were just . . . ." I didn't quite know what we were doing there, though I should have.

"I want to say my morning prayers with you."

"Oh . . . that won't be necessary," Joe groaned.

"Please . . . please?" Misha persisted.

He shook his head faintly. He wanted no part.

Misha nonetheless put the Tefillin on his arm and head and began. I thought he might have been more fervent than usual. Nearing completion, he requested guidance. He wanted to know how to help this man whose vitality and humor encouraged us. How many had he saved? How could we save him so that he could save more?

"What can I give so that he may live? What can I do so that he may live?" Misha asked the heavens.

Misha closed his eyes and stood next to Joe. More and more light was coming in from the slats and the less-than-well-crafted roof. I put a hand on his shoulder. "Let's give Joe some more rest. Come, we'll have to get ready for headcount in an hour."

He caringly removed his Tefillin and kissed them. I could see an idea was formulating.

"I need a knife," he said to the men now rousing and seeing how Joe was. "If not a knife then anything sharp."

Those around Joe had no idea where such a thing might be found. They were contraband and could lead to swift punishment. Nor did they know what Misha had in mind for it. One man stepped forward with a nail. It was old and bent, probably something he'd pulled from a plank while on a detail and kept hidden for one reason or another. Misha inspected the nail but dismissed it. "It's rusty. Far too rusty to make an incision."

The idea of anyone, let alone Misha, making an incision on Joe's chest staggered me. I'm sure it did many others too. Dr Rosen had recommended against anything of the sort; Joe was simply too weak to protest. It could be the final straw for the poor guy, well intentioned though Misha undoubtedly was.

"If it's all we have, then I'll have to use it," he stated with a determination rare in a boy. He ran the sides and point of the nail over the wooden bunk frame. Faster and harder, rubbing off as much of the rust as he could until the metal gleamed, though not entirely, I must admit.

"Big Joe," Misha said leaning over the stricken man, "do you trust me?"

The old man was in and out of consciousness but he found the strength to reply. "Yes, my young friend, I trust you. I place all my faith in you." I sensed he was simply being considerate.

Misha asked a few of the men to hold Joe's arms and legs down. Joe looked incredulously at the boy-surgeon standing above him, a nail in his closed hand. Too weak to protest, his eyes conveyed the unmistakable idea that though Misha was a fine lad, he was no surgeon.

"It's your only chance, Joe," he replied as he jabbed the nail into the swollen blackened mass of his first patient's ribcage and with the palm of his hand, pushed in a half inch before removing it. He then made two more punctures in the same area. Misha placed his hands around each hole and gathered the blood and pus in a motion similar to kneading bread. The pain brought Joe as close to consciousness as he'd been since the day before. Out came a hideous red, black, green, and white fluid, some of which was thin, some of which was thick like paste. As dreadful as that barracks full of filthy men was, the stench of that cheese-like pus hit me and made me gag. Misha continued his work on each of the three punctures until the vile substance stopped oozing forth. The boy-surgeon washed off the wounds as best he could and stood back.

Joe lay back, breathing easier, eyes clearer. Misha put his hand on Joe's forehead and his smile indicated that it was cooler. Joe fell back to sleep.

"Well done, Doctor!" I exclaimed. "We shall soon know how successful you've been. And Misha," I added, placing an arm around him, "I'm very proud of you, Misha. Or is it Doctor Coen now?"

Everyone returned to a little more rest before the guards rudely announced the new day. Some of us wondered if Misha had done any good. There was always the question of whether it was better to live or die.

Joe woke up with the rest of us, put on his shoes, and went out for headcount, albeit unsteadily. An inmate on either side of him helped him along, though any sign of carrying him would have betrayed his frailty and gotten him sent to the condemned group. At work, others took the most strenuous jobs and gave Joe a hand whenever possible. Again, nothing too obvious, but guards look the other way and go off on unscheduled breaks. I saw to that as best I could.

"Thank you, Misha, for saving my life," Joseph later said with profound gratitude. "I truly thought my day had arrived."

"Oh, we couldn't let you go," Misha chirped. "We love you a great deal. Who else can brighten our lives here. Only you, Joe, only you. In any case, it is not me that we should thank. It is the Lord."

"I see. You are certainly right. Then I thank the Lord—and his talented young assistant here before us!"

"Misha," I asked, "what gave you the idea for that operation? Where did you find the courage to see it through?"

"I don't know. I truly don't. I just saw what had to be done and went ahead. No matter. The important thing is that we have Joe back."

Joe thanked Misha again and made his way back inside the barracks. I thought again of Misha's Tefillin.

My relief on hearing a pleasant story must have shown on my face as we walked along Granite Bay once more. A natural question occurred to me and I found the courage to ask what became of Big Joe. Adrian said he didn't know. People came and went, one way or another. He was pretty sure that Joe didn't fail a selection though. His strength returned as best it could and he was one of the better workers. Adrian shrugged his shoulders and said Joe might have been sent off to Monowitz where the artificial rubber was being made for the German war effort. He was a strong and good-natured man. He had that going for him. He also had the prayers that Misha said with him working in his favor.

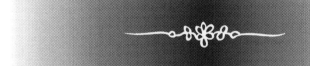

SHIMON

As much as I appreciated the break from the dark stories of cruelty and death that Big Joe's chapter brought, I knew that most of Adrian's story would not have many pleasant respites. It came to me that such events might have been relished by inmates, at least those who had not abandoned hope altogether. It also came to me that Adrian decided to interject a pleasant story into our meetings in order to make the undertaking easier for him. Maybe also for me. We continued the next day.

There was a man named Shimon. He was quiet and kept to himself for many months. You'd not notice him much. Many men were like that. Some because they needed time by themselves to gather their reason and identity. Others withdrew from reality altogether and awaited their fates. Oh, I suppose there were a hundred reasons. One day, Shimon opened up. And Danny . . . I honestly wish he hadn't.

He approached us—Misha and me—and asked if we would listen to him. I suppose in all his silence, things were building up inside him or he was trying to organize his experiences in order to tell them in a coherent manner. Anyway, Misha greeted him and said we would of course listen to his story. He offered no introduction.

"We were humiliated and yelled at as we were herded down the streets of Berlin. They hurled stones at us. They shot some of us down. We were taken to live in an isolated part of the city—a quarantined part, one might call it, as I'm sure many Germans did. Others called it the 'ghetto.' That was a term used for the Jewish part of Italian cities. How do I know this, you might wonder. Well, before all this, I was a history teacher.

"I read and taught of the Caligula and Attila and the Borgias. So I was not unaware of despotic rulers and dreadful people in human affairs. I knew of their murders, wars, and cruelties—and presented them in detail to my students. I must add—I must *confess*—that I taught my pupils that those things were in the past. That we Germans were cultivated, educated, civilized. We Germans—yes, I said 'we.' I considered us Germans. We had assimilated. We had our religion, of course, but we were Germans. Hadn't we read Goethe and Schiller? Hadn't we served in the Great War, in the same trenches in the east and west? Not everyone considered us 'true' Germans. That lesson was taught in 1933, when National Socialism came."

Misha and I looked at Shimon with greater respect. In part, because we were astonished by the abruptness of his opening up to us. In part, because he spoke with such clarity and conviction. There was so much he could tell us. He reminded us of a number of teachers we'd had in Lodz who'd inspired and encouraged us. For the moment, Misha and I were once again being taught, though in a gloomier classroom in a much more challenging school. But let me get back to Shimon.

"I ask you boys this today. Did any of you think that you would have to go through this? Did you ever think that you would be treated like animals? No, worse than animals. Did you ever think that your religious beliefs would lead you to a concentration camp? Of course not. None of this would have occurred to any of us."

Shimon thought that I was Jewish. That happened often enough. I was in a block inhabited mainly of Jews, many Kapos were Jews, the SS treated me only a little better than they did Jews, and I was always with Misha. I think Shimon's assumption made me realize that I felt a deep commonness with the Jewish people. I lived with them, worked with them, felt hunger with them, faced death with them. I even prayed with them. I felt part of a people who had learned to endure suffering.

"We went along with the process," Shimon went on. "We were put in the ghetto. Our jobs were taken away, our belongings, our property, and then our humanity. Losing a favorite coat or even one's home is superficial compared with losing one's humanity. We had our families there in the ghetto. Yes, thankfully we had them. We thought that one day it would be over. One day the war would be over and decency would again prevail. Some of us sensed we'd become sheep and we knew all too well where sheep are often led.

"Rounding us up and forcing us into the ghetto was just the first chapter. Many more chapters lay ahead—chapters that those despots I mentioned could never have imagined. They had their vengeances and reprisals and slaughters, but nothing like our *noble civilization* of today has performed."

Shimon pronounced "noble civilization" with great irony. His face took on aspects of bitterness and despair.

"The ghettoes were then liquidated—a cold term drawn from physics and business. But the word hid murder. Who knows how many. Our meager belongings were tossed into the street and we were beaten and abused as we were driven down the streets of Berlin."

Shimon became emotional, probably from what lay ahead. Misha lay a hand on Shimon's shoulder. "You don't have to go on," Misha said. "We'll understand." But Shimon responded with a fiery glance and an irate voice. "I want to go on! I want you to know!" We were taken aback, but Misha nodded understandingly, and Shimon continued after a few moments.

"My son Yehuda, six years old, and my daughter Rachel, four, both slept in the same bed, in the same *broken* bed. We thought ourselves fortunate. We remained together." He chuckled softly. "Children are remarkable. They can accept hunger and squalor and find new ways to create and have fun. Yehuda and Rachel would run through the muddy streets and alleys, playing games and making them up as they went. A stick or bottle could become props in an impromptu play. It protects them from the dread that haunted us adults.

"A neighbor child would get sick form the filth and crowding. Some recovered but some did not. When we heard of one in failing health and on irreversible decline, we tried to shield our children from that knowledge. But children know. They tell their friends and word spreads. They also have intuition. They sense what a child's absence from play means. They sense what a parent's avoidance of a certain name means.

"A neighbor's boy—Chaim was his name—developed an intestinal illness. Diarrhea and vomiting took a toll. He became thin and breathed only with difficulty. There in the ghetto, it was only a matter of time. One morning, it was little Chaim's time. My children knew him well. They played with him daily. My wife and I initially chose not to tell them, but we sensed they knew. Continuing our silence, though, would weaken the trust that held our family together. We explained to them that their friend was gone, gone forever. A difficult concept to expect children to understand, but Yehuda and Rachel did.

"I was reading to them in bed on the night the ghetto was liquidated. I managed to bring their copies of *Hansel and Gretel* and *The Ugly Duckling* along with us. They loved them. I suppose most children do, don't they? As they felt themselves drowse, they'd reach up to me for a hug then drift off to slumber with happiness across their precious faces.

"Rachel fell asleep first. She usually did. Yehuda held on a few more minutes, though he knew every word of the Ugly Duckling story. He looked up to me and asked, 'Father, are Jews ugly?' Yehuda had heard this from kids before we were sent to the ghetto. It pained me to think he felt the need to ask me that. I told him of course we are not ugly. Of course we are not bad. There are some bad people in every nation and religion. The Nazis, the people who put us here, are bad but most people around us are good. Yehuda found that comforting. He whispered, 'Good people around us,' as he joined Rachel in sleep.

"I heard shouting and screaming. As the noise came closer, I heard orders being given, in German. Not the Yiddish we all knew. German, with all its crispness and cases. I heard people running down the cobblestone streets followed by the heavier footfalls of boots. Shots were fired. People screamed. I looked outside and saw a German soldier shoot a young man who'd fallen down. Another shot finished the job.

"Soldiers were running up stairways, banging on doors, kicking some in. They reached mine and the door flew open with a single kick. My wife screamed and held our children who somehow remained asleep. When two soldiers burst in, I thought they'd be moved by the sight of a mother and father near their two slumbering children. I truly thought that. How could they not be? How could *anyone* not be? Such naiveté, such naiveté. I looked at the soldiers and they at me. I looked for their humanity, a gentle response to the sight of my family. I fixed on one of them, mid-twenties, not much more than a boy, not unlike the boys I'd taught in school. My search for his humanity found only the cold and emotionless eyes of an obedient member of the SS."

'I know you are a good man,' I said. He slowly shook his head and said, 'I am not what you call a good man when it comes to your kind!' He swiftly drew his pistol. I begged him to put it back, to spare my children. I was looking into a cold, impersonal implementer of policy. 'I see two young Jews who must not become adult Jews.'

"The first shot struck Rachel, the second Yehuda. The soldier looked at me and said, 'There. They died in their sleep. A better death than they deserve.' My mind could not comprehend what had just happened. My wife gasped uncontrollably and held her blood-splattered babies. The soldier continued, 'You two will not have such good fortune. You will perform hard labor before you too die.' I looked at my hands and saw *The Ugly Duckling* book was now spotted with my children's precious blood. I kept mumbling the author's name, 'Hans Christian Anderson . . . Hans Christian Anderson.'

"'Raus!' the soldiers shouted, grabbing me and shoving me toward the door. I saw my wife lying on the floor. Did they shoot her too? Did she die of heartbreak? Is she alive somewhere? Please tell me the answer, boys. Please . . . ."

Of course, we had no answer for Shimon.

"An officer shouted out that everyone was to get into the street and walk to the rail station where they would board trains. Some of us actually believed we were being transported to another country where we'd be free. There has been strange rumors of sending us to Madagascar or the Russian steppes. Many people seized upon those rumors to stave off the fear that other rumors brought. Most of us had heard of the camps. Concentration camps, work camps, and death camps.

"I couldn't cry. I still can't cry for my wife and children. I lost them all many months ago and still I can't cry. I lost my ability to feel anything. I work, I eat, I sleep . . . but this is mere clockwork. Nothing exists anymore for me."

Misha and I looked around and saw that a few people had gathered around to listen to the quiet man who'd finally decided to speak. We'd heard similar stories. Similar but not as heart-rending, not as skillfully narrated. To this day, when I see a quiet person, I recall Shimon and I wonder if that person's preference for solitude is borne of tragedy. Perhaps not one as horrifying as the one Shimon told us long ago, but tragic nonetheless—and deserving of our respect.

The men looked on Shimon in a new way. They'd all, to be sure, faced horrors of their own, but hearing of one's children shot to death in their sleep as one watched could still elicit sympathy and understanding from many there in the block. They nodded to Shimon or even greeted him but he remained withdrawn and mute. That was what he wanted and we accepted it.

Most of us anyway. One evening Misha asked him if he wanted to pray with him the following morning. Shimon merely stared back without any expression.

"You know," Misha persisted, "you can pray for something from my Tefillin." Shimon remained silent. "Well, it's not the Tefillin you are asking, but our Lord will listen," Misha corrected himself.

I put my hand on Misha's arm. "Let's leave him. Maybe another time." We looked at Shimon and knew where his thoughts were. I thought that if he had even momentary thoughts of being with his family, in happy circumstances of course, then his state of mind might be a helpful diversion from the present.

Misha finally relented. "Come, Shimon, let's go to your bunk." He was respectfully leading him along the wooden shelves when Shimon unexpectedly spoke.

"Yes, Misha, I would like very much to borrow your Tefillin tomorrow morning. Thank you. You're most kind."

Misha and I looked at each other in surprise. A trace of a smile that only old friends would recognize came across our faces.

"Of course. Tomorrow morning, I'll come to your bunk and you can say your prayers. And ask for anything you want."

"Thank you, young man. Thank you," Shimon muttered as he climbed into the straw of his bunk area.

The poor man. I think of him when I see a young couple holding a their child. Poor, poor man. I'd seen children and even babies murdered. We were required to witness such things to make us immune to such cruelty and perhaps even to attract us to it. I was never attracted to such things. No, not at all. Some of the conscripts were though, I must tell you. They looked on in fascination, as though an older boy were exposing them to the forbidden. They were attracted to it and captivated by it and eager to perform it on their own as part of gaining approval and becoming adults.

I asked Misha what he thought Shimon would pray for. Peace of mind? Vengeance? I sensed Misha had some idea. He was ever perceptive, but he didn't reply.

The next morning, Shimon prayed quietly over the Tefillin as Misha and I stood a respectful distance away. Shimon concluded and returned the Tefillin to Misha. None of us spoke.

We thought we might have opened a door to Shimon and brought him into the small groups that formed in the blocks, though usually only for a few weeks or a few months owing to circumstances. Misha tried to engage him in conversation and I probably did the same though less often, but neither of us had any success. Shimon rose, attended headcount, went out on work details, then returned to his bunk. After telling his story and performing his prayers, he reverted to being one of the damaged ones. Zombies, one might today think of them as. Walking corpses. We accepted them as part of our existence there. There was no choice.

A few weeks later it happened. I think Misha recognized its approach. I should have too. Shimon's wish was granted.

On entering Misha's block one morning, I saw him standing near Shimon's bunk. Men walked by and took quick looks before continuing to prepare for headcount. One or two patted Misha on the back consolingly. I looked into the still dark area where Shimon slept and saw him lying there. Misha said, "He's gone." I knew what he meant. There was no shock. Shimon lay perfectly still, eyes closed, mouth open slightly, a more peaceful expression than I'd ever seen graced his gaunt face. He'd left us.

It was as pleasant a death as one could expect. He hadn't been beaten to death or shot by a gleeful German boy, nor had he gasped for breath as acrid blue fumes surrounded him in a dimly lit chamber. No, Shimon passed away in his sleep. It was not in the fullness of his years; he was thirty-five at most. He was not surrounded by his family, only by fellow scarecrows—many of whom envied him.

Misha looked at our uncommunicative friend and teared up. "That which he prayed for that morning . . . has been granted him," he bravely noted.

I pondered his words and understood them. "But isn't that against your beliefs?" I asked, though it was hardly the time for such a discussion.

"Sometimes death is the best thing that can happen," he replied with certainty and moral clarity. "It was in any case the Lord's will."

I agreed. That bleak thought occurred to all of us. I'd prayed for my own death many times and something—perhaps the Lord, perhaps not—kept me alive.

A few of us carefully picked the poor man up and carried him outside to where the bodies of those who'd died were placed. We might have laid him down more gently than we had for the others. I like to think we did. Then we went off to the headcount. There was a selection that morning.

LOVE ARRIVES FOR MISHA

Adrian was especially affected by the story of Shimon. He suggested that we take a break for a few days. I of course agreed. I too needed time off to take in and better comprehend what I'd heard and relate to the experiences of others I'd known who'd been through the Holocaust, including my father. Two days past, then three, then four. I read a few books and ordered a few more.

Parts of his narrations created dreadful images that haunted my waking hours and stabbed me awake in the middle of the night. I would find myself standing at a barbed wire fence looking at a camp, always from the outside. I stared at the fence and thought of grabbing it and making an effort to get in but I could not.

It was only after a week that Adrian felt up to continuing. Adrian and I sat down and I could see that warm thoughts were dwelling within him that day. I think he intentionally came up with a more pleasant story. I was glad that he did, mainly for him but I thought I might sleep better that night.

Danny, have you ever seen a flower grow from a crack in a sidewalk or in a dung heap? Believe it or not, Misha found love in Auschwitz. I'm glad he did and I'm glad she did too. Yes, love can bloom even there. It's such a powerful force in life. So powerful that it asserts itself in even the darkest places, in even the darkest place. That's quite a testament.

My mind reeled as I imagined two young people finding themselves in that darkest place. Improbable but wonderful, beautiful and moving. "How did that happen?" I asked, almost laughing. I say almost. Adrian shook his head and it seemed that warm memories were surging through his being.

One evening, as Misha and I were walking along the fence near our block, we saw a group of women outside their block on the other side. It wasn't the electrified perimeter fence; it was just an internal one that kept inmates from gathering and making trouble. We heard the strange and appealing sounds of feminine voices as they talked and played. Some were girls, about our age. Younger children, as you know, were of no use on the labor details and sent to the Kremas on arrival. We watched the girls as we would in a schoolyard or park back in Lodz. They were different in appearance from schoolgirls though.

"Their heads have been shaved," I sighed.

"What a cruel thing to do, especially to women and girls," Misha added. "I saw that going on when we got here. Maybe they do something with the hair. Their long flowing hair told people who they were and how they thought of themselves. All gone in an instant. The girls cried. Their mothers too. I remember the weeping."

A girl about our age sat by the fence not fifty feet away. Her head lay low near her knees. She was the very image of youthful despair. Not far behind her were three women looking upon her with concern but leaving her alone for the moment. Misha knew her feelings and wanted to reach out to her. So did I. The fence and our awkwardness with girls held us back, at least until Misha summoned the nerve to speak up.

"Are you well?" he called out in Yiddish.

The girl lifted her head and looked around for the voice—the *boy's* voice. Her hair had grown back a little over the month or so since she arrived, leaving short splotches atop her head. Beneath that, however, were the delicate features of unmistakeable femininity. I'm quite sure that's how Misha saw her then! She looked over to us, then lowered her head to return to her private grief.

"Poor girl . . . ." Misha whispered. "Something's happened to her."

I might have chuckled at that observation. "Something's happened to everyone here, Misha! Do not let the sight of a pretty girl make you forget where we are!" But he showed no interest in my comment. His thoughts were across the fence.

"My name is Misha," he called out, "and this is my friend Adrian. May I ask your name?"

She raised her head again, her face still marked by sorrow. To Misha's delight, she stood and walked over to the fence—to where we were. We could then see her tears and where they'd streaked down the grime on her cheeks. Despite her pain, it was clear that she was very beautiful. Striking blue eyes, prominent cheek bones, and lips that seemed to have been formed by an artist's hands. As captivated as I was by her, it was clear that Misha was even more so.

"My name is Naomi," she said in a soft voice and eastern German accent.

Misha was in a faraway land just then. There is a word for this . . . *smitten*! Yes, Misha was smitten. By this young girl across the fence.

"Naomi . . . you have such a beautiful name." Circumstance had of course prevented Misha from having any contact with girls. He'd never had a girlfriend back in Lodz but that day, his natural warmth came through and Naomi's face reflected immediate appreciation. "Naomi, what is it that makes you so sad?" he asked with obvious concern.

She looked at my Kapo tunic and felt uneasy. I cannot blame her. We were in general a rather disagreeable lot. "What are you doing with him?" she asked nervously.

"Well, that's a long story and our time is short. Adrian is my friend and has been for many years. You have nothing to fear from him. Nothing at all. Please tell us why you are so sad."

Naomi continued to look at me warily but decided to answer his question. Her response was instantaneous and horrifying. "My mother was taken to the gas chamber yesterday."

I defy anyone to formulate a swift reply to those words. It would have been thoughtless and uncaring and trivial. Misha and I were silent. The skies were equally so. I wondered about my mother back in Lodz and Misha must have reflected on his and where she might be.

"I am very sorry, Naomi . . . . I wish there was more we could say." Thankfully, Naomi herself wanted to say more, through a hundred sobs and a thousand tears.

"We arrived here a month ago. I don't know just when. My father was taken with the men and we never heard from him again. My mother and I were assigned to the bakery until she developed a sharp pain in her stomach. It was difficult for her to eat or drink. Nothing stayed down. The women brewed teas from wood and grass or from a nail to put iron in her blood. She continued to weaken and become even thinner.

"Two nights ago, she said to me, 'Do not worry for me, my precious. I'll be alright. You have to take care of yourself though. You are young and beautiful and you have to survive this bad dream. You have to grow and meet the love of your life and get married and raise children. This will end soon, I am sure. I hear people talk about the end of the war coming. You have to make it till then.' She caressed my head until I fell asleep and in the morning I was still in her arms.

"That morning, at selection, the doctor just looked at her briefly and sent her to the sick and weak group. She gave me a last look, smiled, and walked slowly away. She turned once to wave to me. She was happy to go. Yes, she wanted to be with me and watch over me but her health deteriorated and so she was ready to die. In a way, death saved her from so much more . . . though I am not grateful for that. Not at all."

"I lost my father the same way only a few months ago," Misha said, his mind trying to reckon how much time had passed since that foggy morning. "I saw him very sick and weak near that fence by the administration building." He pointed in the distance and after some hesitation, Naomi looked that way. "I am grateful I had the chance to talk with him, to enjoy his smile, and to feel like a little boy again. I thank the Lord for giving me those minutes with him. They are the most precious moments of my life. And then I watched as he was taken with the rest of his group. It was like my being was cut in half. All the memories from childhood came to me. My birthdays, holy days, prayers at synagogue, my Bar Mitzvah . . . ."

The two children cried and held hands and comforted each other. An embrace was impossible through the fence, though I doubt two souls have ever been so close.

"I am sorry," she whimpered. "But Misha, may I ask about your mother?"

"I was separated from her and my father at another place, not here. A transit camp perhaps. I never saw her again and I've never heard anything from anyone in the other blocks about her. There's simply no word."

I think they both wanted to put the dark past behind them. They both felt something attracting them into a future. Naomi acted on the feeling first.

"Where are you from?"

"I am from Lodz, not far from here. And so is Adrian here. He is my best friend, actually more—we are like brothers." Misha clasped a hand on my shoulder. "We lived in the same building."

Standing with the young couple, wearing my Kapo tunic, I felt like an outsider. To Naomi, I must have seemed an enemy. But when Misha placed an arm on my shoulder, I felt a part of the group. I was one of them and Naomi looked at me in an accepting way.

"I worry about you all the time," I said as I mussed his hair. "I'm safe enough, I suppose, but I am always looking out for this guy."

"I thank the Lord every day that he sent Adrian to me. Even if my time should come here one day, I'll die in peace knowing that Adrian was close by."

Those were powerful words to me back then and they have stayed with me. They are among the few good things from those times. Our camaraderie and love for one another had been unspoken. Obvious to all, but unspoken. Naomi's appreciation of our display of friendship touched her youthful heart and gladdened it on that otherwise cheerless day. I saw her beauty more fully at that moment.

"You are so fortunate to have each other here," she said sweetly. "It will help you survive. You can encourage each other until this comes to an end, hopefully soon."

"What about you, Naomi? Where are you from?" Misha asked, obviously pleased by the emerging rapport. We both knew that asking that question invariably led to an account of how they got from their homes to here. Each story was unique, though I'm afraid that many get mixed together over the years. That's unfortunate.

"I come from Berlin. I lived there my entire life. Oh, I loved Berlin so. My whole family was there, my girlfriends were there . . . . It all changed one day when they forced us into the ghetto. People said it would pass soon. It didn't—you know that. We thought if we behaved in a certain way, a respectful way, no harm would come. Not true, not true. It was all chance. Then we were packed into trains and sent to here." A bitter look came across a child's face. So out of place. So sad to see. "I never thought we'd look back on the Berlin ghetto with any longing! Can you imagine that? The Berlin ghetto, a happier time?"

She smiled and the sweetness of a girl asserted its power over the bitterness of premature aging. It was so pleasant to see that transformation, I can tell you. Misha and I felt youth come forth from our beings.

"Here we see the human mind finding new ways to be savage. It takes many days to come to realize we are not in a nightmare, doesn't it?"

Yes, we could find oneness in trying to comprehend the enormity around us. For Misha, her words were vital and he awaited her every syllable.

"But we don't wake up. Everyday, beatings, selections, gas chambers, crematoria. Everyday. It was easier to face these things with my mother beside me."

"It will be different one day," Misha said with more confidence than I'd heard before. "I know that one of these days the war will be over and all this will be exposed. The world will be in shock, I am sure. And it will bring justice here."

"I hope that happens soon. And after it does, I wonder how we will be. Will we be able to go about our lives with our jobs and our families and our concerns of the day? I don't think so. Life as we once knew it as children is gone. There will never be the sweetness and joy and eagerness for the new day and what it might bring. I'm not sure I can ever be what I once was. Worse, I am not sure that I want to be what I once was, with all its foolishness and falseness. This," she said pointing around her, "has made us sour old people—forever."

"You have to keep your will to live," Misha said with determination. "It is commanded in our sacred writings and we must obey. We owe this to our Lord, our forebears, and generations to come."

"These words . . . I've heard them, thought of them, but they are merely words now."

Misha and Naomi paused and the only sound was the buzzing of a floodlight that was now brighter than the fading light of the day.

I remained silent. In part because I had no beliefs to bring to the conversation and in part because this discussion was between a young man and a young woman. But I must say . . . no, I must admit . . .

that I had largely withdrawn from my setting. I was there but merely as an observer. What was going on at that fence and in the camp all around us had nothing to do with me.

I must also admit that this sense of being detached from my surroundings has never entirely left me. After liberation and after the war, it stayed with me. I left Europe and came to America but I remained apart from both worlds.

Fortunately, I had the presence of mind that evening to note that we all needed to get back to our blocks. Misha and Naomi looked at each other sadly at the prospect of parting. Misha handled it well.

"Naomi . . . can you come here again tomorrow?"

"I'm so glad you asked! I'd love to see you again!"

They said good night and went back to their respective blocks. Naomi walked in with the women who'd been watching over from a distance. Two hearts had gladdened more than either could have thought possible that morning. Misha lay in his bunk and looked up at the beams of the roof and thought of the bright occasion that the next evening would bring.

After a dinner of thin soup, Misha went to meet Naomi by himself. As you might imagine, this was according to his request. I wasn't offended. I knew what was going on. I don't know what they talked about that night but they didn't seem to want for things to discuss. I peered out of the block from time to time and saw them chatting and even laughing.

They came to meet every evening after work and meals. Some of the men in the block looked on at the courting by the fence and their hearts too were gladdened. The same thing probably happened across the fence in the women's block. I'll bet the men and women, in the blocks and out on work details, talked about the two love birds who sat by the fence.

Misha asked me to come along every now and then, I think out of friendship. Naomi was very pleasant, a joy to be with, and a welcome break from the drudgery. I enjoyed being with them but I didn't overstay. I was always watching for guards who might come by on patrol who might find some sport in the two soulmates under the light.

"You know, Adrian," Misha said one night as he came back from the fence. "I *love* Naomi. I really do."

I probably wanted to laugh out loud and tell them that everyone in the block knew that—many of them before Misha did. I hope I held it in. "Yes, I noticed that, Misha. You're a completely different person when you're near her. You have a glow, you walk on air."

"She's smart, talented, and beautiful. I love her outlook on life now. It's changed since that first night. Oh, Adrian, I wish she and I were someplace else."

I was afraid he'd say something like that. I wanted to bring him down to earth but it was better they had love and illusion and left what might come for another day, another power. Let them look forward to a time when they could be together as a young couple should be. Let Misha's words be only of her. Let them hold hands through the fence and steal a kiss the same way. I'd watch for guards.

"I want to marry her," Misha announced on returning from a rendezvous one night.

"What!" My exclamation was instantaneous. I was unable to hide my astonishment in the least. As much as I wanted to let him live in their world of perfection and beauty, I knew that marriage was something he could not have and should not try for. Too dangerous. I suppose my response was almost a scolding. "No, Misha, no. First, you are both very young. Far too young to marry. Second, how could you get married? You and Naomi live in different blocks. The guards will never allow you to marry her."

"I know, I know," Misha agreed as the air of his dream deflated a bit. "Still, I want to tell her that. I want her to know that I want her to be my wife."

"I think it will only make you both more miserable," I told him with the blunt frankness of an honest friend. "I think you both have enough misery without creating more on your own."

"We are both almost eighteen and we truly love each other. What can be done?" He looked to me to provide an answer.

"I don't know, Misha, I simply don't." I shook my head to accentuate my bafflement and powerlessness.

Misha and Naomi continued their courtship every night through the fence, despite the fence. "Love makes the world go 'round," he announced to the block one night. The laughter was immediate and genuine and widespread. Some of those who'd been completely withdrawn might have even let a trace of a smile come across their faces as they recalled their own youths. Was there a happier couple in the camp? I don't think so. I determined to help them.

They say that an urgent need will somehow yield a solution. Well, one day a solution arrived from an unexpected quarter. Highly unexpected. It amazed us. It really did.

Adrian stopped and looked at me expectantly. I asked if he wanted me to guess what happened. He said he didn't. I asked if he wanted to end our talk for the day. Again, he said no.

"Well?"

"I think we should have some lunch," he said amused by my bewilderment.

"Easily rectified, Adrian. It's on me."

As we walked to a sandwich shop I imagined falling in love under such circumstances. I thought back to my boyhood and the glorious feeling of being in love for the first time. She and I lived in Haifa and attended the same high school. We took walks together along the Mediterranean coast and every thing and every one seemed more alive. The promise of wondrous things to come was in every ray of sunshine and on every street and on every wave gently touching the shore.

Where was Misha and Naomi's love going? What was to come to the pair? Did they look around them and see beauty, perhaps in the surrounding woods? Maybe the woods held out the promise of escape. Through some miracle they could break out from the perimeter fences or run away together from a work detail and live together in the forests. I've read of the woods becoming havens for escapees. Perhaps Misha and Naomi heard this too.

As Adrian and I ate our sandwiches we talked of new chip designs we'd read of in trade journals. There was interest in those things; we both had to compartmentalize our discussions of the past. Otherwise, we'd have been rather dubious employees. Where was Adrian's story going, I kept wondering. Adrian did close our last session with a smile. At least the arrival of tragedy would not be immediate.

COURTSHIP ALONG THE FENCE

One night Misha and Naomi remained late at the fence. They sat and held hands beneath a weathered wooden post, a light at its top, which buzzed and blinked but allowed them to see the other's face and responses and emotions. I doubt they noticed the noise, not even in wordless moments. I sat about twenty-five meters from them, on guard. I'd signal with a whispered "Hey!" and they'd quickly separate and head back to each's block until the patrol had passed and they could stealthily return.

One night I was drowsing until I heard footsteps and the angry barks of a dog. Coming swiftly on the scene was an SS guard, a menacing shepherd dog stretching out before him on a leash. I thought of "Barry," a vicious St Bernard at Treblinka, and of his equally vicious SS owner who was ironically called "Doll." Here was another guard and dog rapidly closing in on my two friends.

Misha positioned himself as though to defend Naomi and took on a brave face. I must say his effort to look virile and menacing before an armed guard was absurd. Touching, but absurd. I looked for a large rock that I might crash down on the guard's unhelmeted skull. We could hide the body somewhere. Yes, there would be reprisals but what could be done to us that wasn't already ordained? I looked on as the guard and his snapping dog came right up to them. Naomi cried from across the fence, too frightened to budge.

The guard ordered his dog to heel and he immediately complied. Misha and the guard stared at each other and in the flickering light I thought I made out a smile on Misha's face. Yes, it *was* a smile—not, however, like the sort I'd seen on those who accepted imminent death.

"Misha," the guard said. He slung his rifle and held out his arms for a moment to show he meant no harm. "Misha, do you remember me?" The guard lifted his cap higher on his forehead.

"Bruno . . . Bruno Müller. Yes, of course I remember you from that morning. We prayed together, you and I—for your mother."

"Yes, we did. By God, we did. My mother is much better for it," the guard said, looking about for peers. The dog's discretion was assured.

"I am very happy to hear that, my friend, very happy indeed."

I think they wanted to embrace or shake hands but circumstance forbade it.

"You called me 'friend'," Bruno said, shaking his head in bemusement. "It sounds so strange here and now. Welcome? Yes it's welcome. And I call you my friend also, Misha." He turned and recognized me, the Polish Kapo lad who helped bridge the chasm between SS and inmate that morning.

"Bruno," Misha said warmly, "you and I are fellow human beings. Everything else is mere happenstance. It does not reflect our humanity. It will end one day and the world will be normal again. I am sure."

Incredible, absolutely incredible. I saw a Jewish boy and an SS corporal recalling how they prayed together. And the boy called the soldier "friend." Danny, the scene of Misha and Bruno must be one of the oddest incidents of the whole period. Naomi must have been increasingly confused by this encounter across the fence from her.

"This is my dear friend Naomi. Our lives have come together owing to . . . well, to happenstance. We meet most every night. And we are in love. Very much so."

Naomi stood up from the shadows on the other side of the fence post. She was at a loss. She had no idea how to respond to an SS guard. Recognizing her bafflement, Bruno bowed slightly the extended his hand though the fence. "I am pleased to meet you, Naomi." He was courteous and gentlemanly, as though in a Berlin theater.

"It is my pleasure to meet you, Bruno," Naomi haltingly replied. A pleasant smile came to her face. Uncomfortably and slowly, but it came.

Misha saw an opportunity and decided to call in a marker, so to speak. "Bruno, I have a request, please. If you think there is nothing you can do, I will completely understand. I have to ask though."

Bruno was puzzled but a nod told Misha to go on. It dawned on me what he was about to request. Then I thought, no he wouldn't. Well, he did.

"Naomi and I are in love and we want to marry. Is there a possibility such a thing can be arranged?"

Bruno was taken aback. He wanted to oblige, but how? He looked around at the foreboding buildings and wires as he weighed the ridiculousness and wondrousness of the couple's situation. The wondrousness must have won out, though a specific plan eluded him.

"This will take some thinking, my friend. There are cracks in the system and things get done without anyone in the administration building knowing. But this . . . a wedding. By God, this will take some thinking. In the meantime, you have about one hour until I finish my patrol and another guard comes by. Be careful you two—he is unlikely to be as understanding as I am." Bruno bowed and took his leave, his dog trotting alongside. I never knew the dog's name.

Naomi breathed easier. "Misha, you have a Kapo friend and an SS friend. Are there additional surprising acquaintances in store for me? A colonel or the kommandant perhaps!"

"I don't think so," Misha said as the three of us enjoyed her endearing wit. "Naomi," he added as he reached through the fence for her hand, "he will help us. I'm certain of it."

I headed for my watch position and told the lovebirds to remember Bruno's warning of the shift change. Feeling the night chill arriving, I huddled inside my coat. I thought, for the first time in many months, of how fortunate we were. Amid all the barbarity, we were all in fairly good health, two people had found love, and we had a guard looking out for us as best he could. Moments of optimism in a death camp. There were some.

I thought again about the end of the war. Rumors of approaching armies swept through the camp and brought tremendous elation, but they led to unrealistic expectations too. The camp would be liberated in a few days. Next week we'll all be free. Then the elation faded into despair—until the next train brought new word from people who'd heard radio reports from London or Moscow.

Lately, however, I'd heard the SS guards speak of the war not going well. Their faces were no longer as buoyant as they were two years ago when German armies seemed invincible. They were worried. I suspect they were worried not just for Germany but for themselves. Justice would be swift and severe for such men. I'm grateful I saw some of it.

I hoped time would be on the side of my two friends over there beneath the buzzing light. I cleared my throat to remind them of the time and walked back toward the block.

Misha or I would see Bruno from time to time over the next few days and try to make furtive eye contact. He'd cast his eyes downward to show that nothing had yet come up. Nonetheless, Misha, Naomi, and I went about our days with something to look forward to.

One morning, as Misha and I were about to head out of the block for headcount, Bruno appeared at the entrance. The few inmates still inside froze, as the appearance of an SS guard often signaled torment or beating. We knew his presence indicated he wanted to talk to us, so we made our way behind the structure where we stood near Bruno in feigned fear and submission.

"Two weeks from today, a few dozen guards will be away on leave. Yes, camp administration has determined that such respites are good for morale and efficiency. Accordingly," he said with a momentary grin, "we will be woefully understaffed and certain parts of the camp will be empty, including one of the guest quarters."

I had no idea what he was talking about, neither did Misha. Bruno was perplexed and even annoyed by our failure to comprehend his meaning.

"That will present the opportunity," he said, carefully enunciating each word as he looked to his left and right, "for a wedding."

"Oh . . . yes! Of course!" Misha stammered while maintaining a subordinated posture.

Bruno had stayed on top of things!

"I'm not sure if my presence can be assured, my friend, but I want you to know that I've seen a traditional Jewish wedding before."

Another mind-boggling utterance from our acquaintance in the SS. Bruno saw in Misha's expression a call for explanation.

"I attended the wedding of a schoolmate's sister." Bruno enjoyed seeing our puzzlement. "The couple stood under a canopy in splendid attire, obviously deeply in love."

A few inmates walked by and looked at the SS guard and Misha and me, before turning away. I'm sure they thought we'd been picked out for abuse. They could never imagine that the SS guard was recounting his attendance at a Jewish wedding in Berlin. Bruno stopped short. Perhaps it was because he could not be seen chatting amicably with us, but I thought it was because the schoolmate was the same one he'd seen dragged from the classroom and shot in the street.

He returned to the matter of the impending marriage ceremony. There was a small building, set away from the other guard quarters, where members of the staff held small private gatherings. He had arranged to have the rooms to himself for a morning and a small group of people could be spirited in and out without attracting undue attention. Misha, he said, would have to provide a Rabbi to preside over the rite. He cautioned that the decorum might not be entirely agreeable. We didn't know what he meant and we didn't care much about decorum.

Adrian stopped here, leaving me with a number of questions. Did Bruno keep his word? Did anyone get caught? Did Misha and Naomi get married in an SS guesthouse in Auschwitz? Adrian assured me that all these questions would be answered in time. And with that, he pointed to his watch. It was eight pm, night was falling, and staff were vacuuming the offices and buffing the hallways.

I asked once more if he'd told anyone these stories before and he shook his head. He went on to say he didn't think very many people would care to hear about those days and those that did would neither comprehend nor understand. He thought that because my father had been at Auschwitz and because I had grown up in Israel I would though. I suppose that because I had become his friend, I would understand.

NUPTIALS AT AUSCHWITZ

Adrian arrived refreshed and energetic the next day. As usual, I brought rolls and coffee and we roamed down the hallway for a conference room that was not scheduled for anything that day. We did not want to get up and move in the middle of a narrative on account of a meeting for a softball game or picnic. I suppose we would have gladly moved for a bridal shower that day though.

"So the wedding . . . Misha and Naomi's wedding. I've been looking forward to this since last night, Adrian. I love weddings and look forward to those of my friends, and one day to those of my children—when I have them." Adrian smiled and said he was about to tell of an exceptionally beautiful occasion.

Well, Danny, I'm seventy years old and I've been to my share of weddings but none as amazing as Misha and Naomi's—and none as strange, as surreal. It almost seems to be a dream, though no one could have dreamed this. It also seems like something out of a movie, though no filmmaker would try to convince viewers that such a thing happened. But Danny, I was *there*. I recall it in great detail—including the decorum.

Bruno instructed us not to have more than ten people for the occasion but it was difficult to keep the "guest list" down. So on a Friday morning, Bruno marched us over to the SS guest house, which was indeed empty and sufficiently distant from the SS barracks. As we filed along, we avoided any appearance of cheerfulness. We were simply another work detail trudging off to a day's toil under the watchful eyes of a trusted SS guard and a Polish Kapo. Yes, we appeared to be just another kommando.

As we entered the room, the guests almost instantly spotted a table upon which there were liverwurst, potatoes, and pears—all lifted from the SS dining hall. The food was meant for *after* the ceremony but as you can imagine, the priorities of the guests were different and the food was gone in minutes. This might have made for a nicer ceremony as the congregants were sated and even merrier after dining on decent food after so many months of near starvation.

There were two large windows with what seemed to us to be elegant lace curtains, which we closed even though there was no one about. There were sofas, chairs, and tables complete with ornate ash trays and lighters. A glass chandelier hung from the ceiling, gracing the occasion with its delicate colors of the spectrum.

I noticed pictures of rural scenery on the walls. Germany not Poland, I thought. It was very pleasant to see green meadows, if only in pictures, after the daily scenes of grime and death.

On another wall, however, were photographs of German soldiers on the march, rifles slung on their shoulders, unmistakeable confidence and pride on their faces. Nearby were two photographs of the leader the soldiers had taken oaths to obey, even unto death. Yes, his image was there in that room which was about to hold a wedding ceremony. This was the decorum Bruno had cautioned us of.

Oh yes, Bruno brought clean uniforms for the couple. They washed up and changed into them before the ceremony. There was no white dress, bridal veil, or tuxedo, but the change of clothes was welcome.

Though we had the benefit of a Rabbi from an adjacent block, Misha began the rite with a prayer over his sacred possession. "This Tefillin was given to me on the occasion of my Bar Mitzvah by my father who went to his death a few months ago . . . only a few hundred meters from here. He told me to keep the Tefillin with me and to pray with it always. I have kept my father's wish. Every morning over the last few months, I have prayed with my friend Adrian." Eyes turned to me. Everyone there knew me, except the Rabbi. I felt embarrassed and out of place.

The Rabbi began the ceremony and the young couple was as joyous as any I'd seen in Poland or America. Rings skillfully crafted from wire were exchanged, then Misha stepped on the ceremonial glass, leading to restrained applause and exultation. Dancing ensued and so help me, Bruno took part. An SS soldier was dancing at a Jewish wedding. I can still see the images today and will remember them for the rest of my life, strange though they are, inexplicable and perhaps even revolting as they are to most people.

After twenty minutes or so of revelry, Bruno showed the young couple to an adjoining room which was used for visiting officers of significant rank. The room was as well appointed as a decent hotel in Berlin. It had a bathroom, towels, and more relevant to the occasion, a large bed. Misha and Naomi entered the room and we left them alone.

The guests went off to work details escorted by me. Bruno stayed near the quarters to guard against unexpected visitors. Happily, there were none.

That evening, in the block, I met up with Misha. He was in high spirits, as you might well imagine. I was very happy for him and so were most of the men in our block, some of whom applauded his arrival.

There was, if I may be permitted to speak in defense of a member of the SS, a tragic dimension to Bruno. He was a decent man. I truly believe that. Yet he was part of the Reich's death machinery. I make no claim as to the decency of the SS in general or any others in it. Nor can I make any claim as to Bruno's conduct in general, at Auschwitz or elsewhere. However, to me— and to Misha and Naomi as well—he was both helpful and courageous. Perhaps an offensive work routine forces us to make occasional efforts to be kind, if only in small ways. Bruno thoroughly enjoyed the wedding ceremony. He had helped create a moment of brightness amid so much night.

Adrian's voice trailed off and his head bowed down. He excused himself, saying he needed a brisk walk to clear his thoughts. I understood and went back to our office to check for messages. Out in the atrium, I saw Adrian walking among the tables and trees where workers took breaks and had lunch. There were a few people out there, even though the workday was underway.

I don't think they took notice of the balding aging man. He was old, something from the past. He'd soon be gone. That's the way it is now with young people. I doubt Adrian took much notice of them either. Same building, different worlds. I sensed that we were soon to return to the less pleasant aspects of Auschwitz.

SEPARATION

I'm sure it was the happiest day of Misha's life, whether in Lodz or in the camp. He and Naomi—no, he and his wife—continued to meet every night at the fence, beneath the light. How many marriages here in the United States last very long? How could we expect a marriage to last at a concentration camp? A marriage at Auschwitz could never bring anything but a brief respite. Still, I'm glad they had it.

One evening, only a couple of weeks after the wedding, Bruno signaled to meet us behind the block. Oh, he'd walk by and give one of us a surreptitious glance and we'd know he had something to tell us. I'm not sure how Misha felt about the upcoming meeting, but I felt dread. Bruno looked glumly at Misha for quite a while, searching for words. Finally, he announced, "Everyone in your wife's block is being moved to a sub-camp."

Auschwitz, you see, was a whole complex of camps. A few dozen or more. Inmates were moved about as circumstances demanded. Yes, the camp system was run on business principles and the managers had determined that the women were to be sent elsewhere.

Misha, as you can imagine, was devastated. It took a while for him to formulate a response. Poor boy. He could not have known that his question would bring even worse news. "How far from here?" he meekly asked.

"Quite far. But Misha, this is not the truly bad news." Bruno continued. "The women will be working on short-term projects." Bruno saw that Misha didn't entirely understand the meaning. "They are of less value. They will be worked exceptionally hard . . . and then,

146

in all likelihood, they will be sent to Birkenau. Not immediately, but in a few months. I will be able to watch over Naomi from time to time, though I can't be sure how much I can help. By God, I wish I could help more."

Misha heard the same words I did. I think he seized upon "not immediately" and "watch over" and hid from the larger meaning of Bruno's news. Only when Bruno laid his hand on Misha's shoulder did the meaning sink in.

"I am going to pray now," was Misha's eventual, soft reply.

One thing I can tell you, Danny, the next few weeks were heartbreaking. Husband and wife met whenever possible. They held hands, kissed, and embraced as best they could through the wire. Their love was strong and sweet and hopelessly doomed. Could anyone hate a fence? I did. For them, however, I think it was simply part of their relationship, regrettable though it was, and it was also blessed in their minds as the place they'd met.

There was nothing I could do to help Naomi. I determined to strive harder to keep Misha's spirits up. Nonetheless, it is amazing what the human spirit can do when it yearns for something. It is amazing to see what extraordinary courage a person can find to express his love. One day Misha and I had a conversation just before we went nodded off. He'd already met with Naomi that night and I was preparing to leave for the Kapo barracks where I occasionally stayed.

"She told me that they are going to be taken to a new sub-camp the day after tomorrow," Misha told me, his eyes fixed on the ceiling.

"So soon?" I blurted out—unwisely, I know. I realized that several weeks had passed since we'd learned of the move. "I am very sorry, Misha. So very sorry."

I expected a look of profound helplessness or a flash of anger to come across his face. Instead, I saw determination and knew he had something going on in his head—a plan or at least the kernel of one.

Determination in the outside world was one thing. Inside that place, it could be something quite different. It took determination to stand up for morning headcount. It took determination to take a beating. It took determination to grab hold of the perimeter wire. But Misha's face told me he had a plan to be with Naomi.

"What's going on in there?" I asked tapping a finger on his temple.

He smiled slightly and said, "Tomorrow, I'll climb over the fence and see Naomi. I have to."

This was rash. I'd expected more thoughtfulness. I told him the fence was maybe three meters high and lined at the top with barbed wire. He'd be cut, cut badly, and there was no way to treat such wounds. He'd get infections, maybe tetanus. Seeing that this had no effect on him, I tried another approach and said that Naomi would never agree to it.

"Yes, she rejected the idea. So I've vastly improved upon it."

I didn't want to hear it, but there was no way of stopping him.

"Since we heard of the women's transfer, my head has been racing. At headcount, I think. On a road detail, I think. As I fall asleep, I think. I have all the material. Tomorrow night, Adrian, I am going over that fence," he said pointing in its direction. "I'll use that old mattress that belonged to a man who did not return from a work detail two days ago."

"Let me guess. You haven't told Naomi about this improved plan," I said, still eager to talk him out of this.

"Not at all. She would never agree to it. In fact, she'd strongly disapprove of it." Misha smiled cunningly. "But I think my best friend will."

"And undoubtedly you expect this best friend to assist you."

"Your suspicion is well placed. Tomorrow night, you shall be my lookout for any patrol that might happen along."

"Maybe we should ask for Bruno's help?" I suggested.

"I don't want to. That man has already risked too much for us. This exercise we can accomplish by ourselves." Misha looked out into the clear moonless skies. "Tomorrow, I'll be reunited with my love. After all, who knows when I'll see her again."

Tired and weak and hardly in an environment that led to considerate wording, I said, "Yes, who knows when or even if you'll see her again." I immediately wanted to take my words back. If Misha recognized my artlessness, he was good enough to avoid any reaction.

The next night, I brought him an extra tunic and we stuffed hay between two shirts and wrapped his hands for protection from the barbed wire top. He looked ridiculous, part scarecrow, part clown. Off we went toward the fence with that foul smelling old mattress.

"The hay is already driving me crazy!" he said, grinning like a naughty boy and for a moment I saw the young boy I knew back in Lodz. "But it's all worth it," Misha's eyes sparkled. "I'll see Naomi."

We reached the fence beneath the buzzing light and Naomi welcomed our approach with a loving expression. It was for Misha of course but it warmed me too. When she noticed the straw, she showed concern but knew trying to talk him out of it would be pointless.

"Tonight, Naomi, we shall put my plan into operation," Misha announced proudly before kissing her through the fence. I gallantly turned my head and scanned the path that the guards and dogs had made over the years.

"Adrian, please be even more alert than usual tonight," Misha implored. "We'll need every moment of warning."

I nodded and headed about ten meters down the fence line, where I sat low and looked in the direction of a likely patrol and listened for a dog barking in the distance. I couldn't help but turn to watch Misha scramble a few feet up the fence then toss the mattress over the barbed wire. His clothing nonetheless snagged on the sharpened ends and I could see his hands reach about to grab hold without cutting himself too badly. He got his upper body across then holding onto the wire, he tumbled over to the other side, landing on the ground with a dull thump. Fortunately, no guard was within earshot.

"Good work," I thought before looking down the fence line once more.

Misha was rewarded by his wife's loving embrace and they walked hand in hand in the direction of the women's block where a private spot could be arranged.

After an hour or more, I'd neither seen nor heard anything. No patrol, no dog. I nodded off, confident that it would only be for a few minutes. But I'm afraid I drifted off into a deep sleep, better than I might have had in the malodorous block. I was startled awake by a hand on my shoulder. "It's only me, Adrian." It was Misha, fresh from his visit. "Time to get back."

We caught only two or three hours of sleep. Well, I caught that amount of *additional* sleep. At dawn, Misha set down to his prayers as the others exited for headcount. Bruno entered and the few remaining inmates scrambled out. He walked down to where Misha sat and sadly reported that Naomi and the other women were taken away an hour ago. I feared that Misha would run for the fence and make some frantic and foolhardy effort to reach her. However, he turned peacefully to us.

"I know, Bruno, but do not worry. I said a prayer for her now and I'll say a prayer for her every day from now on. She'll be fine. I know it." Misha's confidence was palpable. There was neither fear nor sadness. He was sure that his loved one would be able to face whatever lay ahead for her.

Faith . . . . Danny, I'd never seen such faith . . . nor have I ever had it.

When I arrived at Misha's block the next morning, he wasn't there and no one could tell me where he was. I began to fear that he'd done something rash, despite his faith and prayer. With that thought, I suddenly realized where he'd be and I hurried for the fence. I could see the stillness of the now-empty women's barracks, a door creaking noisily in the morning wind. There beneath the now dim light sat Misha, Tefillin on his arm and head.

There was utter devastation of the soul on his face. His eyes were hollow and tearful, his cheeks sagged in despair. I'd never seen him in such a forlorn state. He was a broken young man.

"No, wait," I called out. We stared at each other for a moment until I found my words. "We must pray together. I'm an outsider. I stand nearby, not understanding the meaning, yet the prayers bring me hope too." I sank into my own sadness and began to cry. "I pray for you and for me and for goodness to return to the world. I pray for the poor souls that pass through this place. The time of prayer was *ours*. You were about to pray without me, Misha. That's . . . that's not fair."

I don't know how long I'd gone without crying but I'd sealed off my emotions in an inner chamber where I thought they'd gone away. I knew then that they hadn't. Misha hugged me and we cried. We cried like children, like children with no parents, children alone in the cruelest of worlds, all alone save for each other.

As we wept I thought back to when we were little kids and tried to find something to cheer us. We'd been exploring the woods near Lodz and happened upon a beehive high up a tree from which honey dripped down to a waiting army of ants. We climbed the tree to get a better share, forgetting that Misha's father had cautioned that where there is honey, there are bees. I saw one bee flash by my nose, then a few more and a few more, until a hundred or more of the irate creatures were swarming all around us, stinging us and sending us scampering home in pain and fear. Our mothers heard our cries and held us, comforted us, and soothed our many stings.

As we held each other along the Auschwitz fence, Misha suddenly asked, "Do you remember when we cried in our mothers' arms after the bees got us?" I told him I'd just been thinking of that moment too . . . and we laughed. We laughed at our plight back then and at our plight there at the camp. We thought that we'd been through a lot together and would continue to do so. Our lives and fates were intertwined.

"Come," he said, "it's time to pray."

And so we prayed. We felt grateful for our long friendship and for our continued presence in each other's life.

We later learned that Naomi and the other women were indeed taken to a sub-camp near Auschwitz. Misha prayed for her every morning. Sometimes at night, just before I'd leave for the Kapo barracks, he'd hug me and weep silently. "I miss Naomi . . . I miss her . . . I miss her so much." The pain of her sudden departure eased in a few weeks but she was never far from his mind. He'd often say, out of nowhere, "She's fine . . . I know it." I believed him.

Misha never saw her again after that night. Neither did I. We never found out what happened to her. Naomi disappeared into the darkness, along with the other women in her block, along with many other people in that camp. It's important to think of a few individuals like her or like Misha, otherwise the entire experience becomes an incomprehensible narrative of faceless and identity-less masses and cold statistics. And the Holocaust loses its enormity.

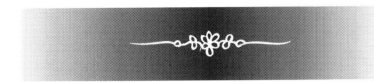

BERTHA

Adrian and I met again the next day, this time in a small coffee shop in Folsom. I thought of the paradox and potential discomfort in being not far from a large and renowned prison, though of course it had little in common with the ones Adrian and Misha had been in. I looked up at the sun and skies and thought that millions of inmates had looked up at the same sight and pondered the meaning of life and questioned the existence of God. I hoped that many of them, at least occasionally, looked up and saw beauty. I wondered if I myself would have had such thoughts and I must say I doubted it.

I'd become accustomed to Adrian's sudden beginnings.

One of the most difficult conflicts that I experienced was when I met Bertha. She was a woman there I became friendly with. Maybe a little more than friendly. I was in *love* with her, Danny. I don't know why I hesitate to say that.

I met her at a dining hall near the guard barracks. The walls had paintings of SS soldiers on the march, conveying power and unity and inevitability. It was noontime. I finished my meal of potato soup and bread with wartime margarine. Yes, we Kapos ate a little better than the inmates did. I stashed some food in my pockets for Misha. I heard a woman behind me bark out, "I need five men to work in the kitchen." It was not the mellifluous voice you hear in love stories. It was a woman's voice but an officer's command.

I turned around and there was a young woman, about five-three, maybe twenty-one, not much older than I. She stood there with her hands behind her back. Her hair was neatly gathered under military headgear with a ponytail peeking out the back—a blonde ponytail. Striking blue eyes, fair complexion, pert nose, and prominent cheek bones. Her lips looked like a small red heart. I almost think she had lipstick on. Absolutely beautiful! I couldn't stop looking at her. She saw this and smirked slightly, as though pleasantly amused by the impertinent glances of a Polish conscript boy.

I was so dumbstruck that it took a few moments to realize this woman was wearing an SS uniform. Well, she filled out that uniform better than anyone else I'd seen. She was an *Obersturmführer*—a first lieutenant in regular armies. I was just a Kapo, a junior guard, a subordinate assistant to any SS corporal or private.

"You! Go get me five laborers," she commanded, this time directly to me. Her officious tone dissolved my amorous thoughts immediately though not irreversibly.

I instinctively conveyed my compliance and was about to grab a few inmates when she ordered me to halt. What did this hold for me, I wondered as she came up to me. "I've seen you before. You are a guard but you are not sufficiently firm with prisoners." Was I about to be reprimanded? Questioned as to my loyalties? She lowered her voice to a whisper. "These five men will get extra food." And, Danny . . . she *smiled* to me. I tell you by then I'd learned to tell the difference between a cruel smile and a human one. This beautiful woman was smiling in a human way. No, in a *feminine* way. This SS officer was showing warmth to me. I rushed out to get Misha and a few others and brought them to the kitchen.

"These pots and pans need cleaning. Get to it," she coldly ordered. "Spotless! Hear me? Spotless!"

Misha and the other guys rushed to clean the dirty pots and pans, scraping off morsels of baked-on food and devouring them in an instant.

"What is your name?" she asked in a softer tone.

"Adrian Nowak, ma'am."

"Adrian . . . . a fine name. I rather like it."

"What is your name?" I found myself instinctively asking, out of bounds though it was.

"Bertha Haff."

Recalling my all but forgotten manners from my youth in Lodz, I said how pleased I was to meet her. She went on to compliment me on my looks—most welcome to a poor lad. "But what do you have to do with these *Jews*? Why don't you treat them the way the guards and other Kapos do?"

I was alarmed by this. Was she going to ask me if any of them were my friends or, worse, was I a "Jew lover"? Was the warmth I saw just a ruse expertly played on a boy with little experience with women? "What do you mean, ma'am? I simply perform my job as best I can."

She turned to the work detail and pointed to one of the men. "Shoot him!" she barked to one of the two guards there in the kitchen. He put down a plate and obediently drew his pistol. She gauged my reaction. "No wait. Shoot this one." She pointed at Misha and I was unable to hide my concern.

"No, not that one. Please," I found myself saying.

"So you have a preference here? Is this Jew your friend?" She was amused by my pleading and I thought I was in store for another experience with SS sport.

I weighed her question for a second or two and slowly, quietly, and quite unexpectedly said, "Yes. He is my best friend." Why had I said that? She could have Misha and me shot on the spot. I might have been more tired than usual. I might have been more frightened than usual. But I honestly think that something compelled me to be honest. Her smile . . . her offer of more food . . . I don't know. She studied my face, weighing some hidden thoughts, Misha's life was in the balance.

"Never mind," she told the guard. "Let him finish the work." The soldier re-holstered his pistol and eagerly returned to his meal.

"What is it you have for these Jews?" she quietly asked, with a puzzled look. You are not a Jew—I can tell that. So how can you have such a vile creature as a friend? No, as your *best* friend, as you admit?"

I told her of Lodz and our parents and our apartment building. She seemed interested. The idea of having a Jew friend disgusted yet intrigued her.

"It is a remarkable coincidence that you are both here and that you are his guard. No, you are his guardian. What a story. Perhaps this can be written down someday. The Kapo who protected a Jew. Quite a story."

I thought that writing such a story was unlikely. There didn't seem to be a large readership for such a topic at the time. She kept looking at me, trying to comprehend this walking paradox, this Kapo who befriended a Jew.

"You are sweet, Adrian. You are a sweet young man."

That was as strange a thing a woman has ever said to me. She went back to an office in the rear of the dining hall and the work detail breathed a little easier. The SS guards were more interested in food than in torment just then. When the pots and pans were clean, I marched the detail out the back where Bertha was signing for a truckload of supplies.

"The prisoners have completed the task," I reported—in a leading manner, I thought.

"That will be all then."

"Yes, of course . . . but there was mention of extra food."

She came to me as would an upset teacher. "You have nerve, Kapo. You should be thankful that I didn't kill your friend there. You know, it may *seem* to you that we are on the same level here but it is certainly not the case. You are as impudent and vexing as can be!"

I knew quite well that, given the circumstances, she was right about my impertinence. So I apologized. She of course could have summoned a guard at any time.

"No extra food for your Jews," she said briskly. It was hard to accept that such a beautiful woman, with such evident warmth, could become so heartless, so suddenly. I felt disappointed in her. I'd expected more. Why had I expected her to be different from the other SS?

I prepared to march the detail back to the block when I heard her voice again. "Adrian," her voice was again soft, feminine, even alluring, "would you like to meet later tonight?" My head reeled as her personality had changed again so suddenly. My German was reasonably good but had I heard her right? Was she . . . how do they say now, coming on to me? I don't know if I spoke or simply nodded. She then suggested meeting her at the rear of the dining hall at seven. "I'll be here," she promised.

No one heard us arrange our rendezvous but back at the block Misha clearly recognized my excitement and asked, "What was going on between you and that SS woman?"

I laughed. My spirits were raised, my masculinity was affirmed, and I felt giddy. What boy with such emotions running through him can keep from talking about what was racing through his mind? I had to talk with Misha about this.

"She invited me to meet with her tonight after dinner."

Misha was stunned but then he too laughed. "She *is* quite pretty. I saw how you were looking at her. I would also fall for her under different circumstances. Go with what your heart tells you." He put his hand on my shoulder. "But Adrian, my friend, be careful."

I released a long sigh and my boyish dizziness diminished a little. "You're right, Misha. We both heard her in the kitchen. One moment she orders someone shot, the next she orders a halt. She's one of them, yet not entirely."

Misha was wise, wiser than I. "Don't make a premature judgment. You don't know her and she may be different. Go and meet with her tonight. *Watch* yourself."

Bertha and I met at the appointed time and place. She was in a fresh uniform and she had a light perfume that reminded me how grubby my life was. Thankfully, I was able to wash up a bit at a guard barracks so I wasn't entirely out of place.

"Let's go for a walk," she suggested, almost as though we were in a city park. I know I chuckled slightly and said it was hardly the place for a romantic stroll. Initially taken aback, she soon enough appreciated my wit—a trait which I think was not in great abundance among the boorish staff at the camp. "You are a clever young man, Adrian. No, this is not a place for walks at sunset. This place would not be my first choice."

"It's what we have for the moment," I added, completing her thought.

"Yes, it's what we have now . . . . Besides, we can stay near the administration building and hospital and avoid the less attractive places. You are different, Adrian. You are different from the other Kapos and guards and staff."

Again, I felt her acceptance so I replied with my established wit, "That's a welcome observation, but of course the camp personnel are drawn from jails and outcasts and the like. So yes, I am different." She did not offer any reply so I invited one. "Am I wrong?"

"No, Adrian, you're not wrong. The staff here do not come from the better elements of German society. Not by any means. Still, I wonder why it is that you are different."

Bearing in mind that I had to watch my tendency for impertinence, I asked Bertha where she was from.

"Stuttgart. My father is an officer, a colonel in the infantry serving bravely on the Russian front now. I volunteered for service in the SS and naturally was sent to officer school. I wanted to be on the Russian front too but I was posted here. I'd much prefer to be on the field of battle, nonetheless our work here is also serving the Reich."

I gave her a skeptical look as I enjoyed the ability to speak freely. "How, may I ask, is this camp serving your country?"

"Oh, you simply don't understand!" she said in amused toleration of what to her was my lack of comprehension. "Adrian, you are not a German. You are not of the Aryan race. I need to teach you about our nation."

"I've heard a good deal about it already. I heard it in the training I received at Treblinka. I heard it from guards here and from some of the other Kapos. The German people are the master race and the rest of us are inferior and of questionable usefulness in German Europe. Isn't that the German view of things?" My voice rose in sarcasm.

"Yes, exactly. So you *do* understand us, Adrian."

She completely missed my point. She deceived herself into thinking that I'd accepted the German worldview—*Weltanschauung.*

"Oh, of course I understand. I understand it to be untrue!" No amount of Nazi indoctrination could have shielded anyone from my meaning then. Anger flashed across her face as she realized she'd completely misunderstood me, embarrassing herself in front of a Slavic lad her junior. Her eyes seemed lethal, like twin sniper scopes aiming at me. Her beauty raced away into an inner place from which I hoped it would soon return. I was sure that I'd just crossed a line and that my life was in peril.

"How *dare* you say that the wisdom of our leaders is nonsense? How *dare* you? They have studied history from ancient times to the present and have given the German people and the world the results of their efforts, which is brilliant and moving as well." Her words came out like venom from a serpent.

Where I found my courage, I know not. I shot back. "I've heard some of the SS people speak of exterminating a race for its beliefs. Is this brilliant? Is this moving? You have to realize what this is." We stopped our walk near the administration building and faced each other. "You are killing hundreds of thousands of men, women, and children. They've done nothing wrong at all."

"Oh, you poor boy, you are so ignorant, so naive. The Jews are a plague on us all. Are you forgetting that only ten years ago they brought an immense depression to Germany and the whole world? They stole our money and jobs. Are you forgetting who ended the depression and brought us back as a powerful nation? It was not the Jews, it was the National Socialists—the Nazis. It was Adolf Hitler, Adrian. It was our Führer."

It was my turn to take on an understanding approach. Mine, however, was sincere. Hers was a mask through which she expressed her disrespect for me—a Polish boy. "I see that you truly believe this, Bertha. But old people, women, and children do not bring depressions. Such people do not deserve those gas chambers and incinerators over there." I pointed to the chimneys in the distance which poured out thick smoke and a foul stench all day. "You bring people who never lived in Germany and who never could possibly have brought down its economy and then you kill them in their thousands."

She was stunned. I wasn't sure if it was from my insolence or my argument. It was an important matter. I didn't back down, Danny. You'd have been proud of me.

I was indeed proud of him. Who else do I know who argued against Nazi propaganda with an SS officer, albeit a fetching woman SS officer?

We began to walk once more, now in the direction of the staff hospital. Had we stayed in the same spot, our differing opinions could have led to shouting and worse. Walking had a soothing effect, I think.

"That's all there is to it. Your people went through a terrible experience in the 1930s. So did everyone in Europe, everyone in the world. Out of that terrible experience came terrible men with terrible plans. There are many Germans who do not believe your leaders. They are too frightened to speak out. They know what will happen to them. I am just a stupid Polish boy. My views are meaningless—as is my life, it seems. I simply perform my work here and no one even knows of my existence or cares of my opinion."

She stopped again. I didn't know what was coming.

"You know, Adrian, you indeed are a stupid Polish boy." Her voice became stern and each word was spoken slowly and clearly. "You must be more careful how you speak of the Third Reich. You see my uniform. You see the skull and lightning bolts of the SS. I am *proud* to be a National Socialist."

I looked into her eyes and yes, I *saw* a National Socialist. A Nazi soldier who took part in the camp's operations and was proud she did. But I also saw femininity and emotions. My next words came less from a rational assessment of the moment than from an emotional response within it.

"Yes, but you are also a woman . . . a *beautiful* woman."

The sharpness of our debate flew from us and we giggled like children, perhaps by the foolishness of my previous words which every boy and girl had heard in many a film and radio drama. I took her hand. So help me, Danny, I took her hand. I took the hand of Lieutenant Bertha Haff, daughter of Colonel Haff, who was then serving in a regiment to the east.

"I liked you from the moment I first saw you," I whispered, my eyes not far from hers.

"I've seen you about the camp for many weeks now. There was something *delicate* about you that I found attractive. I wanted to meet you and I had to create an excuse to meet you. I freely confess that to you here tonight." No whisper ever had such feminine wile. "I do not care for your opinions or friends though." A feigned look of ire came and went.

"We will not agree on our politics or our friends then, it would seem."

"This weakness you have for Jews . . . it's part of a larger aspect of you that I like—a softness, a tenderness."

We stood silently once more. Something was balanced in the moment but thankfully it was not my life.

"Will you come back to my room?" she asked almost shyly. "There's a shower . . . you can freshen up."

The prospect of a shower was almost as appealing as the implied benefit to follow! My look must have betrayed my concern with getting caught.

"Don't worry. The girls bring men to their rooms all the time."

We laughed and headed for "her place," as they say.

Her quarters contained two twin beds separated by a table with a radio. The walls held photographs of Olympic athletes, dark forests, and a Wehrmacht officer I presumed was her father. "I have no roommate now," she whispered. It tells us a great deal about my living conditions that my desire to take a shower took precedent over any other. After my quick reacquaintance with soap and warm water, she served a beef and potato dish she'd prepared at the dining hall kitchen. A few bites of the stringy meat and I stopped.

"What's wrong, Adrian?" Her expression was of concern.

I shook my head and looked about at the surroundings. They were humble by, say, middle-class styles, yet to me they were palatial. I could not have expressed my feelings at that moment. Fortunately, she could.

"You don't feel right enjoying my food and drink accommodations while your friend is placed in one of the blocks."

How to describe this? Perceptive? Yes, she was that. I think that's one of the things I appreciated about her and one of the reasons I fell in love with her. Yes, we succumb to more than beauty and charms in women.

"Well, Adrian, if it will ease you conscience, I can put some of this food in a bag and you can bring it back to your friend over there."

It was bewildering, at least to me. She was cold and warm. An SS officer and a woman. She was my superior and about to be my lover. Well, we looked intently into each other's eyes and I told her she was a good woman who could read my feelings and respond to them. She replied that she appreciated the protectiveness I'd shown. She thought of it as a feminine characteristic, even a maternal one, but that it nonetheless fit well with the rest of me.

We embraced and I could not hold myself back anymore. We kissed and kissed and kissed more. Older and more experienced than I, she directed us to the next levels of passion. We made love all night. She was my first, Danny.

Of all the special and loving and awkward and humorous first experiences I'd heard of, this was certainly the most unusual. This man's first woman was an SS officer—a true believer in the Reich and its objectives. Many things in life just force me to shake my head.

I loved Bertha. Most every night I would find a way to slink over to her barracks then into her room and into her arms. She had no roommate for many weeks and later, when she did have one, there was an understanding.

My affair, if that's the word, with Bertha meant that Misha and I spent less time together. He understood. My evening departures must have made him think of Naomi. That saddened me, though I know he was happy for me. "I knew young love and remember the beautiful feeling," he used to say. "I am still in love with my wife and I always shall be."

Bertha and I discussed politics every now and then. That is to say, we discussed Nazi ideology and its practice. I was never able to change her mind, nor could she change mine. She saw my protectiveness as a positive thing in some ways. It made me affectionate and loyal and that endeared me to her. She indulged me by giving me food to sneak back to the block. My protectiveness was, however, a flaw in most other regards. It held me back from seeing the superiority and strength of German culture and how it was destined to spread over the weaker people and destroy some of them.

I told her that the flaw in her cultural-superiority philosophy was easily refuted by a quick look at the train depot, the selection yard, and the chimneyed destinations of the weak. I never made any progress with her. Well, at least that's what I thought. I don't know how to say this without sounding sympathetic to her, but dwelling inside her, beneath those dreadful ideas, was a loving woman capable of kindness and compassion. Yes, it's true. I almost wish I could tell you that she was simply a Nazi robot. She wasn't. She just wasn't. As the modern expression goes, we agreed to disagree and we dwelled on the positive things we shared.

Well, one day there were signs of change in her. Where did it all lead though?

I sensed that Adrian had grown tired so we called it a day. He also seemed quite burdened when he stopped, which made me wonder what was to come. I had much to think about. A Nazi with a heart of gold? There are indeed complexities in people that perplex us and annoy us. In any case, Adrian was by no means defending her beliefs. In talking to him, I was always impressed by his honesty and decency. I hope that people back then were similarly impressed.

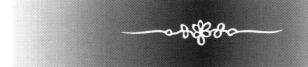

REDEMPTION

I used to tell Bertha that other people's beliefs constituted the bases of their lives and many had a longer and more distinguished heritage than the beliefs then fashionable in Germany. I might have expressed this more delicately than I do here though. The beliefs of others gave them strength and hope and constituted no threat to her own beliefs or those of her country. I wanted her to see this for herself. So I asked her to come to one of the inmate blocks—Misha's, as you might have already guessed. I didn't expect a sudden change, only a sowing of the seeds of doubt. I'd certainly have welcomed that.

I awaited her one chilly mist-shrouded morning. You couldn't see more than a hundred meters ahead. The inmates were mostly out for headcount and I'd explained to the guards that an SS officer was arriving soon for Misha and me to do work in a mess hall. Do you know how much the guards feared officers? It was almost comical.

An hour went by but at last I saw someone gradually appearing from the fog. A woman, in uniform. Yes, Bertha was heading toward us. No, we didn't display any form of personal interaction on her arrival.

"Come," I said as though we were discussing a small matter about a work detail, "I want to show you something inside." She looked disinterested but in we went and there was Misha on his bunk. I handled the awkward introductions as well as could be imagined. Misha said that I'd told him many good things about her and she smiled, though I'm not sure precisely why. She did not speak. I suspect she was revolted by the sight of this grimy Jewish boy in a row of fetid bunks.

She and I watched silently as Misha bowed and began his prayers over the Tefillin. His dedication and fervor were obvious, seemingly filling the empty dank barracks with warmth and life. It dawned on her, she later admitted, she'd never met a Jew before, at least not in any meaningful sense. She'd only seen them on the streets of her hometown and of course here at Auschwitz. They were faceless abstractions without any human connection to her. All the easier, then, to believe the worst about them.

As he prayed fervently, I told Bertha about the Tefillin, about how his father had given them to him five years ago in 1939. I said that Misha did this every morning and that others joined him, often when they were near despair. I went on to say that they weren't always Jewish and that at least one German Lutheran had prayed with him. I shouldn't have said that but Bertha was too absorbed by the ritual unfolding before us.

"These prayers give people here hope, Bertha. Hope for a better day. Even amid all this. He prays just as his father did, and his father before him, going back thousands of years."

Bertha spoke not one word. Her eyes were fixed on this boy before her, this boy who didn't fit well with her worldview, this boy she could have had killed a few weeks ago in the kitchen. An occasional glimmer of compassion came across her face, soon followed by revulsion. But revulsion of what? I don't think it came from the sight of a hideous Jew. No, I think she was sickened by Misha's tattered clothing, the cold filthy interior, and the stenches that came from within the block and from without.

Misha kissed the Tefillin and looked over to Bertha and me, a look of serenity on his face. Bertha shuddered slightly and excused herself. "I have much work before me today. *Aufwiedersehen.*" Misha and I thanked her for coming. Misha wondered aloud what would come of this morning. We recognized that there were risks but Misha said that he trusted my judgment and that everything would be fine. "Our hearts tell us the right things to do," he said.

I thought of the possibilities. She could respond angrily, either from her convictions or from the blow to them. She could brush it off as the quaint rite of a strange people. Did she still think this strange people had to be wiped off the face of the earth?

I sensed that she was deeply affected by that morning, though I didn't see any change, at least not in the days immediately following. We didn't discuss the matter. We went on as before and I was beginning to think that whatever the experience had meant to her had been short-lived and she was back in the comfort of her beliefs.

Several weeks later, as were asleep in her quarters, I felt her trembling and thought she was having a bad dream. When I held her, she awoke but the trembling continued. In fact, it worsened. She was out of breath, sweat streamed down her forehead, and her heart hammered almost audibly. She tried to speak but was only able to emit gasps and sobs. It was a panic attack, common enough in the blocks. Inmates with medical training taught us how to respond by breathing calmly along with the afflicted ones. I held her in my arms, rocked her back and forth, and breathed slowly with her until she calmed.

"I don't know what happened to me, Adrian. There was a dream and I awoke and . . . . I've killed people, Adrian!" She started to shake again, though not as badly. She wanted to continue. "I've killed many of them on many occasions . . . in training, in work, for no real reason."

I didn't know what to say. I couldn't tell her things I didn't believe. I couldn't tell her that she was mistaken or that she had meant well. I thought it best to simply hold her and comfort her. Coming to grips more fully with what she'd done would have to wait for another day. She eventually fell back to sleep.

I didn't though. I remained awake all night and left early in the morning. There was little in the way of a farewell that morning, but we had parted ways. Bertha had murdered people. I didn't know precisely how but her panic suggested they were dark events. I kept making up excuses for not meeting with her. Misha of course noticed something.

"What's happened between you and Bertha?" he abruptly asked one night.

"Nothing . . . nothing at all." I tried to brush the subject aside. I failed.

"Did you have a fight?" That was a reasonable suspicion, not far from the truth.

"No, everything is fine. We just haven't had time to meet for a few days." I failed again.

"Adrian, *what happened*?" My friend's eyes demanded explanation.

"She told me that she'd killed people, Jewish people." Misha nodded silently. I suppose the thought was not as foreign to him as I'd suspected. After all, his view of her was never clouded by romantic notions. "It was on more than one occasion . . . in training . . . other times too. She woke up in the middle of the night and admitted it to me. No, she *confessed* it to me in a blind panic. You've seen it here before."

"So the matter has great emotional power inside her. It's not just a distant event."

"I think so . . . . I'm not sure where she and I are anymore. I'm not sure I can see her anymore."

Misha said that my reaction was understandable. He showed considerable concern for my wellbeing. He offered no specific recommendation. He told me to look inside her heart and see if there was true remorse. He urged me to bear in mind that she had grown up in a certain way and been taught in a certain way. He thought that my relationship with her had caused her to reexamine her beliefs and that this was good. He went on to say that change never comes easily or quickly and that he was always ready to listen to me and help in any way.

I think Misha would have made a fine Rabbi.

One evening, a sudden silence outside Misha's block announced the arrival of an SS figure. I suspected who it was and when I turned to look, there she was. Men skulked away fearfully. I wanted to do the same, though I feared much less. I didn't know what to say or do. Misha greeted her—rather graciously. "Good evening. Good to see you again." Bertha was uneasy about being there and Misha's elegant manners utterly disarmed her. She thanked him. Her voice was soft and feminine, as though at a family dinner.

"I've come to see Adrian Nowak."

I nodded to her as though in obedience and told Misha I'd see him in the morning and went off with her, our hands occasionally brushing, eager to do more. Our feet took us, naturally enough, back to her barracks. We embraced, expressed our regrets at not seeing each other, and made love. A few hours later she was again stricken by a fierce panic attack. I calmed her again and she said that she was having the attacks every night. Meeting Misha in the barracks that morning had brought them on. Wisely or not, I promised to be with her.

And so our separation was over. I fell in love with her all the more, as her needs drew me in. As she once observed, I had a protective nature. It manifested itself toward Misha and also toward a guilt-ridden SS officer.

Our nightly meetings, though always inside the fences, were temporary escapes from Auschwitz. She was not German and I was not Polish and the world was not amid a catastrophic war. We even found a place to walk that was as far from death as possible. We talked about our childhoods and what plans we'd made in those days. She'd wanted be a performer. She enjoyed music and dance and hoped to apply to a conservatory to pursue those interests. Then the war came and she like millions of people had to change her plans. I envisioned her in that conservatory and in time becoming a talented performer, traveling about the continent, renowned in cities from Warsaw to Paris.

One night she asked me what I was going to do after the war. The question caught me by surprise. It made me realize how my life and hopes had been confined since conscription. I sighed and answered that I saw no point in making plans until the war was over. She said that the war would end someday. All wars do, even immense ones like the one we found ourselves in. I said that even when the war ended, we would never be able to put all this behind us. It would dwell inside us forever—reminding us, haunting us, maybe even tormenting us. *Forever.* I said I'd be angry if the world simply put the war and the death camps behind them. Not everything is meant to be forgiven and forgotten. There would be investigations and trials and judgments.

Bertha remained silent. Again, I wanted to take back my words even though I'd never spoken more truthfully and sincerely. Everyone knew the war was not going well for Germany. I had heard guards say that the Treblinka camp in northeastern Poland was being dismantled because the Russians were nearing it. The gas chamber was being taken down brick by brick. I expected an explosion from Bertha. I got a whimper.

"What will become of me?"

I must confess that my visions of postwar justice often included gallows and firing squads but at that moment I banished them from my mind. I needed to tell her something. I said that the judgment would be shaped by the testimony of prisoners and that any guard or Kapo who'd shown mercy would be shown mercy himself—or herself. Oh . . . I don't think I truly believed that. I just wanted to give her hope and a reason to listen to the warmer parts of her soul.

It must have been several minutes before she spoke.

"Yes, I truly believe that those who show mercy shall be shown mercy. There is a poetic quality in those words which appeals to my sense of right and wrong. But Adrian, what about your words of all this dwelling inside us, haunting and tormenting us, in every waking hour and at unexpected moments of our sleep. Will the testimony of inmates free us from our own consciences?"

I thought of that SS guard who shot himself in the head and recalled that Bertha had a pistol in her room. She continued.

"Our own conscience is stronger than the opinion and judgment of another. Those who do evil will have to live with themselves. Today, they can blame others and go about what they see as their duty. One day, those excuses will disappear or they will be shattered. And those who do evil will be pursued relentlessly by their consciences, by themselves, by voices within."

We never raised the issue again but it was with us every moment. It weighed on Bertha more than it did on me, as I wasn't there on my own will and I was closer to an inmate than to a guard. I should think I was far closer to an inmate, though not above blame and not beyond the reach of conscience or later judgment. It weighed more heavily on her with each day. She became withdrawn and joyless— even embittered. I tried to show her a good deal of affection but it helped only a bit and only for a while. Our relationship used to lift us above the dread of the camp but now it seemed that death was closing in on us—more on her though.

Adrian put his head between his hands and cried. I'd seen him become emotional at several points in our meetings. This was something different, something more overwhelming. I kept my silence and thought it best to continue anther day, but then Adrian spoke.

I loved her with all my heart . . . and I'm pleased that I found good in her. But bringing out the good in someone in a place like that . . . well, it can have unfortunate consequences. She kept it all to herself and I never imagined that she could do what she did. It was utterly unimaginable.

Bertha had about six SS guards assigned to her mess hall who watched over inmate laborers and even helped out with the food at times, probably because it gave them first shot at the pies. A new guard was assigned to her mess hall one day. His name was Alfred and he was a mean bastard. No other way to put it. Even by SS standards, he was exceptionally cruel. We'd come to see mealtimes as a break from hard work and abuse, but not with Alfred around. No, not with Alfred around.

When assigned to supervise spooning out the soup to inmates, he'd have his sport. He'd swat an inmate's bowl so that some of the meager portion splashed onto the floor and the poor inmate's caloric intake plummeted that day. Sometimes Alfred would knock the bowl to the ground and crush it under his thick leather boot. Well, if you lost your bowl, you lost your meals and that meant inevitable deterioration. Alfred knew that. Of course, he knew it.

He more than most also took pleasure in beating people. No reason. I recall one time Alfred studied a group waiting in the chow line until one poor guy stood out for some reason, then he began to club him with the butt of his machine pistol—a Schmeisser, as it's known. Over and over, the chest, groin, stomach, and head, until he was dead. He wasn't the only one to die at the dining hall. We came to call this guard "Mad Alfred," though needless to say not in his presence.

I was standing on the side of the mess hall one evening, more or less supervising the line of tired men shuffling slowly ahead to get a serving of watery potato soup which would sustain them another day, if only barely. Some of the younger and healthier men were speaking to one another, others were simply too exhausted or resigned. I was looking outside and saw more lines of tired men when I heard a blow land and a cry of pain.

Mad Alfred had struck Misha.

My friend picked up his bowl and prepared to leave the mess hall without any food. That was one way of avoiding Alfred's unreasoning rage. Just leave. Better to be hungry than beaten or worse. Perhaps Alfred had seen enough of this tactic or perhaps he just wanted more sport that evening, but he clubbed poor Misha across the head with his machine pistol. Such hatred on his face. I can still see it. Misha fell again to the ground.

"Stand up, you filthy Jew," Alfred shouted at the top of his lungs.

I instinctively went over to protect him, though I had no idea how this might be accomplished. My mind raced. How could I get Misha out of this? There was no way to calm Alfred, yet I had to do something. Misha climbed to his knees and I sensed another blow was about to come down on him, but Alfred wanted to protract the moment and savor it. He determined to accentuate things with a little more verbal abuse before returning to the physical.

"You are the scum of the earth! You do not deserve to live!" Alfred's face reddened and twisted into a hideous sneer. "What do you have to say in your defense, Jew?"

Misha remained quiet. He knew all too well that no matter what he said, Alfred would respond with more hatred. This was not a conversation or a debate. It was a sadistic game. Silence might other times have had a calming effect as the tormentor saw his mastery and was pleased by it. Bruno was not in sight; his corporal rank could have silenced this loutish private. Nor was Bertha around; her officer status would have had the same effect.

"I'll ask one more time. What do you have to say, Jew?" Down came Alfred's machine pistol across Misha's skull and once again the poor lad cried out in pain.

Someone shouted, "Don't do that again!"

It took me a moment to recognize that I had been the one who barked out those words, more forcefully than I thought myself capable of. My hands were formed into fists and I was poised to fight Mad Alfred.

"What did you say, Kapo?" Alfred was almost as astonished by my words as I was. His attention turned fully onto me.

"I said don't do that anymore," I repeated in a quieter though determined way. I think the dolt's head was spinning.

"Why not? He is a mere Jew—not a human." He checked my patch and determined that I was a Pole not a Jew, and this was made my boldness all the more incomprehensible to him. He found himself reacting to my words. He was on the defensive. "What concern is this to you, *Polish* Kapo? You Slavs are almost as worthless as Jews!" He laughed, turned back to Misha, and announced with satisfaction, "And now, Jew, you will die."

I leaped toward him and grabbed hold of his machine pistol. Our faces were inches apart. His eyes showed complete hate and his foul breath struck me. His mouth shook as we grappled over the weapon. The inmates stepped back, sure that no good would come from this, rewarding though it was to see someone fight Alfred.

"What are you doing, Kapo?" Alfred said haltingly, his face grimacing from exertion. This Polish boy was putting up a stronger fight than either one of us thought possible. But older, stronger, and better fed, Alfred won out and I fell to the floor. He leveled his machine pistol at me and the other guards leveled their weapons on the inmates lest there be an uprising like the one they'd heard took place in Treblinka a few months ago. Misha pleaded with Alfred to kill him and spare me. Alfred turned to me.

"Kapo, you care for a Jew's life? I always thought you Polish Kapos had enough sense to at least hate Jews. Ha! Now this is something I've never seen before . . . and I will ensure that I never see it again. I'm going to kill you both." I looked down the barrel of his weapon. I saw cruelty in an abstract form that was no longer part of a man. It was some sort of evil essence that roams the earth and inhabits people from time to time and this night, it had settled inside Alfred. I was sure I was about to die and I felt that at least I would perish while doing something good. I prepared myself fro whatever death would bring.

I heard a sharp crack—a single shot—but didn't feel anything. Would fierce pain suddenly hit me? Was I already dead and beyond pain? I looked up and saw a hole in Alfred's forehead. A perfectly round hole that changed from black to red. Alfred had a stupid, stunned look on his face as blood poured from his wound and he crumpled to the ground, a faint look of consciousness still visible.

"This . . . you deserve, private."

It was Bertha's voice. It was Bertha's shot. She stood over him, her Walther P-38 in hand. The other guards raised their weapons but they were in a quandary. One of them had been shot dead but by an officer—a woman officer, someone of greater authority than theirs. I'm sure their minds reeled. So did mine.

Bertha stood near me but addressed everyone in the hall, especially the SS guards, who were still unable to comprehend how to respond. The inmates, though glad to see Alfred die, thought there might be a mass reprisal right there in the mess hall. They looked warily for the doors but most were reluctant to flee.

"I've killed many innocent people, just as this thug was about to kill these boys. It was wrong! *All this* is wrong!"

I alone there understood how the guilt and shame had been building in her. It had tormented her, torn her in two. She'd been searching for a way to put an end to her nightmares and panics. She no longer thought that postwar justice would be lenient and she sought her own justice, her own redemption, and a punishment of her choosing.

"You men," she shouted to the guards, "look around you. What do you see?" No reply came, though she was an officer and an officer's words ordinarily demanded a reply. "What you see are innocent people."

One of the guards, a corporal, finally spoke. "Come with us . . . come with us, please." Getting no response, he spoke louder, though still respectfully. "Come with us, Frau Oberleutnant."

Bertha turned and spoke softly to me.

"I want it to end this way, here and now. They'd hang me after the war, I know it." My mind raced trying to understand where this was going. "Even if I lived, my mind wouldn't give me a moment's peace. There would be nothing but torment—ceaseless and growing torment."

She smiled in a strangely serene way and checked her pistol.

"I can do nothing about past murders, but I stopped one tonight. Why don't we see our mistakes earlier?"

Her serenity and clarity indicated she knew her course and I knew this night would not end well. "Bertha . . . don't . . . please don't."

"Goodbye, Adrian," she whispered. "I love you."

She raised her Walther and fired two shots into the stunned corporal. Most of the guards were too dumbfounded to respond but two of them fired their weapons into her. The fusillade was deafening in that enclosed hall. Smoke filled the room and dust flew from the lighting and window sills. Inmates hurled themselves to the ground, some fully expecting a massacre to follow as killing had been set loose. Two or three bullets ripped into Bertha's torso and arm and she fell to the floor like a broken doll. The reverberation of the gunfire faded into silence.

Most of the guards scurried for help and for an officer to tell them what to do. What had just happened was well out of the ordinary and well beyond ability of simple guards to deal with. A single guard sat down at a table, fearful of what might happen for shooting an officer, sickened by the idea of having killed a German woman. His machine pistol lay uneasily before him.

I crawled to Bertha and held her. Misha stood just behind me.

"Bertha! Why did you do that?" I demanded as my anger mixed with pain. I could see her life slipping away and I started to cry. "I love you . . . I love you."

She weakly clutched my arm and spoke as best she could. "Do not be angry . . . I couldn't continue. It's good you are here with me now . . . a better gift I could not hope for."

She was shivering. I wanted to warm her but with what? All I could do was hold her. I tried to pull her close but the motion only tore into her wounds and caused her to cry out. My tears fell onto her tunic and mixed with the blood pulsing from her chest. I bit my lips to prevent breaking into childish sobs, so much so that I cut into my lips.

"Adrian . . . ." She tugged on my arm and our eyes met for the last time. Beautiful even in that state. "Don't cry," she whispered faintly as her hand brushed away my tears. "Don't cry, Adrian," she repeated. Then her hand fell to her side and life escaped from her eyes.

I held her lifeless form and wept. I'm not sure for how long. It was Misha who showed sense. He put his arm on my shoulder and said, "Adrian, we have to go. There will be trouble here soon."

Most of the inmates had already scurried back to the blocks. Misha and I could hear whistles and barking dogs and we knew that in a moment a full squad or two of SS guards would be on the scene. I replayed what she'd done and said, unable to comprehend that it had truly taken place. The acrid smell of gunpowder had a convincing effect and I came back into the moment. I folded Bertha's arms across her front then got up and walked out of the mess hall.

No one ever asked any of us for accounts of what had happened that night. I presume they grilled the guards who'd been there, but it was an embarrassment to the SS and they probably covered the incident up. After all, an SS officer would never have questioned the operations of Auschwitz.

The joy and optimism I'd known over the last few weeks were gone and I slid back into despair, accented by countless replays of the shootings that night. The next morning as Misha and I prayed, I asked God to have mercy on Bertha, but I wondered if he had any reason to listen to me.

I suggested that Adrian go home and rest. He sat in the room a few moments then left. I think he'd been praying.

MAX

Adrian and I spoke only about work matters for well over a week. I knew by then that he'd pick up again when he saw fit. I knew he wanted to see this through, painful though it was for him. I can say, without slighting Adrian's pain, that it was often unpleasant for me as well. My dreams were haunted by images of trains and fences and smoke.

I thought about these images my soul kept showing me and concluded, or at least suspected, that the fences represented the divide between those who were there and those who were not. As much as we read and listen and think we understand the period and place, we do not. We do not and we cannot. It's absurd and insulting for people to think they do.

My dreams of looking through a fence at crowds of people were unpleasant but they were also reminders, cautions. They announce to me, "Danny, you were never here with us."

Adrian and I sat on a balcony after work and enjoyed the gentle warmth of the late-afternoon sun. We'd had a long day. Many problems surfaced in a design—fuse effects, antennae. Oh, but that's technical talk and suffice it to say we made headway in fixing them and the design would be on time after all. We were tired and eager to relax. I said that after such a hectic day, it was good to have some pleasantness. How could that be a cue?

You know, the sun shone and momentary joys came, even in Auschwitz. Impossible though this sounds, we found such moments. I've mentioned Naomi and Bertha. Nonetheless, it was chiefly a long period of darkness . . . . You know, Adrian, we had a pet dog.

I might have chuckled a bit at this too. A pet dog. It was very much part of war movies for the guys to adopt an orphaned pooch, but in Auschwitz?

Yes, his name was Max. I have no idea where he came from. Maybe he ran off from the SS kennel or he just wandered in from the village of Oswiecim or the woods. Anyway, he was an amazing little guy.

One morning, after we completed our prayers and started to prepare for the day, we heard a high-pitched yapping. Misha and I looked at each other in amusement—and in boyish expectations. A puppy? Here? Another yap came. We looked outside and noticed a little pooch looking around sadly. Black, brown, and gray fuzz. He was a shepherd. What you call a German shepherd. It was love at first sight. We gave him water and a little bread and he began to hop around and lick us as though he'd found new friends and a welcoming home. He had.

"We're keeping him," Misha announced.

It was my thought as well, but I asked how we'd accomplish that.

"We'll tie him under the bunks while we're out. We'll leave him enough water and food to hold him for the day."

"Alright, Misha, alright. Do you have a name for our new friend?"

"Maximilian. Max for short."

"Max, young man, welcome to your new dwelling, humble though it is!"

Misha rolled Max onto his back and rubbed his tummy, much to the pup's delight. Misha pressed his nose to Max's and there was an immediate bonding. So we had a new friend there in the block, a wonderful little guy named Max. He showed up not long after Misha lost Naomi and I lost Bertha, so it seemed like he'd been sent.

Everyone enjoyed Max's presence and most were kind enough to bring him a small bit of food so that feeding him wasn't too burdensome on Misha and me. He established himself as a negotiator and peacemaker, at least within the block. If two guys started to get into an argument, and especially if it looked like a fight was about to break out—yes, that happened even among inmates—Max would race between the two guys and bark at both of them. I like to think he made them both feel foolish. Misha would underscore Max's message in case it eluded the men: "If he tells you to stop, you should listen. Don't we have enough trouble here without fighting each other?"

Max developed good instincts. The approach of a guard sent him scurrying under the lowest shelf. But Max had limits to his judgment and tolerance and we were always worried that he'd be discovered. Well . . . .

I sensed from Adrian's long sigh and lowered eyes that the heretofore cheerful story was about to change. The sun was going away and a dark cloud was rolling in, so to speak. I'd become accustomed to sudden changes.

It was summer, and exceptionally hot. We completed a morning work session in the mill and they marched us back to our block until later that afternoon. Odd, but we were occasionally given rest time and even extra water. Initially, I thought it was some calculation of work schedules and death rates. That is, they had certain goals to reach and if the death rate exceeded a certain level, the goals would not be reached.

But a guard told us a while later the true reason. The guards disliked having to deal with a large number of corpses in the hot weather. Decomposition . . . stench. They didn't want to be around them, not even to supervise us hauling them away to a pit or crematorium. I suppose the odor stayed in their uniforms and upset them as they dined.

So we were lying in the block waiting to be taken off to more work when a guard came in. No, I should say he *staggered* in. Very soon we could see that he was drunk. I've wondered if some of them found refuge from their consciences while intoxicated. Anyway, the unexpected arrival of a guard, drunk or sober, was a bad omen. This fellow stumbled down the center aisle, looking back and forth for someone to heap abuse on.

Most of us were awake—resting, quiet, though awake. As required, we stood up smartly as the guard entered. One chap, however, had fallen asleep and the guard hovered over him, irritated by his breach of SS protocol and perhaps also by his peaceful look. He stood over the man and shouted at the top of his lungs,

"Achtung, Jude!"

We stiffened our postures of attention. Incredibly, the man dozed on, oblivious to the angry shout only a few feet away. A beating or worse was about to take place.

"Achtung, Jude!" he again shouted. This time, the man woke up, scrambled to his feet, and assumed the position of attention as best he could.

A rustling could be heard from under the shelf—Max. Even though the guard was forty feet away and preoccupied for the moment, Max's behavior was worrisome. Our pooch was annoyed, upset, on the brink of barking—his established way of imposing peace and quiet on the unruly.

The guard put his face next to the now awakened man and once more shouted the old Nazi cry of warning and intimidation: "Achtung, Jude!" It was no longer an effort to waken or startle him. It was an attempt to get him to show resentment or weakness or anything that might be interpreted by a drunken lout as reason to become violent. The guard saw something or maybe he didn't, but he suddenly struck the man hard across the face.

Max peered out from the shelf, his eyes fixed down the aisle, nostrils flaring and a soft growl threatening to become louder. The guard's victim was always affectionate toward Max and often brought him potato morsels. Max was surely about to bark to defend his benefactor. Misha and I tried to glare him back under the shelf and offered "Shhh's" to encourage silence. I caught his eye and mouthed, "*Still*" and he comprehended my German instruction to be quiet.

But the soldier hit the man harder and he fell to the floor. Max again growled softly. This time Misha shushed him. But the soldier started to kick the man. The blows and the man's groans caused enough noise to allow us to be more assertive toward Max and with the guard's attention fully on his victim, I was able to lean down and nudge Max back under the shelf. He looked at me in confusion. A friend was in need. Why not protect him? Excellent reasoning, but not there and then. Nonetheless, Max obeyed. He huddled back under the bunk while the beating continued. At length, the guard had sated his thirst for cruelty and stumbled out of the block.

Some of the men helped the poor guy to his bunk and checked for broken bones and deep cuts. Fortunately, there didn't seem to be any. Max looked out from the bunk and wanted to see his friend and with a nod from Misha, he scooted down the center and leapt atop the man. Max looked at the poor fellow with canine compassion, which never lacks for sincerity or helpfulness. The man was still groaning but the sight of his friend's concern lifted his spirits.

"Hey, little friend, it's so good to see you."

We let Max stay with him for a while. It seemed that his presence really helped the man.

The thought of dogs helping people convalesce or get over hard times rang true with me. I've read of nursing homes letting a dog have the run of the place. The dogs seemed to be able to recognize which patients were in need of attention and which ones soon no longer would. Dogs . . . . I have a Labrador.

THE GYPSIES

As I'm sure you know, Danny, not all the inmates in Auschwitz were Jewish. There were Polish political prisoners, especially in the early years, Russian prisoners of war, homosexuals, and Gypsies. Yes, the Nazis persecuted the Gypsies and if I'm not mistaken that group suffered the highest percentage of their people killed in the extermination program. There were whole stretches of Gypsy blocks at Auschwitz I and II. Perhaps their aloofness from any fatherland and dark skin made them particularly loathsome to the Third Reich.

Misha and I noticed a new group filing toward one of the blocks that had laid empty for a week or so. It was about a hundred meters from us, on the other side of our block from the women's block with the buzzing light. We moved closer to see this group in the off chance there was someone we knew. We wouldn't have called out to anyone we recognized. That could set a guard off. But we would have taken note and made later efforts to make contact.

The group filing into the barracks was rather large, well over five hundred, meaning that they would be packed into the block even more tightly than we were. As they grew nearer, we saw their colorful bandanas and skirts and determined they were Gypsies—a common enough site in Central Europe in those says. There were men, women, and children in this new group. Yes, there were some blocks where families were not separated. In some cases, they were required to write letters to those back in their village or town telling them all was well in their new locale.

A few nights later, we heard guards shouting from the Gypsy block. Then we heard shooting and screaming. Misha and I looked out and saw muzzle flashes as the guards were simply shooting the Gypsies down. Some were able to get out of the building but we saw flashlights train on them and bullets cut them down. There was nowhere to run or hide. It was a slaughter.

"Those poor people," Misha whispered.

We saw three or four children make a run for it together—brothers and sisters, I thought. A guard emptied his machine pistol into them and made sure they were all dead after inserting another ammunition magazine.

"Little children . . . liquidated," was all Misha could say, using the SS term for murder.

We'd heard the SS refer to their work as their "duty"—*Pflicht* in their tongue. Some spoke of performing their duty without pleasure or satisfaction. It was simply something they felt bound to do and they should take no more pleasure in it than they would in killing off insects in a field of corn or in a neighbor's house. I heard one of them proudly quote a superior on that point as though the words contained profound wisdom. Well, there were many of them who performed their "duty" in that impersonal way. But often, and most notably that night, I could see that they were having fun, enjoying the murder spree. Misha and I could hear a guard delight in finding a Gypsy or two huddling at the fence then train his rifle or machine pistol on them and perform his "duty," though not in the impersonal manner consistent with the instructions of that SS commander. The screams and pleas of women that night were particularly heartrending.

At such moments of sickening helplessness, Misha and I would talk about how close the Russian troops were. A year or two ago, we might have discussed the possibility of the Third Reich winning the war and then Auschwitz would continue its work for years, decades, and even generations as new fields and buildings were found with more bugs to exterminate, deeper inside Russia and Africa and all of Asia. Or maybe the SS would build a dozen or two dozen additional extermination camps in freshly conquered lands. Maybe this was how the world would end, with selection and gas.

But at that time, we'd heard that the Russians were nearing Poland and that the Germans were losing ground every day. We would talk about how these SS guards would face justice when they arrived. Some of the men spoke of legal proceedings, others hoped to see the SS lined up and shot or packed into one of the Birkenau Kremas. Misha and I avoided the darker discussions as they meant giving in to the Reich's way of thinking. He more than I, though.

Misha and I turned away from the massacre and went inside the block, passing a few saddened faces who also looked on helplessly. Perhaps some felt a sense of commonness with Gypsies for the first time in their lives, but there were many who were so accustomed to such things that it was almost as though they were watching a play they'd seen before many times and didn't appreciate much the first time.

I awoke a few hours into sleep by my little shepherd friend who needed a little time outdoors. So, after determining that the SS had gone from the area for night, I slipped out with Max. He sniffed about, did his business, and trotted about playfully until he looked over at the sight of the ill-starred block. He stood still. In the moonlight we could see various clumps on the ground. Some of them huddled in bunches, especially in corners where the fences intersected and boxed the poor people in as the hunters closed in. A bandana fluttered in the light wind from the head of a woman. How terribly still they were.

I saw something scurrying among the corpses and suddenly realized it was Max. He'd shimmied under the fence. The sound of footfalls froze me. I turned in fright but it was Misha. "How did he get over there?" he asked. I didn't know. We made soft calls to him and lured him with a crust of bread I had in my pocket. No luck. Max continued his exploration of the horrible place and then trotted into the block itself. We had to go get him.

We found a small hole under the fence where Max had snuck though. After looking around for a patrol and seeing none, I held up the fence wire as Misha scooted underneath then he did the same for me. Staying low to the ground, we slinked toward the block, passing close to the hapless Gypsies strewn about and scores of rats that had recognized opportunity. One poor man had been shot in the skull and brain tissue oozed from a hideous wound and lay on a patch of bare ground. We only looked down to mind our steps. A stench was beginning to rise.

We heard a few whimpers from inside the block and thought Max was in trouble. Inside we found more corpses and more pools of blood. Some were near windows and there were signs they'd tried to break out and make a run for it. We heard more whimpering, soft, muffled. Max pointed us to an area beneath the row of bunks and there was a bundle of clothing. Inside of it was a baby, no more than four-weeks old. There were other whimpers from other areas beneath the bunk rows and to our dismay we found two more babies wrapped in colorful peasant swaddling, all of them calling for nourishment, calling for their mothers. Sensing impending slaughter, the Gypsies hid their newborns as best they could, in hope of . . . in hope of what? An SS guard on a murderous spree suddenly finding compassion dwelling within? In hope of some improbable miracle?

Oh, we saw strange things in an occasional repentant guard, but in point of fact it was we who had come across the three babies. They were calling out to us, pleading for milk. And it was we who had to decide what to do. We had three babies on our hands in the center of the most heartless place in the world.

Amid all the cruelty and insensitivity there occasionally arose within me the need to do good, to show the world and myself that yes, there was humanity still dwelling inside me. That need was stronger in Misha and so was recognition of limits to humanity in present circumstances.

"We can only take one," he murmured.

The unspoken question was obvious enough. The answer was only a little less obvious but agonizing to express, let alone put into practice.

"We have to choose one," I said, "and quickly."

We placed the three babies next to each other on a dry area of the floor. It was soon apparent that one, a boy, was not well. He did not respond to touch or sound or any stimulus, try though we did to attract his attention and look into his eyes. My God, what we were doing. The remaining two were both girls, both angelic, both gifts. One began to cough then cry. She coughed more and more. We knew of respiratory infections that spread in the cattle cars and blocks. We knew that they would not be treated and that any baby with such an infection would be prone to coughing fits and more difficult to conceal in our block. That helped us in our painful and paradoxical decision.

The little girl opened her dark eyes and smiled serenely at us. We naturally enough smiled back. She held out her little hand and we each took a finger or two. There's something magical about interacting with an innocent baby. It's like the entire hell around us had vanished and all that remained was the two of us and this little baby—this new life. We knew that we had to save her. We had received a sacred mission to save this life and we were determined to do it, risky though it was. I wrapped her in her clothes and cuddled her in my arms. This one would come with us.

We wrapped the other two back in their swaddling and placed them under the row of bunks. We placed them side by side, so they would not be alone. Misha prayed over them and we left the block and made our way across the field of the dead. Behind us we heard the two babies crying. We heard them back in our own block. I heard them for many years after that. I'll hear them again tonight.

THE MADONNA AND CHILD OF OSWIECIM

The next morning we awoke with our new ward. The reactions of the other men were mixed. She was cute but she would become too much of a burden on everyone with continuous demands for food, water, and attention. We couldn't simply hide her under a bunk row while we were off on labor details. Furthermore, there was the matter of the guards finding her. They might well punish the whole block and the idea of what they might do to the baby was appalling to consider.

"Misha," I said as he held her in his arms, "we can't keep her . . . not even for a day." Misha was too practical a young man to offer rebuttal. A slow nod told me that he'd come to the same realization and I was thankful of that. "Maybe we can ask Bruno for help on this. Adrian, you have to find him . . . soon. We have to get her out of here."

Misha and I suddenly realized the baby needed attention. She needed a certain kind of attention that most men knew nothing about in those days. The baby needed changing, or what would have to pass for it in the block that morning. As we unwrapped the girl we found a small purse, the sort one might keep change in. But inside there was a thick roll of currency tied together with a small string tied into a bow. The family had put all their hope in that bundle of clothing we'd found. We untied the bow and found a number of bills in Hungarian *pengo* and in *Reichsmarks*—the currency of Nazi Germany. It was probably the equivalent of a hundred dollars. That was quite a bit of money back then; in Auschwitz, it was a small fortune.

There was a lively black market in the camp with goods and services traded between guards and inmates, though not openly of course.

Some inmates worked sorting through the belongings of those right off the cattle cars at a place over in Birkenau nicknamed "Kanada" and they'd occasionally come across a ring or watch, which they'd put into their pocket and later exchange. Misha and I beamed at each other as we unfolded the money. We knew that the money greatly increased the baby's prospects of getting out of Auschwitz. I set out to find Bruno.

He was at the enlisted men's mess hall. I stood in the doorway until I caught his eye and we met in the back. As he pretended to scold me in order to allay suspicion, I asked him to come by our block later in the day.

"Yes, of course. Is something wrong?"

"It's something rather urgent and we need help—Misha and I . . . and, well, someone else. Not another dog," I added.

Misha and I hid the baby with Max and went out for the day's labor. I think we worked the train tracks again that day. All the while, we worried about our charge back under the bunks. It would be unusual for a guard to go into a block during the day. There was nothing there to steal and the smell was off-putting to say the least. Nonetheless, we worried. Like parents, we worried.

Bruno entered our barracks and came to the rear where Misha and I were—along with Max and our bundle. Bruno greeted Max and commented on his rapid growth.

"By God, he has grown . . . and he's certainly a very bright young dog," Misha said trying to lead into the matter at hand. "He found something the other night, over in the Gypsy block." Bruno's expression became quite grim as he knew what had taken place—without his participation, I can only presume. Again I was struck by being in the presence of a member of the SS, yet confiding in him, trusting him, and placing hope in him.

Misha pointed to the little bundle on a bunk and opened it to Bruno's astonished eyes. He stammered and struggled for words—and for the most part, lost the struggle. The darker complexion and mention of the ill-fated block eventually told him all there was to know, including why we'd asked him there that night.

"It's a girl, Bruno. We gave her a little bread and water," I noted, "but she'll need more attention than we can give."

As though on cue, the little girl looked into Bruno's eyes. He was momentarily captured by her but he quickly recovered. "I don't know what to do . . . how can we . . . it's far too dangerous."

"We want her out of here, Bruno," Misha prompted. "Far away from here, out of the camp." He held up the roll of bills.

Never have humanitarian and monetary interests come together in a more timely manner. I don't know which figured more highly inside Bruno at that moment and I doubt he himself could have meaningfully calculated each factor's weight just then. Misha and I looked intently to Bruno and I think Max was probably looking up as well.

"Max found her," I said. "He went into the block and found her under a bunk. We can't save everyone here, Bruno, but we can try to save this little girl. She's an innocent baby—a new, pure life. We can't leave her to die in here. It would be against nature. *Please* help her."

Bruno leaned down to pet Max and murmured, "What have you gotten us into, Max? What have you gotten *me* into?" The humor made us think that Bruno had been won over. "There's a woman from my church in Oswiecim," he soon said. "She's older . . . very kindhearted, no children of her own. She can help. Yes, Elsa will take care of her. What's the baby's name?"

"We don't know her name," I replied as Misha and I looked at each other, "and we haven't come up with one in our short time together." Misha looked at me as though coaxing something out of me.

"Rosanna . . . how about Rosanna?" I stammered. Misha and I knew that to be my mother's name and I think for a moment he thought of his own mother.

"Rosanna, it is," Bruno announced. "Well, young Rosanna, it is my sincere hope that you grow up in a world very different from the one we find ourselves in this day. And our first step toward that new world must begin right now. Let us get you away from this place and into Elsa's home."

We wrapped up Rosanna as though she were a precious gift, kissed her goodbye, and tucked her between Bruno's arm and tunic, as though he were taking a package over to the church. "Little Rosanna, you are in excellent hands," Misha said as they headed away from us.

"He who saves one life, saves the whole world," I whispered, recalling a proverb I'd heard Misha's father say. And at that moment, I felt the truth of that saying. I felt that we'd done a wonderful thing, one that might counter all the bad things I'd done since the war began.

All this vanished as we saw, off in the distance, that Bruno had run into an SS officer. Misha and I walked over in that direction, getting close enough to hear the exchange and looking occasionally in the general direction.

"What have you got there, Corporal Müller? Or should I still call you Bruno as I did in school?" The officer's voice seemed good-natured but hard experience had taught that cruelty could lie just beneath a smile and a kind word or two. Indeed, it was part of the guards' routine as they toyed with inmates before unleashing their cruelty.

Bruno and the officer exchanged desultory salutes then fell back into chatting. That is, until the officer's eyes shifted to the bundle, perhaps brought on by a muffled whimper or unexpected motion.

"What is that under your arm, Bruno?"

Yes, even we heard Rosanna cry as she needed water or more air in the swaddling. Bruno couldn't dismiss a question from an SS officer. And as if to underscore the power relationship, the officer said, sternly, "Corporal Müller, I asked you what you have under your arm and I will have your full answer."

We noticed some slurring in the officer's voice and an unsteadiness to his attempts at a stance of authority. He was drunk. That posed opportunities and difficulties. He might be too drunk to pursue the matter or he might be in the mood for sport.

"While on a pleasant evening walk, I found this Gypsy baby, Herr Hauptsturmführer, and I was going to toss it into the pit we've been using while one of the Krema is undergoing repairs."

"Ah, one of those Gypsies!" he said, now wobbling noticeably. "Bruno, my old friend," he said looking down to Rosanna, "we are old school friends and can dispense with the Corporal-this and Hauptsturmführer-that, at least for the moment. Can we not? For this evening, please call me 'Fritz' as in the old days back in Berlin."

"That is quite kind of you, my friend. How is it you find yourself here at Auschwitz? And how is it that I've not had the honor or serving under you?"

"I was at Monowitz for many months now but I'm here for a few weeks now. Bruno," he said in a mock scold, "only a corporal? Ah, but you never had my ambition, my drive, my thirst for command. So it is destiny then that we are here, I a Hauptsturmführer and you . . . a Gefreiter. How fitting, how very fitting."

There was a definite sneer in his voice now that didn't bode well.

"Good for you, Fritz, good for you! By God, the entire school I'm sure is proud of you. Perhaps we can talk about old times some other time, and in some place where old friends can speak again without regard to rank."

"But Bruno, old friend, what did you say you have tucked under your arm so delicately this evening?" He chuckled sloppily. "I'm in a rather inappropriate state, I'm afraid. A baby, you said?"

"Just a Gypsy baby that I found in the field outside the block they were in. It must have eluded our men! I'm taking it to the pit where the rest of her kind are now."

"Bruno . . . Bruno . . . Bruno," he was once again chiding him in demeaning way. "You have no ambition and you have no thoughtfulness either. A baby—Jew or Gypsy or Russian—can serve a purpose."

Misha and I froze. Bruno looked into the officer's face for a sign of an answer but none came. I'm sure all three of us knew something bad was in store though. Bruno continued to search for an answer; the drunken officer provided one.

"A baby makes an excellent target! We can hone our marksmanship skills." With those dreadful words, he reached into his holster. "By chance, I was just issued a new Walther P-38." He pulled the slide back, chambering one of the 9-millimeter bullets. "I'm eager to get some practice with it."

Bruno looked for a sign of humor or of a test of some sort. There was none.

"But Fritz, even a baby is such a large target. No challenge in it. Surely we can do better at the firing range another day. Perhaps tomorrow."

"Yes, you're right. It is a rather large target and it would not be sporting." Bruno's ploy seemed to have worked. The officer rolled his head back and forth as though thinking the better of it, but then his eyes lit up. "Bruno, you will throw the baby into the air and I will demonstrate my keen marksmanship to you, even in my present condition!"

"Oh Fritz! Far too dangerous. You might miss and hit someone else," Bruno objected cleverly. "You might hit me! Better I take the pile of rags to the pit."

The officer looked around and found an open area to the south. "Bruno! You can toss it up here! In fact, Gefreiter, I order you to do as I say!" He then aimed his pistol at Bruno. "Now!"

Misha and I were disgusted. We'd saved Rosanna only to see her shot by a drunken SS officer who happened by. What diversion could we attempt? What diversion would not get us all shot? Neither Bruno nor Misha nor I dared speak. There was, fortunately, someone who did. Max began barking as he ran to the officer. Would he shoot Max and then the rest of us? He lowered his pistol and looked to Bruno. "Your dog, old friend?"

"I'm afraid not. He's the prized pet of a senior personnel officer in the administration building. The man is a Sturmbannführer and he lets his dog run about in the evening. He's a prickly sort and everyone likes his dog— or else! And Fritz . . . I'm not sure how he responds to loud noises!" The officer holstered his pistol and tried to befriend Max but to no avail. He kept snarling and snapping at the drunken lout.

"Another time, Fritz! You and our canine friend must to try to become better acquainted another evening."

"I'm sure you're right, Bruno. Another night and this fellow and I will get along splendidly."

"Undoubtedly, Fritz."

The SS officer yawned and teetered about uneasily. I think he was afraid of angering this senior personnel officer Bruno had made up out of thin air. Such people were helpful in promotions and had been known to send troublesome guards and officers to more "challenging" work in Waffen SS units fighting the Russians.

"Kapo!" Bruno called out to me. "Come here now and help the good Sturmbannführer back to the officers' quarters. He's a bit under the weather and needs a hand. Be quick here, Kapo!"

I started to run over but Fritz waved me off. "No, no. I need no help. Not from anyone, let alone a Polish conscript boy. Bruno, my friend, we must talk over old times some night."

"That is my hope, Fritz. I look forward to it."

Then a cocky smile came across his face as his idea recurred to him. Reaching again for his Walther, he said, "Bruno, old friend, I've changed my mind once more. I will demonstrate my marksmanship to you this night. Toss the baby in the air."

Bruno's expression changed. He seemed to accept Fritz's idea of sport, though I discerned some anger as well. He wrapped the baby carefully in the cloth—in a manner that puzzled Fritz.

"Do you care about this baby, Bruno?" he asked in a disgusted way. "Do you really care for this subhuman trash?" He shook his head few times. "I'm afraid that's the case here. Oh, I feel sorry for you, Bruno, but then you were always weak and stupid. That is why you'll always be a lowly enlisted man, humbly following orders from your betters. After I dispose of this pile of rags here, I will have you tried and punished for your despicable sentimentality. Really, Bruno, there is no place in the SS for such weaknesses."

"That won't be necessary, Fritz." A broad smile came across Bruno's face, as though he accepted the officer's will and beliefs—or more likely, he was acting to save his own life. "Yes, Fritz. I'll toss the baby into the air for you."

"He has a plan," Misha whispered to me. "I know he does." I had my doubts. It appeared we had only given Rosanna another few hours of life. Misha and I held our breath as Bruno stooped down then launched the little package high into the air—ten meters or more. Fritz aimed his pistol unsteadily into the sky, trying to place his shot on the moving target. We flinched as a shot rang out. To our astonishment and relief, we saw Rosanna land lightly in Bruno's left arm and chest as he held a smoking pistol in his other hand.

Fritz had a look of surprise on his face as his pistol fell to the ground. Only then did Misha and I see the dark spot spreading across Fritz's tunic. Who was more astonished by this, me or Fritz, you might wonder. I think it was Fritz. He looked around for help but realized, as did we, that a shot was nothing out of the ordinary in the rows of inmate blocks. Summary executions were common enough and that ironically meant no help was coming for a dying SS officer who'd wanted a little sport to cap off a night of drinking.

"You . . . you shot me . . . ." Fritz said falling to his knees. "For a Gypsy baby's life?" He was incredulous.

"Yes, I did just that," Bruno calmly replied with no sense of pity or remorse, his P-38 still at the ready.

"Well, one of us aimed well."

"I did well in marksmanship, Fritz. But that has no bearing on my worth as a man."

"So . . . right here and now, tell me what makes you of more worth." His slurred speech was increasingly laced with sarcasm. "Educate me, won't you?"

"Think, while you can, what goes on here." Fritz was slumping lower as his strength was leaving him. Bruno continued with his lecture to the small class. "Selections? Gas chambers? This is mass murder. You must see that now."

"But . . . our Führer has said . . . ." he murmured weakly, grabbing hold of what was a powerful idea to him.

"What if another country conquers us and deems us weak? Then would you have them put your family into a Krema?" He was like a prosecutor breaking a lying witness on the stand.

Fritz simply shook his head in disbelief. I thought he was about to drop dead but he was summoning his final strength for a few more words.

"You know, Bruno, you are not stupid." He laughed phonily and bitterly. "But you have lost your mind. You have saved that baby but you both will pay a price later." He choked and spat blood then fell down to the ground.

"I am sorry for you, Fritz. I hoped you would have a moment of light before you left us. By God, I did."

Fritz's body spasmed slightly a few times before becoming still. I've wondered what went through Bruno's mind then. After all, he'd just killed an old friend and the prospect of retribution was very real. But Rosanna was crying loudly and he had to tend to her.

"You did a very brave thing today, Bruno," Misha said. "But how will you explain this?"

"I'll hide his body. An investigation will determine he was quite drunk and suspicion will lead to a brawl with another guard. It has happened before, it will happen again. I hoped Fritz would feel regret before death . . . but he did not."

We stood there a while, looking at Fritz's body, until Bruno handed us the baby for another goodbye. We kissed her and wished her well then placed her again under Bruno's arm and watched him head off to the main gate. He was waved through at the checkpoint and walked off in the direction of the village of Oswiecim, to the church, and to Elsa.

I leaned back in my seat and breathed easier as I envisioned Bruno carrying Rosanna to an old childless Polish woman who lived on church property a mile or two from the perimeter of Auschwitz-Birkenau. I imagined the congregation knew what was going on there. How could they not? Train after train of arrivals and no departures. They'd seen the work kommandos. Emaciated men and women. Then there were the occasional escapees who made for the forests but might have come into the church for food. I wonder if they received any.

I asked Adrian if he ever got any word about Rosanna. He said that he and Misha prayed for her and that Bruno said that Elsa took her in without any questions. The congregation loved her and helped in raising her.

A Gypsy baby, dark of skin, raised in rural Poland amid a devastating world war. I thought of a famous Polish icon I'd seen in an art book in college. The Black Madonna of Częstochowa, it was called. Maybe Rosanna reminded the congregation in Oswiecim of the Black Madonna's infant and saw her as a miracle. How could anyone think of her as anything else?

DAVID AND NISIM, THE SEPHARDIC BROTHERS

Trains arrived almost every day. People disembarked and went through selection. Some passed and were sent to one of the blocks. There were always open bunks as there were always deaths, which of course you know. One morning, after an absence of a day or so, I came to Misha's block and saw several new people. The previous weeks' work had been especially hard and many men and boys died on work details, in their bunks at night, or walked off to Birkenau after failing morning selection.

Among the new people were two brothers, Nisim and David Abadi from Krakow. It was difficult not to notice the pair. Their camaraderie and joyfulness was obvious from the very first. Nisim was the younger of the two, about twelve, and despite the conditions he was a bit on the plump side. David was older by two years and quite thin. Yes, David gave his younger brother some of his rations, though nature played the larger role in accounting for their physical differences. Misha and I thought of them as kids, though we were only seventeen or eighteen at the time.

The two brothers, like Big Joe, the powerful fellow who hoisted the boulder, could maintain their spirits amid the worst of it. Such people were important. They gave others hopefulness and appreciation of life whether the others realized it or not. The brothers' complexions were darker than most and their accents differed from the dozens we'd come to recognize from Central and Eastern Europe. In time we learned that Nisim and David were Sephardic, originally from Spain but raised in Poland.

What a misfortune, I thought. Spain was friendly to Nazi Germany but neutral in the war. Spain did not take part in the extermination process as did many countries such as France and Poland. Better they'd stayed south of the Pyrenees than come to Poland just before the war. But life tosses us around the world, doesn't it.

"As long as we're together, we are content and we shall go on," David said as he placed an arm around Nisim's shoulder. "And soon, I shall see that my brother has his Bar Mitzvah. Whether it's here or outside these damn fences!"

One morning David came up to Misha as he was praying over his Tefillin. I stood nearby, listening, praying, and having my own conversation with the Lord. David was surprised to see the sacred boxes. Surprised and delighted. It was like seeing a vestige of home and community.

"What does 'Nisim' mean?" I asked the younger one, curious about what was to me an unusual though intriguing name. I'd heard many German, Polish, Hebrew, and Russian names, but his was unfamiliar to me.

"It has a very special meaning," Nisim said beaming with pride. "It's the Hebrew word for 'miracles'—plural, more than one!"

"Ah, that is a very beautiful name you have, Nisim."

The SS usually separated brothers on arrival at the ramp, so there had already seen one miracle since they detrained at the Auschwitz station. Another was their assignment to the mill, which was not the hardest work at the camp. I knew they would need more help from above.

We came to know their story. They were from a small village in northern Spain where the small number of Jews were descendants of those who went into hiding when Spain expelled the Jews in the fifteenth century. Some Jews left Spain, others converted to Christianity, others still hid their faith and secretly raised their children in the venerable traditions.

Their parents died, both of natural causes. A Polish Rabbi—a Rabbi Lieder, by name—heard from a neighbor of the boys' sad plight and wanted to help. The Rabbi was childless and had recently lost his wife. He prayed a great deal on the matter and then traveled to Spain to bring the brothers back to Poland where he raised them as his own.

I asked if Rabbi Lieder was in the camp. I was curious and thought I might be able to help, if only to get word to him that the boys were well and perhaps to arrange a short meeting at a fence or workplace. The boys said they were separated from him in Krakow long ago.

"He was taken from us and pushed onto a truck. 'Watch over your young brother, David,' he called out. 'Stay together and never lose faith.' Then he summoned the will to bravely smile and wave goodbye to us as the truck careened off. We heard he died in a transit camp and know he loved us to the end."

I knew enough to know that a Rabbi could have been singled out by SS tormenters and shot. Or maybe a Rabbi could be seen as offering hope and unity to inmates, and for that reason he'd be eliminated as soon as possible. Some survived though. There was the one at Misha and Naomi's wedding.

"After a few days in the ghetto, they put us on trains and that's how we came here," David said in closing.

"And then we came here and met Max—and we love him very much!" Nisim said as he hugged our shepherd friend.

Max was growing into a large, lovable, and powerful dog. The intelligence he showed as a pup developed apace with his other attributes. He sensed we were all in a dire predicament and that his role was to help us as best he could. He recognized when one of us descended into failing health and tried to cheer him and encourage him to go on. I truly think he saved more than one life in our block. He sensed the limits almost as well as the rest of us did.

They were wonderful boys and they brought great joy. Nisim and David loved Max and played with him as often as they could. He'd snuggle with them sometimes at night before padding his way back to Misha. Well, people who love life also love dogs.

I smiled on hearing those words. I'd had the same thought. I said that it sounded as if the brothers formed part of a community in the block.

We all knew the physical realities. We had to stay physically strong and mentally alert. Otherwise, we'd lose out one morning. But the spiritual realities were there as well. I saw Misha, Max, David, and Nisim as a heart of sorts for the block. Their hopefulness and courage inspired many around them and provided them the will to get up again. You might think that one block at the camp was just like every other, but it isn't so. There were blocks with no such spirit, with no such heart. And you could see it. People in some blocks were all in utter despair, lifeless, hopeless. You could see it at morning formation, you could see it at the selections. And you could see it in the morning when the dead were stacked outside.

Well, some things happened in a very orderly manner—morning formations, work, meals. But there was the unpredictable too—beatings, executions. Yes, I've tried to tell you of occasional acts of kindness, even from unlikely places, but of course the cruelty was far more present.

When a guard decided to kill a prisoner, there was nothing we could do but lower our heads and hope that we would not be next. Even though I was a Kapo and part of the camp staff, I was not so important as to be excluded from such acts. When I heard a blow strike someone, I thought I might be next. When I heard a rifle shot, I thought the next bullet might strike me. My breath would stop and my heart would race.

One afternoon—it was in early 1944—just before we trudged off to eat, a guard came into the block and shouted for ten of us to follow him. We were to shovel the snow at the main gate which had accumulated since the kommando had cleared it in the morning.

He pointed to people one by one, Misha and David among them. I volunteered my services in order to watch out for my friends. So off we marched, through the falling snow and cold, to the infamous main gate over which the sign "Arbeit Macht Frei," meaning of course "Work is liberating," hovered like a cruel joke. A truck arrived with shovels and we began to clear the road—I in a supervisory position. We were making good progress and hopeful that we'd be done quickly. We'd then get some food before returning to the relative comfort of the block.

Outside the gate, nearing the checkpoint, came three cars. They were staff cars, big Mercedes Benzes, the kind high-ranking officers enjoyed as a privilege. I called out to the men and boys to let the cars pass, so they stepped back and leaned on their shovels, judiciously avoiding eye contact with the men in the cars. The first car drove by, then the second, both making crumpling noises on the frozen ground. The third came through the gate but came to a halt not far from us.

The black Mercedes was not ten meters from us, idling roughly and sending thick exhaust smoke into the frigid air. I could barely make out the forms of two people in the front seats and saw the embers flare from a passenger's cigarette. I felt dread come over my soul. I heard the engine roar and the wheels spin before getting traction and lurching forward. The car came roaring through the gate, heading for a group of my kommando standing on one side of the road. They cried out in fear, tossed their shovels aside, and dived away, but the Mercedes slammed into several of them before halting again. Three men lay on the ground—one motionless. The car maneuvered in the snow and proceeded to run over the motionless man before backing up.

A rear door opened and the guard who'd brought us to the gate hastened to it and stood at attention as an SS colonel got out and looked at the carnage illuminated by the headlights. He was wearing a greatcoat and a hat with the death's head symbol of the SS both of which were becoming flecked with snow. He laughed and said, "Disappointing . . . . I hoped to kill more. I'll have to train my driver better! Continue clearing the snow, corporal." He got back inside and the car drove off toward the administration building.

I raced to the man who'd been run over, and though it was someone we knew—Menachem was his name—I confess my first reaction was relief that it wasn't Misha.

"Get back to work!" the guard shouted. "Someone will remove the body in good time."

We completed the task and headed for the mess hall. We had to hurry as the mess hall would not stay open for a single work kommando on a snowy night. Food was very important after strenuous work, particularly during winter time and after a grim death. We needed every calorie. I wondered why the cars hadn't arrived ten minutes later. It would've made no difference in the world to anyone but poor Menachem.

We returned to the block and tried to warm ourselves in huddled groups. Max trotted over to me and I gave him a piece of bread with a little jam from my Kapo portions. Nisim came over to Misha and me, a look of concern on his face. "David didn't eat. I don't think he's well. Can you look at him?"

David lay on his straw, eyes closed until he sensed someone nearby him. His eyes were red and swollen, not from tears but from pain. A crust of bread was in his shaky hand. "The car . . . that car . . . it hit me."

We pulled up his shirt and saw a large bruise forming on his abdomen. No external bleeding, but that meant little. We'd all seen those bruises spread and bring fever and decline. I shuddered.

I hadn't noticed that he was injured. I guess my mind fixed on poor Menachem and I assumed that the other two men weren't seriously injured. I'm sure now though that David hid his injury at the gate. A brave display? Fear of being put to death on the spot?

"I ate the soup . . . it was good," David whispered in obvious discomfort. "I just couldn't eat the bread. Chewing hurts. Nisim, *you* eat it." David tried to sit up but a sharp pain sent him back down promptly. "I'll be fine by morning. I just need rest." David tried to smile though without much success.

"I'll be near you, David," Nisim promised. "We can strengthen each other."

"Yes, Nisim. Thank you . . . and I love you," his brother bravely replied.

It was a hard scene to watch. We'd seen it before, but not with boys their age, let alone with brothers. We made crude compresses as Doctor Rosen—then long gone—had prescribed before for someone. It was out of our hands though. I think Misha and I both knew that if David were to die, Nisim would fall into depression and follow not far behind. Max hopped up on the bunk and lay between the brothers. Misha and I thought that a good omen.

"Max will watch over you, David," Misha offered hopefully. "And in the morning, we'll pray together."

I told Misha that I'd be staying in the Kapo barracks that night. Too much time away from my supposed colleagues could lead to suspicions and rumors and in time to accusations. We agreed that we'd better know David's prospects in the morning. He'd either benefit from sleep or the swelling would have worsened and made him incapable of work.

"He's in good hands," I said.

"And in good paws!" Misha added.

I laughed as much as circumstances permitted and bade him farewell until the morning.

Misha was awaiting me when I returned, his face forewarning bad news. We walked down the center of the block, past the shelf-like bunks, until we came to where David and Nisim were lying next to each other. Max was distraught. On closer inspection of the young boys, I could see an unusual stillness in David. Yes, he was dead. He had passed away silently in the night, as best as one could hope for in that place.

Sensing our presence, Nisim awoke, breathed in deeply, and as he began to stretch, he saw our somber looks. He looked over at his brother's peaceful face and let the reality of the situation sink in. We expected him to cry out, refusing to believe his eyes. Tears and soft sobs ensued from all three of us. I think Nisim saw that his brother was at peace and a feeling of relief exceeded his grief. Perhaps David had had a long hour or two before falling off to sleep and come to the firm decision within his being that drifting away in sleep would be the best thing.

A few men walked by and quickly comprehended the situation. Misha found words. He put his hand on the boy's shoulder and said, "Nisim, my friend, today you shall say the prayer over the Tefillin."

Nisim slowly nodded his head, accepting the situation, accepting Misha's offer.

"Our adopted father, Rabbi Lieder, told David and me something long ago when we commemorated our parents' memory. When someone dies, there is no reason to be sad. On the contrary, it should be a happy event. We were puzzled but he went on. When a person dies, his soul goes into the heavens and is closer to the Lord. That's what our Rabbi told us. He asked us to be happy when he died. David and I remembered his words the day we were separated from him and also the day we heard of his fate. So how can I be anything but happy on the death of my brother David? Yes, I am sad that he is gone. I can no longer talk with him or play games with him. He will not be here to help and protect me. But the Rabbi's words echo within my soul, even this sad morning."

"Nisim," Misha offered, "your brother will always be with you. He'll be in your heart. You'll always be together."

Nisim hugged his brother silently as Misha and I looked on. I think the Rabbi's words found a place in our hearts as well. We knew that there was no time for extended grief. Misha handed his Tefillin to Nisim and the boy began to pray for his brother. Afterwards, we went out for headcount and assignment.

REVOLT

I asked Adrian if there were ever escapes from Auschwitz. He replied that there were quite a few, though he had no personal experience with any. There were a number of kommandos that worked on the fringe of the camp and even several kilometers away, often near woods. I'd read that escapees would run deep into the forest in hope of finding partisans who'd protect them or in search of a hillside where they could dig out a cave. From there, they'd eke out their survival on berries and nuts until the Russian army reached southern Poland.

When I asked if punishment was meted out to anyone deemed responsible for an escape, whether a Kapo or other inmates, Adrian nodded and drifted into the past for several moments. "Everyone," he eventually whispered. "They'd kill everyone in the escapee's block. It made a point."

Yes, yes. Well, there is more to the story of the boys and men of Misha's block. Yes, I'm sure you've wondered what became of them. It was a few weeks after David's death from that hateful colonel's car. You know, Danny, I've searched for accounts of what I'm about to tell you. There were similar cases that I've read about at other camps but I've found nothing of what I'm going to tell you. By the demanding standards of World War Two and the Holocaust, it was a small event, smaller than a parallel event at Treblinka, in the Warsaw Ghetto, and at one of the Kremas in Birkenau, where people rose up. Nonetheless, it was a decisive event in those of our block and I want to make sure that someone knows that it happened. This will ensure that the event and those who took part in it have some mention in history and a measure of life that the SS denied them.

I shuddered at those words and all that they suggested was to follow. Adrian smiled. It was a sardonic smile, one that blended bitterness with a trace of fondness for those involved.

I suppose you could say it happened because of Max. Yes, none of this would have happened. Or at least it would not have happened that way, on that day. I don't blame my little friend. Naturally, I blame the SS. I love Max to this day.

In early 1944, rumors were rife that the Russian army was nearing the Polish borders. We could hear aerial bombings, especially at night when the ambient noise was low, and wondered if the Russians might bomb the munitions factory at Auschwitz I or the artificial rubber factory at Monowitz. During the day we would occasionally see a plane streak overhead, a red star on its wings. A Yak, not a Messerschmitt. Russian, not German.

The prisoners looked at the Russian planes with joy and hope, but they had to hide it. The guards looked up fearfully, as well they should, but they could *not* hide it. I think some of them became less cruel, thinking we'd speak up for them and save them from Russian justice. I, a conscript, looked up with the same emotions of the prisoners. Nonetheless, I wondered if the first Russian troops through the gate might simply shoot all the guards, all the staff, and all the Kapos. It wouldn't have been the worst injustice that took place inside the fences of Auschwitz.

It was a cold morning with the added burden of snow which made the ground muddy though on the verge of freezing. We stayed inside the block until the guards got word of what labor we were to perform that day. Shortly after noon a pair of guards shouted for us to assemble and led us to a yard not far from our block where we were to lay a foundation for a new building. Yes, the Russian army was getting closer every day, nonetheless plans had been made and schedules had to be met so the construction went on. Two trucks came up with shovels, hammers, and wood, but we had to wait for an engineer to arrive as the guards had no idea how to do anything but shout and kick. The men stood about in the cold snow, stamping their feet to try to keep them from freezing.

Not all the guards had become less cruel with the reports of the approaching Russians. Not by any means. A second pair of guards showed up and almost immediately began to torment the inmates. They hit men, shoved them, laughed at what they'd done. It was getting nastier and nastier which we all knew could lead to worse things. One guard swung his rifle with all his strength and hit a man across the face, sending him sprawling to the ground. The guard then chambered a round and shot the poor guy in the chest. He gasped, spat up blood, and died in a few seconds. His blood stained the snow but began to be covered by fresh flakes drifting down. I looked around and saw Misha not far away, safe for the moment.

An engineer was driven up and issued the plan and the kommando set to work digging in the hard ground to place the wooden beams forming the foundation. I walked about, seemingly purposefully, swearing only somewhat convincingly at the men. I heard one of the new guards shout, "You! Come here—now!"

He wasn't addressing me or Misha, who was aligning a beam in the freshly dug ground. Someone behind us had been summoned but I dared not turn suddenly.

"What is this? A boy?" Astonishment and annoyance were in the guard's voice. "No children are supposed to be here. You should be in the showers. Come with me!"

"Please leave him with us. He's a hard worker," I heard a man intervene.

I was turning my head cautiously to see who the brave man was when I heard a loud staccato burst from a machine pistol and saw a man fall to the ground dead. I don't recall his name but I think he was from a salt mining town near Krakow. Then I saw the boy being dragged away by the ear as he screamed and begged then fell to the ground.

It was Nisim.

"Stand up," the stout soldier commanded. Nisim was too scared to comply, so the guard grabbed the back of the boy's tunic and dragged him away toward the selection yard where a group of frail people awaited their last walk. I can still see the guard's boots glistening from polish and melting snow as he marched off with his helpless quarry. Nisim tried to right himself but stumbled and fell. "No!" the boy shouted in outrage, stunning everyone there. "I can still work! I'm strong!"

The guard was probably more stunned than the rest of us. He grabbed Nisim again but again Nisim broke free. "No! I'm not going there! You've already killed my brother. That's enough! I can work, I tell you!" The guard was dumfounded as Nisim continued his rebuke. "You have brothers and sisters, don't you? Don't you understand? Can't you imagine someone dragging one of them off to death?"

Every shovel stood still as the drama unfolded. The guard was taken aback by such unexpected resistance. "Ha! I will not argue with a Jew. Now come with me."

"Yes, I am a Jew. I am a boy like your brother. Would you let someone treat your brother this way? *No one* should be treated this way!"

I expected the sound of gunfire at any moment, from the stunned guard or one of his less dumfounded compatriots. Instead he began to rain blows down on the boy. Nisim began to cry out and scream.

I walked then trotted to the scene not fifty meters from me. I didn't know what I was going to do but I was going to try to stop this. The closer I got the more I realized that I might get killed for my effort, nonetheless I kept up my pace in the snow and mud. My boots made sucking sounds and I almost stumbled to the ground. I thought to myself, "I'm going to *kill* him!"

I heard sounds from behind me, from the direction of the block. Then I heard barks and snarls as I stumbled and fell onto the muddy ground. Max had run out of the block. His strides were amazing. All four of his paws rose off the ground at times, his eyes were fiercely lit and his fangs showed brightly in his black muzzle.

The guard was too busy delighting in beating a young boy to see the danger. Max set upon him like an avenging angel and fastened his jaws around the neck of the now startled guard. His fangs sank deep into the flesh and ripped four deep punctures that must have opened an artery. The guard fell to the ground and clutched his neck, trying to stanch the flow of blood but shock soon set in and he went into ludicrous convulsions.

The other guards were strangely motionless. They must have wondered where this beast had come from. Was he from the camp's kennel? Was he the pet of a high-ranking officer? They simply watched the guard on the ground bleed profusely and shake uncontrollably.

One of the guards made some sort of calculation and aimed his machine pistol at Max who glared at him and snarled menacingly. For all his canine wiles, he knew nothing of the power of 9mm bullets. I cried out "No!" and I think Misha did the same, but in an instant the machine pistol had spoken and four or five rounds slammed into poor Max. The first two brought sharp cries from the poor fellow, but that was all. A second burst needlessly tore more holes into his lifeless form.

Misha and I felt rage. Others did too. Forty or more men from our block defiantly came over to the construction field. They looked about and seethed with anger—no, with hate. There was hate in their eyes. Where I'd seen a sigh of hopelessness, I now saw a thirst for revenge.

They'd seen many men killed—one only minutes earlier. They'd seen friends and family members sent off to the line that led to the Kremas, yet something was different that day. The abuse of a young boy and his courageous resistance? Max's desperate attack? The uncertainty in the guards' eyes as the Russian army neared? The shovels and pickaxes in their hands?

Something had changed in the men's calculus. Something had even reversed. The inmates sensed when guards were escalating their cruelty and someone might die. That afternoon it was the guards who sensed that events were escalating out of their control and they looked around at the prisoners' numbers and then at their own, which had become one fewer as the wounded guard continued to gasp violently and look around frantically.

One man hefted a pickaxe and stealthily came upon a guard from behind. With a mighty cry he raised his weapon and, as the guard turned about in horror, he sent its metal shaft deep inside his chest just below the collarbone. It was the first time I heard an SS man scream—and Danny, I welcomed it. I think we all did. The remaining three guard's shot him dead and formed a small perimeter from which they poured out fire into the host of men descending upon them with shovels, pickaxes, and bare hands. A dozen or so inmates were shot down in seconds but the rest overpowered the SS guards and began to hit them over and over with the implements. I've never seen such furor and never want to again. Danny . . . arms and legs were hacked off. The machine pistols now in the hands of inmates were emptied into corpses.

A detachment of guards—a dozen at least—raced to the scene firing their rifles and machine pistols into the crowd of frenzied inmates. Another detachment came from another direction. Inmates were mowed down like wheat before a scythe. In just a few moments the uprising was stamped out. Surviving inmates, including Misha and Nisim, stood with their hands up before being marched back to the block. A Kapo was assumed to have played no part in this. I hadn't, but of course my sympathies were with the inmates.

I looked down at the hacked up torsos of the guards, their arms and legs and even their heads lying around in the red-splattered snow. Soon enough, a group of SS officers came to the scene, looked at the mayhem, and listened to reports from guards. A reprisal I knew would come and it would be fearsome.

Adrian paused and breathed deeply, staring intently to the floor and into the dark past. A look of bitterness came across his face and slowly merged into simple sadness.

Reprisal . . . . I'd read of Nazis avenging the killing of a few soldiers by wiping out an adjacent village which they presumed had been responsible. It happened in the French village of Oradour-sur-Glane in 1944. The village still stands as it did that day. Buildings in ruins, burned out cars in the quiet roads. A show of will and power and pitilessness. Suddenly, I feared for Misha and everyone in his block.

Yes, there was no way back. The SS officers looked about at the carnage and I believe came to a decision. I heard no words, though I saw grim faces become determined ones. I saw heads nod and with that the meeting concluded with a few salutes. Off they went back to their offices and their dining halls and their girlfriends in the barracks. It took several days though—over a week, I think. I don't know why. Maybe they felt they needed approval from the kommandant or an overseer in Berlin. But it came, it came. Yes, the reprisal came with all its fury.

I looked at him searchingly, almost pleading for him to go on. I felt that any question I might pose would sound childish, like a boy asking his father of his war experiences. I had some faint hope in a less than appalling conclusion, but that slipped away as I looked into his melancholy eyes.

I alone am escaped to tell thee, as the book says.

WAITING

After killing the guards, especially in such a grisly manner, the men in the block had a sense of resignation. Greater resignation, I should say. Death was no longer something looming in the distance. It was now something imminent. They returned to their drudgery, though without the companionship of their courageous little friend Max. Misha and I went on with our morning prayers.

One afternoon, there was an unexpected selection. I say it was unexpected because they were always in the morning. The guards, with no medical officer present, quickly chose a few dozen people and told them to prepare to leave for a sub-camp. Nisim was among those selected to go and we said our farewells.

"You'll be fine, Nisim," Misha said to encourage the disheartened boy. There's always work at the sub-camps. You'll be much better off at one of them. Here . . . you never know."

Nisim could not be consoled. "Still, I'll be *alone*," he whimpered. He was still a boy of twelve and even the hardening of the last few months could not stamp out his need for friends and family, such as they were in the block.

"No, Nisim. Many of your friends here are going with you. And there will be new friends at the sub-camp. Remember your promise to your brother, that you will have your Bar Mitzvah when you reach thirteen. That is a promise you must keep."

Nisim nodded amid some whimpers. "Yes, I will keep that promise. I will enter our faith as a man."

The shouts of the guard came and there was no more time for encouragement and goodbyes. When we say goodbye here in America, we promise to keep in touch. Of course, there was none of that in those days. We all hoped we'd see each other again someday, preferably far from Auschwitz, though the prospects we knew were slight.

Off Nisim went with the others. They assembled just outside the block and were marched in a ragged formation. I followed behind. I saw them trudge out the gate then to the right, away from Birkenau and in the direction of the Monowitz sub-camp. We could only hope for the best. What Misha said about the work at the sub-camps was true, usually. There were no hard rules there. There was always a change in the camp's priorities. And of course there was always the chance of a murderous guard having sport with you.

Then, on the next night, came the horrible orders.

Adrian stopped, more suddenly than other times. I thought he'd continue in a few moments. He did not. I offered to get coffee or water. He simply shook his head back and forth in short motions, almost as though shuddering, and held his hands out, palms first as though reaching for something or pushing something away. I don't know which.

"I want to go home now," he murmured, turning to his desk and shutting down his work station.

"Of course, Adrian, of course. We can continue whenever you wish." I smiled—comfortingly, I hope.

"We'll see . . . we'll see," he said, standing up uneasily. He headed for the door but stopped. He turned to me and said wearily. "You know, Danny, I feel old. All of a sudden, I feel very old." He then went out into the quiet corridor and headed out into the evening.

INTERLUDE

Adrian's words about feeling old worried me, as did the look of realization and unhappiness on his face as he turned to me and spoke them. We all know moments when we suddenly realize we are not children anymore, or that we are no longer teenagers, or even young. Well, Adrian was realizing that he was old, no longer feeling challenges or looking for answers. He knew he was old and in inevitable decline. One day I will have the same realization. We all will. And when it comes to me, I will think of Adrian Nowak that evening in Folsom.

I read a lot in those weeks when Adrian and I were meeting. I read of an uprising at Treblinka, the death camp in northeastern Poland. There was a kommando assigned to extracting the gold from the teeth of the dead. They secreted away a few pieces and traded them for various items with the Ukrainian guards. A measure of cooperation developed and the Ukrainians came to exchange more and more items for the gold. At one point, the Ukrainians even traded weapons which were then used in an heroic short-lived revolt.

I also read of an uprising at one of the gas chambers in Birkenau. The kommando that worked the chamber and crematorium—yes, inmates worked there too—learned that they would soon be sent to their deaths in the very building they labored. They overpowered a couple of guards and fought for a few hours. Again, the revolt was heroic but short-lived. In an extraordinary twist, there was a group of inmates inside the gas chamber when the revolt began and the procedure had to be stopped. A few made their way back to the blocks and managed to live out their days after liberation. Another miracle.

The SS wanted the mass killing to go on in an orderly manner, in an efficient manner. Protests, disturbances, attempts at escape—they all wasted time and slowed down the machinery. There were inmates whose jobs was to make the procedure go smoothly. They chatted with the condemned, at least those who harbored illusions that there truly were showers awaiting them. They asked where they were from. "Oh, I know Breslau well," they might affably reply. "A tailor, you say! We need good tailors here!" Then there were the lies of a nursery near the showers. Yes, tell the mothers that there was a schoolroom up ahead with building blocks and storybooks. The condemned were given towels and bars of soap as they neared the chambers and told to hurry because the hot water would soon be exhausted. It kept the illusion alive. I imagine the men who came up with those ideas thought of themselves as innovators, much like the man who made them run to the chamber so they were out of breath and they'd inhale the gas more quickly. Keep them moving. Keep them calm. Keep the procedure efficient.

One of the soldiers gave a speech before they went inside.

"On behalf of the camp administration, I bid you welcome. This is not a holiday resort but a labor camp. Just as our soldiers risk their lives at the front to gain victory, you will work here for a new Europe. How you approach this task is entirely up to you. We shall look after your health and we shall also offer you well-paid work. After the war, we shall assess everyone according to his merits and treat him accordingly. Now, would you please all get undressed. Hang your clothes on the hooks we have provided and please remember the number of the hook. When you've had your shower there will be a bowl of soup and coffee or tea for all."

How many thought him sincere? How many grasped hold of the lie to stave off insanity.

Adrian didn't come to work the next day. I was worried, naturally, so I called. He was pleased by my concern and said that he just needed a few days of quiet and rest. I agreed and tried to cheer him with talk of restaurants and weather, though it was perfectly obvious what was hanging over us. I waited patiently another two days and Saturday morning, he called.

"Are you ready to hear the rest?" He asked in a manner that implied he sincerely thought I'd had enough or knew what was coming.

"Yes, Adrian. I'm ready. In fact, I've been waiting for your call."

"Then let's meet in the same coffee shop near Granite Bay. But Danny . . . this time let's see if we can have a table on the upper floor, where we can see the lovely sky. Is an hour too soon?"

REPRISAL

One night a soldier woke me up, along with a few other Kapos, to assist in an urgent matter. It was well after midnight—highly unusual. We gathered at an end of the building with a few SS guards from another part of the camp. A young Obersturmführer—a lieutenant—launched into a briefing.

"We have all heard of the murderous uprising at the new buildings. We lost several fine men in that unfortunate incident. We've finally received approval for our response."

My heart sank. A strange meeting in the middle of the night? Approval for a response?

"We've made time in Krema I. We will take the population of the guilty block there this very night."

Adrian looked at me to discern if I knew the meaning. I did. A Krema was a building with a gas chamber and ovens. There were four of them in Birkenau, though one was destroyed in that uprising. So I knew that everyone in Misha's block was being sent to their deaths.

Yes, I realized then who the other SS men were. They were from the Krema. The officer went on in a crisp professional way, as though outlining a plan to load a truck convoy or repair a railroad track. "You men will assist in this operation. I'm sure you will perform your duty in exemplary manners. It might have been you that was hacked apart in the snow that day."

My throat became tight. If I had been ordered to speak, I would have only made incomprehensible gasps. I was close to vomiting. It was all underway in a moment. We marched to the block to begin the night's dreadful work. I went ahead and found my way to Misha's area on the bunk shelf. The strange hour, the look in my eye . . . Misha knew something dire was afoot.

"It's the reprisal, Misha . . . tonight . . . right now."

He nodded. He was just out of sleep, but he understood. He understood completely.

"Adrian, I know you've tried to help all you could."

"I'll keep trying this night too."

Misha smiled boyishly and tapped my arm. "I'll see you later, my friend." There was no fear in his eyes.

A few men in the block woke up and sensed something coming. Some might have understood completely. I don't know. The guards crashed in and roused the inmates, some four hundred of them, from whatever sleep they were having and took them outside, where they were formed into two groups, each with two ranks. Had I resisted or tried to help with an escape, it would have failed and I would have been shot down on the spot or given a special place in the ranks. They were my friends, my family; but I was a Kapo, and I was going to march them over to Krema I.

It was a hellish scene. The guards and Kapos steadily shouted at the men, more than usual as they were exacting revenge on those who'd killed their fellow guards. They might, at least in their minds, have been reestablishing order and meting out justice. They all had machine pistols and they were deployed around the groups in a manner such that their fire would not hit one of their own, only the condemned who had nothing to lose.

It was cold and dark, with only the lights on the fences and guard towers offering brief glimpses of the two groups stumbling ahead. We went out the gate of Auschwitz I and trod over the railroad tracks that separated I from II—Birkenau. Entering II, we saw the Krema out ahead, well illuminated as it operated continually, with crews working shifts—guards and inmates. Herd them into the chamber, seal the doors, and drop the gas canisters. I recalled guards pointing to trucks coming into camp and saying they were loaded with Zyklon B, a rat poison. Some joked about the chemicals being used on other forms of vermin.

My mind raced. I'd read of Zyklon B and seen piles of empty canisters in the Holocaust Museum next to heaps of eyeglasses and combs and purses. The canisters were dropped from above, down a mesh wire column that prevented the people from attempting to stop the billowing discharge. I'd also read of the burns the gas's prussic acid made on bodies, searing them blue. The walls of remaining chambers have blue marks on the walls to this day. There were several chambers, each with a different capacity and layout.

I was at a gas chamber once . . . yes, during an extermination.

I must have gasped when Adrian said that. No, I'm sure I did. I'd wondered if he had seen the operation of a Krema but dared not ask. There are limits. One doesn't ask soldiers if they've killed or taken dreadful souvenirs. A door had been opened though and Adrian went on without any prodding.

After they were inside, a guard closed and sealed the metal doors. He signaled the chemical handler, put on a gas mask, and climbed the stairs to the roof. I watched from below as they cautiously removed the Zyklon B canisters and dropped them down hatches into the panicking mass of humanity. Yes, I heard the screams and shouts. But the SS were prepared for that. An immense diesel generator was switched on and its unmuffled, jackhammer-like noise overwhelmed the poundings on the doors and walls and all but the shrillest of screams. I looked around at the guards and inmate laborers— the *Sonderkommando*, the "special detail" that operated the death chambers and crematoria. They stood about casually. Some smoked cigarettes, talked about dinner, and cursed the cold weather. It was a job. Soon there would be another group to run through. Efficiency. Yes, the place had its own efficiency.

But back to the night of the special operation, the liquidation of the block that had killed the SS guards—the block with my friends.

"I have to take a leak, urgently!" I exclaimed to an SS guard. I ran off before he could say anything. I turned back and slipped into Misha's line, moving among the throng in the dark, a hundred meters or so inside Birkenau, until I found him. When we saw each other, we were strangely joyful. It was like running into each other after school.

"I'm happy to see you, Adrian," he said in pleasant voice as though nothing extraordinary were happening. "Have you any ideas?"

"No, Misha, not yet. The guards are watching too closely."

Misha remained silent as he was moving forward with the line. "Can you find Bruno?"

"I thought of that, Misha. I don't know where he is. He was transferred to another part of the camp a few weeks ago. I haven't seen him since."

As I slowly trudged ahead just outside the throng, I felt the fingers of panic creeping upon me and cold sweat dripping down my back. I kept thinking of my resourcefulness and how it had won out in the past, saving Misha from the first selection with a clownish pratfall into the slime. It was simply a matter of looking around and thinking fast. The night was dark and the guards none too bright. Something would come to me. Yes, it had to.

I walked along, though at moments I wanted to run away. I could occasionally see light come across a few faces I knew. I wanted to pull Misha out of the line and run off with him through the gate, into the village where the Gypsy baby was or onto a train as it pulled away for

Krakow. I even had thoughts of joining my friends for the final walk but only fleeting ones. I'm not that noble.

"Keep them moving, Kapo!" a guard yelled, strengthening his command with a nudge from the muzzle of his machine pistol.

I could pull Misha from the group and insist that I'd received an order from an officer. I could then put my friend into a block holding a newly arrived group. He could be another face in the block. When I apprised Misha of this idea, he looked around and shook his head. "They won't believe a Polish Kapo. They'll shoot us both."

I pleaded with him to give it a try but he simply walked ahead, his face in deep thought yet calm. After a dozen steps, he turned to me, sighed, and said, "We have to accept some things." His boyish cheerfulness was gone. There was no fear or despair in his eyes. It was acceptance.

"Kapo!" a guard shouted as he shoved me from behind. "Is there a problem here, Kapo?"

I shook my head, half expecting a fist to crash down on me. "Not at all. I have everything under control here, *Gefreiter.*"

He gave a through look at Misha then at me. "Keep the line in order. We want this to go well."

"*Ja wohl,*" I crisply answered and he went off to shout at others.

Misha looked at me almost to say, "I told you." But then he did speak. "Adrian, you are my brother. I was fortunate to have you with me. You made my time here better. Having you to protect me was a gift from on high. I'm certain of that."

"You're not going to die this night, my friend. I'll get you out of here!" As I looked about for an answer, I felt like a trapped animal. I looked at the faces of the others in the group. None had any illusion of showers and a hot meal awaiting them. They knew that they'd be sealed in a dank room and shortly later blue smoke would billow from canisters inside mesh columns.

We were about a hundred meters out when Misha reached into his shirt for something. It was too dark to see what it was. As a glimmer of light came through the group from a fence light, I saw the delicate fabric of his Tefillin. His father's gift, Misha's morning ritual, our block's source of hope.

"Adrian, when I left the block tonight I wanted to take my Tefillin to the end but now I want you to keep it. There is a story in these sacred boxes. I wanted to tell it one day but I cannot. I want you to have my Tefillin and tell the world of the light it brought us. You've witnessed their work. I want the story told. And I want them away from this place."

I could not bring myself to reach for them.

"Take it, Adrian. Please take it. Please take my Tefillin before a guard sees it and grinds it into the mud with his boot. I want it free of this place!"

I surreptitiously reached to him and felt the smooth pouch and its contents. I thought back to the day Misha's father showed them to me and for an instant I was back home with Misha, safe. Only for an instant. Now the Tefillin was in my hands less than seventy-five meters from Krema I and its tall stout chimney.

"I promised your father I'd protect you."

"And you did so very well, Adrian. I'm grateful . . . so very grateful. My father would be as well. I know that, Adrian. He would be *proud* of you."

The shouts of the guards and other Kapos grew stronger and more frequent—standard procedure as a group neared the end. Everyone I could see accepted his fate and walked along. I saw courage and nobility in them. They had endured so much since they detrained at the ramp. I wondered that night, and I continue to wonder to this day, how they looked back on the uprising and the killing of the guards. How many of them saw it as a last expression of their dignity as human beings and accepted the consequences without regret.

Misha furtively and briefly clasped my shoulder. "We've been brave through trying times, my friend. A few minutes more, that's all. A few minutes more of helping each other to be brave. Promise me that you will help me face this and that you will find your way through this."

I promised those things—and I did so in strong voice, though I thought myself no longer capable of one.

Misha began to pray.

"I have faith in the Lord, I have faith in the good, and I have faith that good will overcome evil . . . . I have faith in the Lord, I have faith in the good, and I have faith that good will overcome evil."

I repeated the words along with him.

"Death brings us closer to the Lord . . . Death brings us closer to the Lord . . . I am ready . . . I am ready."

Not far ahead, the first of the group had reached the back of the Krema and were being ordered to disrobe. I'd seen the final routine before and I vowed never to go near a Krema again. I started to tremble. Misha did not. I no longer focused on the others. I was cold, not from the weather but from a weakening pulse. I became dizzy and disoriented and fell to the ground.

"I have faith in the Lord, I have faith in the good, and I have faith that good will overcome evil . . . . I have faith in the Lord, I have faith in the good, and I have faith that good will overcome evil."

I heard the clumping of a hundred men's feet and the murmuring of a hundred fervent prayers.

"I have faith in the Lord, I have faith in the good, and I have faith that good will overcome evil . . . . I have faith in the Lord, I have faith in the good, and I have faith that good will overcome evil."

I looked up as best as I could and saw Misha walking forward. He looked back at me and our eyes caught each other's for the last time. He turned back toward the brightly lit building and went on. I breathed in quickly to clear my head and avoid crying like a small child.

A detachment of SS guards ran up from the rear. Two of them peeled off and came over to me. One laughed and said, "What's the matter, Kapo, no stomach for this sort of thing?"

Rage built inside me, the same rage these inmates felt when they rose up. My hands made fists and I was determined to strike back at the bastard. I'd punch him, strangle him, whatever I had to do to avenge this night. As I stood up more firmly I felt the Tefillin inside my tunic and came to a stop, once again overwhelmed by dizziness. In one guard I saw cruelty, but not in the other. I felt a strange gentleness come over me, one that could have no psychological or physical basis I can think of. I had to get through this night. I had to see good prevail over evil.

The second, somewhat older, guard chided his detestable companion. "It's have been a hard night for everyone. The poor kid probably didn't get any sleep. I'll take care of him." With that, the older guard walked me away from Krema I. As we neared the brick opening to Birkenau, I heard the deep, cruel roar of the diesel generator. I clutched the Tefillin beneath my tunic and prayed. I didn't pray for anything in particular. I simply prayed.

And that was the last time I saw Misha. After so many months together, after all my efforts to look out for him . . . there was nothing more I could do. Events were out of my hands. No cleverness or guile could have saved him. I couldn't do anything . . . I couldn't do anything. The operation came too swiftly and there were too many guards. It would have taken a miracle . . . but the heavens were impassive that night, as they so often were during the war.

I went back to Misha's block in the morning. Empty, silent—devastatingly so. It made me realize how much life Misha and Joe and Nisim and the others had given the bleak place. I was overwhelmed by feelings of being alone—alone in life, alone in a dark place far from anyone I knew. If I had uttered some small or great remark, no one would have heard it. If I had fallen on the cold floor and wept for hours, no one would have cared. If I had been struck dead, no one would have mourned me—or prayed over me.

I sat on a bunk row and thought of times Misha and I had talked and laughed there. Right there, on that wooden shelf or near the back. Two boys had found the will to go on. I reached for the leather pouch and held the Tefillin more reverently than ever. Recollections of our morning rite raced through my mind. I wrapped the leather around my arm and head—clumsily, I'm sure—and started to recite the prayer. I had prayed along with Misha many times and thought I knew the words but I then realized I was simply following along with my friend and without him, there would be no prayer, only indistinct and halting mumbling. Still, I felt I was with Misha. I felt a sense of communion with him. I felt he was nearby, smiling and assuring me that all was well, and urging me to hold on to hope and to life.

I placed the Tefillin back inside the pouch. I couldn't cry anymore. I was exhausted. But I had one thought—a determination, really. I had to keep faith with my friend and go on. One day more, then another, then another. I determined to go on. For Misha and the rest who had tried so nobly to do the same but could not. I had to tell the story of what I'd seen.

I stood up, took a last look at the block that strangely had meant so much to me over the last year, then trudged back to the Kapo barracks. What will happen now? I'd be assigned another block of inmates to supervise and we would go out on work details. Yes, I would go on.

The day was nearing its end and the room was darkening as the sun retreated. Suddenly, Adrian shook his head and came alive, as though he'd woken up from a refreshing rest.

LIBERATION

As I thought, I was assigned to watch other inmate groups. Without my friend, I retreated again into my belief that events around me were not truly taking place and that some cruel entity was forcing me to see these ghastly phantasms and stark buildings as part of an incomprehensible illusion. It was comforting but I was able to discern that a dementia was setting in. Certain events, however, caught my attention and took me out of my dissociating refuge from Auschwitz.

Trains were not coming in nearly as often then. The Kremas closed down in the fall of 1944 and the SS tried to hide other signs of their work. We could hear the muffled rumbles of distant artillery, especially at night when most of the camp noise was down. The guns were what? Thirty kilometers away? Ten? The Germany military, the once invincible Wehrmacht and Waffen SS that had rolled over France and Poland, was on its back foot and on the verge of collapse. I yearned to see the day.

The guards were nervous—some even frightened. They didn't seem to take as much interest in their work as the prospects of promotion or punishment were all but gone. There were fewer of the guards too. Some had gone off to the west as the Russian advance neared us. One day, thousands of inmates were marched into Germany, hundreds of kilometers in winter. Remaining workers no longer labored on railroad lines or in the sawmill. They tore down buildings and loaded truckloads of files from the administration building. The rumble of artillery came closer still and prisoners were either elated that liberation was in the offing or frightened that a mass slaughter of remaining inmates was at hand.

One January morning most of the remaining guards and staff vanished. They were gone! I walked toward the main gate and saw soldiers off in the distance. They were stepping warily toward the checkpoint, looking side to side, receiving hand signals from behind. Rounder helmets, not the German ones with the rear sweeping down over the ears and neck. They were Russians. They fired a few bursts into the checkpoint at the gate but it was empty. I retreated to the block I'd been assigned to where I knew people would speak up for me. The Russians walked about the camp expecting to find prisoners of war, Russian, British, American. Instead they found thin, sickly, filthy stickmen. The soldiers were dumbfounded.

A Russian entered our block, his burp gun at the ready. He had a fur cap over his head, not a metal helmet. He too was filthy and unshaven, but from who knows how many months and years of hard fighting along the huge eastern front.

"You are free," he shouted in Russian, which is fairly close to my native Polish. He had the toothy grin of a young man who'd grown up hard in a peasant village on the steppes. He then slung his burp gun and opened his arms as though welcoming us back to life. We shook his hand and danced with him.

This is it, I thought. The day has come at last. I had longed for it so long but had no idea what to do or think when it arrived. All the death and suffering were over. Danny, we hope and pray for things yet are stupefied when they come. Some things come to us from angels, others from Russian soldiers! The only regret I felt that day was that they hadn't come ten months earlier, when Misha was still alive.

The Russians found bodies that had been taken out from blocks in the morning. One soldier came running down, his face horror stricken. He told the others of thousands of more bodies on the other side of the tracks. These soldiers had seen death on an immense scale on the Eastern Front but they were not prepared for what they saw that day.

There was a film crew there photographing and filming the place. Soldiers and inmates—*former* inmates—were taking remaining file cabinets from the administration building. The SS, in their rush to flee, had left many records behind. Thousands of pages. Ah, I thought, the world will see the Germans' own documentation of their dismal work here.

Generals came to see what young officers had reported up the chain of command. Every one of them was astonished and horrified. There was simply nothing in their experiences to prepare them for Auschwitz. Some could not bear it and needed to be helped away. Misha had foreseen this—how stunned the world would be on seeing Auschwitz.

Oh, and not all the Germans were able to get away. The Russians, shall we say, did not give them candy. Some were beaten and kicked to death. If former inmates pointed out an SS guard and said he'd tortured or killed a friend, the Russians would shoot or hang him. For the latter method, they'd tie his hands behind his back, place a makeshift noose around his neck as he stood on a chair beneath a tree or light post, then kick the chair away. No long drop to snap their necks and kill them instantly. They strangled slowly, twenty minutes or more, twisting and gagging hideously. Most of us thought this appropriate. I did. I must confess I thought it the right thing to do. I'd seen their daily beatings and murders, I'd seen the Krema operate that day. I'd seen men, women, and children go there. I'd smelled the smoke from the chimneys. Yes, the bastards deserved it.

Some former inmates, however, didn't think the SS guards deserved it. They shook their heads and looked away, thinking that the place had made monsters out of us too. I've read that the British and Americans treated the SS guards fairly well, according to the rules. I preferred Russian justice that day.

Many Kapos were interrogated, taken away, or hanged slowly. The Russians came to recognize the Kapo patches and a couple inspected me rather roughly. Many men from the block I'd been assigned to immediately attested to my decency, saying I helped them as best I could and was different from those fellows strung up across the camp. With a gruff motion of a rifle muzzle, I was let off.

We were given food, Russian army rations and things taken from abandoned houses in the villages. It was not the best cuisine that Europe had ever offered but it was well received by the grateful clientele, though we were unable to leave a tip. The portions were comparatively generous and we could see health returning to all but the sickest. Medical units arrived and helped those they could.

I walked about the camp cautiously. It was surreal, dreamlike. No guards, no selections, no stench. Many were downright giddy, walking freely and without fear for the first time in years. They hoped to find friends and family members. Some had luck in that regard, most did not.

I passed the guard dining hall, the guest rooms, bakeries, brothels, kennels, and the swimming pool. Auschwitz was a small town. I realized it all the better that day. There were aspects of the camp that I hadn't known about, such as where the medical experiments took place. The people who ran that section must have been inspired by the devil himself. I walked across the railroad to Birkenau and saw how immense it had become in the last year. In one area there were immense piles of belongings taken from people just off the cattle cars. There was row after row of warehouses, some burned now, filled with eyeglasses and purses and overcoats, and even crutches and artificial limbs. The women inmates who sorted through the belongings and stored them called the section "Kanada."

There was one section of blocks that the Russians had surrounded with wire and guards. There were Germans held there. They'd not been judged by the makeshift courts that sprang up and I suppose they were awaiting investigation. I looked about for Bruno in the hope I could provide some testimony as to his decency. I didn't see him though. Would anyone have believed the wedding and Gypsy baby story anyway?

I avoided the Kremas. Yes, for several days I told myself never to go near one again. I'd seen one, I knew what they did, and there was nothing more to know. But after a few days, I walked past the grove of trees where mothers and children had waited. I stared at the large metal doors of Krema I. Misha was right. It was best that I did not continue with him. I imagined him inside there and I shuddered and gagged. I didn't go in. Some former inmates did though. Many came out weeping uncontrollably.

"Adrian? Is that you, Adrian?"

The voice was familiar and for a ridiculous instant I thought it was Misha. As wondrous as those days after liberation were, I knew it wasn't the case. I turned and saw Nisim, one of the Sephardic brothers from Spain. I was drawn away from my sickening grief and into a cheerful reunion. Yes, it was Nisim. Gaunt, eyes hollowed, but able to smile.

"Nisim, you are alive!" We hugged for a long while and cried out of happiness and relief. I'd never thought there could be such spontaneous joyfulness from me again. "I'm so glad to see that you made it. Where were you?"

"Oh, Adrian, it's a gift to see you again. I was taken to a sub-camp to work in a pharmaceutical factory. The work must have been important. We were treated well—you know, well by this place's standards. I was lucky, very lucky. Where are the others from our block?"

My joyfulness evaporated and I told him of the killing of the guards and the reprisal against the entire block.

"Oh, I see, I see." Nisim mumbled, looking behind me at the Krema and nodding his head in acceptance. "And Misha?" he asked with a little hopefulness.

"Him too . . . ."

"I'm so sorry, Adrian. He was your best friend . . . from Lodz."

"Yes, we were both from Lodz."

Nisim tried to keep a brave composure but memories of our friend and the experience of freedom and openness made us both bawl again, shamelessly and protractedly.

"Misha was calm as he walked to this place," I in time explained. "His faith in the Lord was strong. He said that he'd be fine. I believe him, Nisim, I believe him. He is at peace."

"Yes, I'm sure he is. So is my brother David. They are both at peace, far from here."

Nisim and I stood there only a few yards from the metal doors of Krema I, thinking of our losses and the losses of so many others. I don't think we knew how many. Hundreds of thousands? Over a million? There were also Treblinka and Sobibor and Belzec and Dachau and Mauthausen and Belsen and Buchenwald. And poor people lined up outside their villages on the steppes and shot in the back of the head. All those poor people, all those poor people. Yes, I've already mentioned what I thought of Russian justice.

Memories of Misha and Nisim raced through my head. One of them brought happiness, at last. I clasped my hands on Nisim's shoulders and shook him. "You, my friend, shall have your Bar Mitzvah, just as your brother wanted! You will enter adulthood in accordance with your family's wishes." I tousled his hair and expressed my congratulations.

Nisim smiled, though with a quizzical look. "You're right. My family's hopes will be realized. The light shall be passed on."

"David will witness the event, I'm sure of that," I added.

"Yes, he'll be there too . . . . So what are you going to do now, Adrian?" Nisim asked, wiping away tears realizing the bewildering implications of freedom. We now had to think about the next day, plan for it, see it through.

"Oh . . . oh. I'll to go back to Lodz once the German army has fallen back far enough. My parents are there . . . they *were* there, I should say. The German army was in Lodz, now the Russian army. I'm sure the world has changed and little Lodz has changed with it. What are you going to do, Nisim?"

"I'm going off with some of the men in my kommando. We're going to search for our families as best we can. As you said, the German army, then the Russian army."

"That's good, that's good. I hope you have good fortune in your efforts—all of you. But we all know that we have to prepare for the worst. Even I have to do that."

"I know. We've all reached the same conclusion in the last few days. But we've seen the worst life has to offer. No doubt about that."

I agreed. I still do. There was nothing life could offer that would be worse than what we'd seen as boys. Nisim seemed ready for whatever lay ahead and he gave me a brave smile. We hugged for the last time and went our separate ways. As he walked away I was reminded of something.

"Nisim!" I called out.

"Yes, Adrian?" Nisim turned around and looked at me.

"Doesn't your name mean 'miracles'?"

Nisim beamed boyishly and nodded. "Yes, it does. Plural, more than one!"

I watched him walk away until he disappeared into a crowd of a few dozen inmates—*former* inmates. What an amazing young man. Thirteen, and he'd endured all that. The human spirit is a remarkable thing. We went from acceptance of death to planning for tomorrow. It was strange, bewildering, and so beautiful.

I stayed a few more weeks around the camp. Oddly enough, it was hard to leave. Auschwitz had been my world, my home, for three years. A horrible home, yes of course. But it was where I learned to live and help friends and hope with them and face the next work day. It was where I'd met Bertha. Now, I had to do everything alone. No Nisim, no Bertha, no Misha.

I found some civilian clothes in Kanada and walked out the main gate of Auschwitz. I truly was free. My destination was Lodz, two hundred kilometers to the north. I walked and hitchhiked. Russian soldiers asked me directions and gave me a lift here and there. They'd heard of Auschwitz and asked if it was true. It was, I told them, it was. They nodded their heads silently and gave me rations. Local peasants gave me bread from time to time. Along the journey I could see hundreds of abandoned farmhouses and desolate villages. My hopes of finding my family grew dim as I crossed the war-ravaged landscape.

When I finally reached my neighborhood in Lodz and came to our building, it was clear my parents were no longer living there. I recognized former neighbors and with a little explanation, they recognized me. They informed me that the Germans had taken my father away in early 1944, though no one knew why, and my mother had died in despair not long thereafter. I was alone, more so than I'd thought. You'd be surprised how the faint hope of finding your family dwells inside you and when that hope is gone, the feeling of emptiness and vulnerability becomes overwhelming. I sat in a park and wept.

Germany surrendered in May 1945 and the guns fell silent across Europe for the first time in six years. I stayed in Lodz a few years, thinking I could rebuild my life there. I was able to lay claim to my parents' dwelling and their modest savings. I worked as a handyman—a very reserved handyman, one who never discussed the war years. There were many such people in Poland—many more in Germany, I'm sure.

One day I decided to leave. There was nothing there but distasteful memories. I decided to leave for good—Lodz, Poland, maybe even the entire continent of Europe and all its periodic bloodletting. I sold my parents' place and all my meager belongings and traveled by train to Italy. I stayed in Naples for a few weeks and thought what to do with my life. I befriended a fellow Pole who'd lost his family in the war. His name was Danke, from Lublin, and we decided to go to America. We arrived by ship in New York City with many other immigrants but soon went our separate ways.

I went to college and graduated with a degree in electrical engineering from CCNY. While working in New York, I met a woman my age— another immigrant from Poland, another waif from the Second World War. Opportunities elsewhere arrived and we took advantage of them. We lived in Texas for many years. Consulting takes me to many places. As you know, Danny, as you well know.

So, that is my story. I've never told it to anyone. A few episodes here and there perhaps, but you are the only person to hear the whole long and woeful confession. I don't know what inspired me to tell you all this. Probably your father's experiences at Auschwitz. Who knows, maybe I saw him there. Who knows.

I thanked Adrian for telling me his story in all its painful detail. I told him that I felt honored to be the repository of his life events. And I made a point of shaking his hand. Over the years I've been fortunate enough to have received a few honors—diplomas, professional awards, plaudits here and there. None, however, approaches the honor of being told Adrian's story and being entrusted with it.

Adrian smiled humbly and said there was one more thing. A frail hand offered me a small silken pouch, faded and worn in most places from what must have been the legacy of many years. It must have been from Poland, before the war. I looked closer and discerned the Hebrew letter "Shin" (ש) sewn into the material. It too was faded by time. As it rested in my palms, I felt something inside. No boy of my faith could fail to know the contents.

"Tefillin," I whispered.

Adrian nodded and I delicately tugged on a fastening which only grudgingly gave way and revealed two small black boxes encircled by leather strips. The boxes and strips were of course quite old but they'd been preserved with linseed oil. Their look and touch made me think them the work of a town artisan, long gone now, proud of his craft. I turned them about in my hands and the light hit the areas where two more of the same letter Shin (ש). To our people, observant or not, the letter is recognized in holy places to symbolize the Lord and our scripture.

I looked to Adrian with wonder and awe as I contemplated the all but impossible provenance of this sacred object. "Tefillin," Adrian murmured, "Misha's Tefillin. He gave this to me that night as we walked toward Krema I in Birkenau."

I was holding a piece of history. Polish history, Jewish history, world history, sacred history. This Tefillin had been there, in the camp, where Adrian's stories had taken place. Misha recited his prayers over it and gave it to Adrian who kept it and cared for it since 1944—over a half century ago. I ran my fingers across the surfaces and thought of Joe and Nisim and David and Naomi and Bruno and his mother, and all the others in the block who'd prayed in that dank block in Auschwitz. And of course I thought especially of Misha.

DEPARTURE

A few weeks later, our contracts with Intel were up. Management wanted Adrian to stay on and offered him a new contract but he had other ideas, other plans. I tried to change his mind over breakfast at the cafeteria, mentioning that another project would start in a few weeks and that he was well respected and even admired here. I might have conveyed that I thought highly of him as a person and cherished his wit and spirit. Anyway, I hope I did.

"I need some vacation time, Danny." He nibbled a bit on a croissant and looked at the morning light illuminating the atrium. "I need to be outdoors, in the sun. Beautiful warm sunlight. Humans were meant to be outside, Danny. Offices are not natural environments. I need more light . . . ."

His expression didn't suggest eagerness for vacation. It was sad. Yes, he wanted to get away, but not out of joyful expectation of walks in nature. He wanted to get away because Folsom was where he'd revisited his past, where he'd gone back to Auschwitz.

"So it was the story then," I finally said.

He nodded.

"Well, I'm sorry I had you go through that again, Adrian. Maybe it would have been better—"

"No, no. Danny, you are a good friend. I thank you for the opportunity you gave me to tell my story. It was dwelling inside me, kicking about, demanding release. But I just couldn't find the right time and place, not even with people close to me. Not even my wife and son. I could never tell them that story! How would they think of me? How would they think of their husband and father after hearing that?"

"It was an honor to hear your story, Adrian. Truly, an honor. I feel that something important has been passed on to me."

"Now I can rest . . . for a while. Now I can think about retirement and what I'd like to do once I leave Folsom."

A warm smile came across his face and lingered longer than I'd seen before on him. A burden had been lifted from him.

"This is it then? Are you retiring, for good? The industry will lose a master. You still have much to offer."

"Oh, the industry will get along fine. They managed many years before me and they will manage many years after me. From the perspective of the people up there," he pointed to the upper floors where the top figures had spacious offices with commanding views of the lake and mountains. "Everyone is replaceable. Some people leave, new ones come in. In a way, Danny, I'll be starting a new life. It's just beginning."

I smiled and made a note to remember his words for when my retirement comes.

"So, Adrian my prematurely retiring friend, what you are going to do in this new life?"

"Well, I always wanted to go on fishing trips, *long* fishing trips. Just throw the hook into the water and sit there, alone on the watery expanses. Another old man and the sea—one who has already found a Hemingway to write his story! I'll listen to the birds chirping, to the crickets and grass hoppers. I'll listen to nature. It will be so beautiful . . . ."

"There's so much beauty in the world," I said while nodding. "And perhaps the more horror we see in life, the more we appreciate the beauty. At least, I hope that's the case."

"Yes . . . yes . . . the horror was long ago. I'm ready for nature . . . and beauty . . . and the sea . . . . Danny, you will remember to write all that down someday—to pass it on to others."

"Of course, Adrian. I will put it down in print, faithfully."

"I want to read it, you know."

"You will, Adrian. I promise you."

His final day came. He gathered his desk material and mementoes into a box. There wasn't much; he was tidy and simple. He had a large calculator from the 1970s or so—the kind I used in college and graduate school, primitive by today's standards. There was a notebook—not a small computer, a paperbound book, another throwback to my schooldays; and a salad plate which he kept an orange or two on. He said the plate was made in Walbrzych, not far from Lodz. And there were small portrait photos of his wife and son.

We sat in our office awaiting a man from security who would escort him to the lobby where he'd turn in his badge. Without it, he'd be a stranger, an outsider, someone out of the system. It was all routine—a cheerless one, I thought. More than cheerless, it was insensitive, bureaucratic, and even cruel.

Adrian looked to me and murmured, "I have a sense that we will see each other another time, my young friend." He then smiled in a fatherly manner, which I very much appreciated and still cherish.

"Yes, I think so too. I certainly hope so," I replied, only barely believing my words.

A light rap on the doorway. "Mr. Nowak?" It was security, uniformed and impersonal. At least he was on time.

"Yes, at your service." Adrian was strangely upbeat.

"Have you gathered all your personal belongings?"

"All of my real estate is in this small box," he said tapping with a single finger on the cardboard file box.

The guard let a slight grin come across his face, which was probably not according to protocol, then he looked around the desk, which presumably *was* according to protocol. "Yes, it looks like you're all done here. Mr Nowak, do you have your badge on your person?"

"Right here," Adrian used the same finger to point to the green badge clipped onto his shirt pocket.

"Danny, it has been a pleasure working with you."

"The pleasure has been all mine." We hugged and as we separated I saw his eyes had moistened. I knew mine had.

"Let me know when you find time to do a little writing. You know, the reminiscences of an old Polish man you once knew."

"I'll be certain to do that, Adrian. Yes, I'll make a point of it."

Then he nodded and walked out of the office with the guard. I heard their footfalls fade as they passed down the corridor. I sat back in my chair and stared at the empty work station.

I gave Adrian a call about two weeks after his departure. He sounded well and in good spirits. He was doing some fishing and looking into purchasing a small boat. A few weeks later, he called me at my home and we had another pleasant chat. This one, however, was briefer. I sensed that our conversations would become less frequent. I was right.

Work became hectic. The new project was a short one and nearing a close. Problems remained, others popped up. How many hours a week was I working? Seventy? But we got the chip done, more or less on time. After that, we could relax. Most people took time off and headed up to the mountains. Some colleagues invited me to come along but I declined. I spent my last few days sitting in my office, alone with my thoughts—alone with Adrian's thoughts, I should say. Every now and then I'd hear a train whistle in the distance.

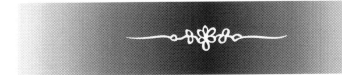

A TRIP TO POLAND

The dullness of sitting around the apartment waiting for the next project to begin was intermittently broken by reflections on my conversations with Adrian. Well, there were also bouts of empty gloom that are par for the course after finishing a big project. I spent five or six hours a day—oh, probably more—reading books on Auschwitz, the Holocaust, and World War Two. Such murderousness all around the world. I felt I had to understand the overall setting before I went to work on writing out Adrian's story. The subject was overwhelming, the challenge daunting. I knew it would take many years to even begin to write it out.

One morning, a former colleague called—Ramy by name. We'd worked on a chip together in Haifa about five years back and kept in touch, mostly on trade talk but occasionally personal updates. Eager to climb out of my dreary state of mind, i asked about his family and thought how my father always asked me when I was going to start one.

"Everyone is doing well," Ramy replied cheerfully. "My wife is with friends today and my daughter Shoshanna is on a trip. I'm in between assignments and I thought I'd see what you were up to there in the heart of the semiconductor world."

"Hah! I'm in between projects too but we're starting another one soon. I presume a family man like you wouldn't want to come here short-term."

"Afraid not. Travel's been forbidden—by the boss."

"Where's Shoshanna's trip taking her?"

"Poland—she's taking part in the March of the Living at Auschwitz. Your family has a connection there, as I recall."

"Yes, it does—and I've learned a lot about Auschwitz in recent weeks, as I hope to show you and the world someday. That's another story though. The March your daughter is taking part in is as I recall a commemoration of the victims of the Holocaust. It must be a powerful experience."

"Powerful and moving. I did it as a boy. I'm very proud of her."

"As you should be, Ramy, as you should be." I imagined young people taking part in the March but images of earlier marches swiftly took their place. I saw boys in their teens, emaciated and cold, walking across the tracks through the foreboding gate of Birkenau. Such images still came to me in sleep, though not as often and not as jarringly.

"Danny? Are you still there?"

"Yes, yes. Still here."

"Ah, that glumness after finishing a big design. I know it well—too well. Why don't you take a trip. Come back to Israel. You know, Danny, our people stopped being nomads long ago. You know, Egypt, Exodus, Moses!"

"Yes, a trip back home would be nice. I'll do it. First, I'll wander through a desert for a while."

Chopin Airport is near Warsaw. There might be another airport named after a musician and it would be wonderful if there were, but I don't know of one. I landed at Chopin and rented a car for the drive down to the village of Oswiecim. Green farmland and old villages along the way. A train would chug nearby—a modern train with freight cars and scores of automobiles headed for eager buyers.

Oswiecim itself had a surprising number of new buildings. By new, I mean built after 1945. Mostly unimaginative concrete buildings from a Soviet blueprint. There were older areas, including a medieval church. I was sure that Elsa worshipped there, maybe Bruno Müller too, and I wondered if Rosanna the Gypsy baby had been baptized there. I admit I was looking around for a dark-skinned woman who'd been born around 1944. No, I didn't see one. If I had, what would I have said to her?

I didn't spend a lot of time in the village. My time in Poland was limited. I didn't even stop in Lodz on the drive south. So, after pondering the congregation of the old church, I walked south toward the worn down railroad tracks that separated Auschwitz I from Auschwitz II. I turned and walked under the gate that led into Auschwitz I—*Arbeit Macht Frei*. I knew people who'd walked through here long ago. Adrian likened the inscription to a "cruel joke."

The blocks—the long barrack structures that each held several hundred emaciated inmates—were strangely clean and silent, separated by well-kept lawns. The floorboards creaked eerily as a few people and I walked through them, never once looking at or speaking to one another. I thought I'd want to be as alone as possible but I was glad I wasn't. I might have been overcome by the malevolent spirit that pervaded the place.

Some visitors had Israeli flags draped across their shoulders, some were Israeli soldiers in crisp uniforms. There was row after row after row of blocks. The arrangement spoke of planning and efficiency and bureaucracy. What took place here was not a pogrom, it was systematic mass killing.

Adrian had never come back here. I understood when he told me, though not as well as I did right then. Something was wrong here. Evil had been here. That was clear. That malevolent spirit was in every block, every field, every fence. I'd seen films and documentaries, I'd read books and articles, but their effects were paltry compared to looking around that place. The silent old planks tell more than the best made films.

I looked along the fences and thought of a young couple finding love beneath a light. There was a red rose placed in one part of a fence—tribute from a recent visitor, I guessed.

People were gathering outside and I joined them. The March of the Living was about to begin. There were policemen, soldiers of several countries, young people on school vacations, and many older people—some of whom I could see had tattoos on their left arms. People from many parts of the world had come that day to take part in the commemorative walk from Auschwitz I into Birkenau. There was about a thousand of us—an average day back then, I thought.

Word was given at the head of the group and the silent walk began. We left a large yard, perhaps one used for selections, and marched out the gate and across the tracks. There before us was the menacing railroad entrance to Birkenau with the ominous brick tower atop it. It ordered us in, dared us to think we understood, then harshly reprimanded us for our superficiality and presumptuousness. I defy anyone to look down the track that leads into the gate of Birkenau and not shudder, and not hear ghosts, and not feel relief and maybe a little guilt that they may turn around and leave anytime they want.

We marched on, through the gate and rows of blocks, and up to the chimneyed buildings where the gas chambers were. I stood there and felt ill. Many people did as well. Others wept and hugged each other, imagining how loved ones had come to this place and disappeared from the world except in the memories of the living. I didn't go in the chamber. Many descended the stairway that led to a disrobing room then to the chamber itself. I could not.

Afterwards, I was worn out. Tears were welling in my eyes and I admit a few streamed down my face before I could get out a handkerchief to wipe them away. I saw a few of the soldiers do the same. Fortunately, I'd brought bottled water. I drank gratefully and looked up to the cheerless sky.

I drove back to Warsaw and stayed the night before catching my flight out of Chopin in the morning. I wasn't heading back to California that day. I was going to Israel. I was going to see my father, the most precious person in my life.

ISRAEL

The flight to Ben Gurion wasn't long, three hours at most. I sat in my cramped coach seat and took out a pen and notebook, thinking I'd write some notes or even a book outline. I still didn't feel I had a grip on the subject though and I wanted to talk about it with my father, an alumnus of that dreadful Polish campus. He met me at the airport, just outside of Tel Aviv. We hugged joyfully and after picking up my baggage at the carousel, we headed to his car.

"So you visited Auschwitz, eh," he said as he opened the trunk. "I went back there about ten years ago. I remembered every building and block and I remembered the feeling of being there—a feeling of desperation, a feeling of doomsday, a feeling of hopelessness. I could still smell the smoke from the crematoriums."

"An older coworker told me an extraordinary story," I said, unsure just how to broach the subject.

"Well, you have plenty of time to tell me. We'll be hitting Tel Aviv at rush hour. It's not California, at least not yet, though we are closing the gap and we'll be in traffic for quite a while. So hop in and get started with your extraordinary story."

You notice changes in people you love after not seeing them. My father was in his seventies then, a little less hair, a few more wrinkles, a facial mole was a little wider. His eyes still displayed life and vitality and inquisitiveness, not the vacant acceptance I see in many people his age. Perhaps that was due to a career in military intelligence—discipline, attentiveness to detail, careful grooming. And of course there was the expectation of those attributes in his son. Well, I did my military service, then went to graduate school.

"So what's new?" he asked pleasantly enough, before adding, "When was the last time you had a haircut? California lifestyles are too soft, Danny. Israel requires firmness in its children." I didn't get a chance to answer, which was fine. "A girlfriend? Anything in the works?"

"No, nothing in that department, dad. I've been very busy with work. But that story I mentioned earlier . . . it's about Auschwitz."

I expected a reaction from him—a flinch or a groan or a sigh. Nothing. He'd been at Auschwitz as a boy in his teens and almost never mentioned it to the family or to anyone as far as I know. Whenever the subject was raised, he listened but never provided much information from personal experience. Here and there, he'd say something about a person or a field or a fence, but no more than a sentence or two, usually delivered quietly and without invitation for elaboration. Whatever thoughts came from my mention of Auschwitz had no effect on his face or voice.

"Fire away, Danny. Isn't that what they say in America? Yes, fire away."

Tel Aviv traffic is clearly catching up to Bay Area traffic, though both trail behind that of Los Angeles, thankfully. So I told him Adrian's story, at least its general contours. Lodz, Adrian, Misha, the arrival of the SS, the camps, and the end—and of course the Teffilin.

No facial change, not even at the mention of SS cruelty or the walk to the Krema. Had he put it all behind him or were the memories there but only as quiet, harmless ghosts? I doubted it. I'd seen how Adrian was still carrying the pain.

"An amazing story," was my father's reaction. "I can tell you this Adrian fellow's account rings true with me. He went through what many of us did. I'm glad he survived. Very glad. He's my age . . . I wonder if I ever knew him or saw him. I recall many Kapos. Jewish ones, Polish ones. Some cruel, some much less so. I can't recall names though and a face after so much time would have changed greatly. Usually for the worse," he added as he glanced at the rearview mirror.

We arrived at home in Netanya and despite my protestations, he carried my garment bag into the apartment. A bite to eat, a little more conversation, and I had to head in for the night.

"Danny, Danny, why did you get up so early? You're on vacation, aren't you? Sleep all you want," he gently chided as he tossed another teabag into the pot.

"Oh well, I slept quite a bit on the plane and besides, I'm still on Silicon Valley Time, which means we work all hours then get up early, no matter what."

"Yes, yes. You work so much that you forget other things—such as starting a family. I woke up earlier than usual myself. What shall we do today? And how long are you here for again?"

"Three week. I'll be here for three weeks."

"That's what I thought you said."

"I keep thinking about the story Adrian told me."

"Yes, Danny, it caused me to think a bit as well."

A momentary vacant look made me think he'd dreamed of those days, and that saddened me.

"There are so many things yet to be learned," I said, hoping to elicit a recollection from him.

"You can still call Adrian, can't you?"

A skillful deflection.

"Yes, of course I can call him. But there are things he can't answer, loose ends, things to look into. There's more to the story I should know."

"Yes, every answer leads to more questions. But I see your mind is looking in a certain direction," he noted leadingly as he poured the tea.

"Well . . . coming back to Israel, where there are so many connections to those events of long ago . . . ." My mind ran about, trying to formulate a question or a dozen questions. "I wonder what happened to Misha."

My father arched an eyebrow. "You said Adrian was with him until he reached the Krema."

"Yes, Misha insisted that he leave. Adrian did not see him go into the Krema or learn anything more of him. Is it possible . . . ."

My father exhaled audibly and shook his head. "Danny . . . we all held out hopes for loved ones after the war and the absence of solid evidence caused many people to cling on to their hopes. After many years, though, they had to give up those hopes. Nonetheless, strange things happen, even at places like Auschwitz. Maybe *especially* at places like Auschwitz."

He paused and looked at me, weighing something. "What is it?" I finally asked.

"Danny, long ago, at that place, everyone in my block was sent to the death chamber—Krema I, believe it was. We were mostly in good health, by the lax standards of the day, so it wasn't a matter of failing a selection. It was policy that if an inmate escaped, everyone in his block would be killed as a warning to others. But that wasn't the case with us. No one had escaped from our block. I don't know why but we were just marched up to the Krema."

I was astonished. My father had never told any of us in the family of this. I sat back, frozen, eager to hear more.

"We waited near a clump of trees. A strange place, almost pastoral despite its proximity to a death chamber. I've seen a picture of women and children waiting in the shade, peasant bandanas covering their shaved heads, a child looking into the camera."

I recalled the photo from a book I'd recently read.

"An SS officer strode up to us, two guards in tow. The officer's uniform was crisp and well tailored. He was a man proud of his position and work. He looked at the group and picked a few of us out for a special detail. I, for one reason or another, was the first one he picked. The others . . . well, they went to their deaths. But a few of us were spared, at the last moment. So, Danny, strange things happen."

"But why? What was the special detail?"

"Danny, the better question is who was the SS officer." He paused for a moment as I fixed on his question. "He was a doctor—a medical doctor. It was Josef Mengele."

I gasped. My head rolled backward. Josef Mengele, the Angel of Death, the man who presided over countless selections and decided who lived and who died. Mengele decided that a boy who later became my father would live.

"And the special detail," my father went on, anticipating a question forming in my mind, "was his medical experiments. I was one of his more fortunate objects of study, as I'm sure you must realize, as your existence indicates. So, yes, very strange things happen—from the unlikeliest people and at the last possible moment."

I was speechless, completely speechless. The irony, the paradox, and the miracle—the miracle I was indirectly a part of. The Angel of Death was part of my family history.

"Adrian asked about Misha when he returned to Lodz after liberation. He held out some hope but after a few weeks he concluded it was pointless."

"Danny, you're here for a few weeks, right? There's a museum in Jerusalem a Holocaust museum called Yad Vashem. Oh yes, you've been there. Did you know they have immense archives and databases? Do you know Misha's full name and place of birth?"

"Yes, Misha Coen, from Lodz." I replied as my mind was planning a drive to Jerusalem.

"Then your day is planned," he said, patting me on the back. "As for me, I'm off to parliament."

"Parliament?" I asked in puzzlement.

"That's what my old friends and I call our morning gatherings where we talk of vital issues of the day, just as they do in the Knesset and other parliaments—without reaching many conclusions, I must note." With that he donned a crumpled gold fisherman's cap and started off to give and listen to speeches in parliament.

"Oh Danny, one more thing. One of my fellow members of parliament—a man I never knew until a few years ago—has the same distinctive tattoo that I have," he said with considerable irony as he pointed to the numbers on his wrist. "Our numbers are only three digits apart. What are the chances?"

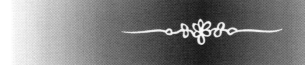

JERUSALEM

The drive along Highway 1 to the holy city of Jerusalem took me through pine forests and villages dating from ancient times. Some places along the way are graced by historical markers indicating that a battle took place there or a prophet delivered unheeded warnings there. As you leave the forests and begin the ascent to the old city, the scent of pine lingers for a few kilometers. As much as I thought I'd be thinking of nothing but what Adrian had related to me, I found myself reflecting on the history of the area.

Jerusalem sits on an elevated area where fortress cities were built in Antiquity. It has been fought over for thousands of years—Israelites, Egyptians, Babylonians, Persians, Muslims, Crusaders . . . . In the 1948 War of Independence, the road to Jerusalem was blocked by the Arab Legion, denying it supplies and reinforcements from the coast. A winding path was made by an American officer serving with the Israeli forces and the siege of Jerusalem was ended. The winding supply path is now a hiking trail. Just to the west is Latrun, a dry hilly area fought over from Joshua's time to the 1967 war. Charred tank hulks and turrets are still strewn about as monuments and reminders.

My historical reflection ended as I came upon traffic on the outskirts of Jerusalem. So much for Joshua and his chariots. At least the drive over to Yad Vashem gave me a glimpse of the Western Wall of the old Temple.

The museum had changed remarkably since my last visit twenty years earlier. Smaller monuments made in communities around the world had been placed all about. One of them honored Oscar and Emilie Schindler who had been central figures in the film *Schindler's List,* which had been released five years earlier. I wondered why I hadn't asked Adrian if he'd seen it. He probably hadn't.

The crowd was small and reverent. You don't go there for a pleasant afternoon. It's a place to remember and reflect. I wonder if that will change. If it does, I hope I'm long gone.

There were piles of prayer books, hats, and shoes—material that had been handed over right after getting off the train and taken to a sorting and storage area. Adrian had mentioned it was called "Kanada." I read that this was because the country to America's north was considered an attractive land of abundance and working in Kanada afforded the opportunity to find food. There were also artifacts from the inmates—spoons, bowls, and hats. I stood for at least twenty minutes in front of a display case with a tattered, striped, pajama-like shirt. It was smaller than anything I'd wear, more like something worn by a young man or a boy in his teens.

I looked around at the photographs and the several older visitors and wondered if they'd known my father, or Adrian, or Misha. A chance meeting, a relative, or a friend of a friend.

A row of computers offered access to an immense database and a few people were entering searches, looking for ancestors or just exploring the archives. I found an open terminal and typed in my father's name and hometown but didn't get any results. I felt disappointment. Then I remembered that my father had a European name then, so I entered it and waited a few seconds for the results to come up. His name appeared in soft green letters, standard PC interface in the 90s, and next to it: **SURVIVOR**.

My heart warmed with pride. It was wonderful that a family member's name was part of the story there at Yad Vashem. He was one of them, one of those who had been through the camps, who had been through Dachau and Auschwitz, and who had lived. I entered another name.

"Misha Coen—Lodz, Poland"

After a few seconds: **No Records Found**

Nothing. He was not listed as a survivor or as a victim. I was disappointed again, and a little confused. He should be in the database. I reentered the search terms and quickly got the same blunt response. I exhaled noisily and a few people stared at me.

"Danny? Danny Rittman?"

A familiar voice came to me in an unfamiliar setting. I turned and saw an old friend I hadn't seen in years. I was surprised he recognized me.

"Ofer! Wonderful to see you!" I said, holding back my elation in the somber setting. We grinned as pleasant memories from college flooded each of us and we shook hands vigorously.

"Good seeing you again, Danny. I've been working here at the museum for many years now. Last we saw each other, you were off to graduate school in America. Are you living here now?"

"Afraid not. I'm just back for a visit."

"I'm sure you will come back for good someday—and stop all this traveling the world."

"Yes, I'm told our people stopped being nomads long ago."

"So true. Anyway, I see you're looking through our database. Anyone in particular? Well, of course there usually is here. Perhaps I can help?"

"Indeed you can, old friend, indeed you can. I'm trying to find out more about a young man from Lodz who was at Auschwitz and who perished at Birkenau in early 1944. I can't find him though, which makes me wonder how up-to-date and inclusive the system is?"

"Danny, you may be sure that our database is the largest of its kind. It's updated daily from museums and research centers all over the world," he answered with obvious pride. "Any search done here goes through the other systems as well."

"Most impressive, nonetheless I couldn't find this one young man anywhere. Why would that be?"

"Oh . . . that's hard to say. There were so many people and so much disorder. Let's go back to my humble office and see what we can do."

I gave a quick account of Misha's story as we entered a side door near the entranceway and headed down a corridor lined with black-and-white prints of Eastern European *shtetls*, concentration camp scenes, and the early days of Israel. We came to a cramped, untidy office with a small Moroccan wall hanging and a desk with piles of papers and two bulky CRT displays. Ofer keyed in the data and went to work, checking the update logs at sister branches and reentering alternative spellings of Misha's last name, such as "Cohen" and "Kahan."

"I've done everything possible, Danny. No records on this fellow, nothing at all. Sorry. Our friend Misha Coen might be what we classify a Non-Recorded Person. There are quite a few, more than we would like. Many people from Europe changed their last names, you know. Haim Brotzlewsky became Haim Bar-Lev—and a general too."

"And if Misha did that without also entering his previous name, we have little chance of finding him," I reluctantly concluded, leaning back in disappointment and exhaling noisily again. I envisioned Misha walking into darkness.

"We can search for your father, if you like—but I suppose you—"

"Yes, I searched for him first thing and I'm pleased that he's there."

"Then I'm happy we've been of at least some help."

"Can we try to search for other people? I have a few more names. One—and I know this will sound strange—one was an SS guard at Auschwitz. Do you have databases for the guards?"

"Yes, we do—especially if they were accused of crimes and put on trial."

I gave him the name Bruno Müller from Berlin and told him the story of Misha's wedding. Ofer stared at me and asked if I was kidding. After I assured him I didn't play jokes at Holocaust museums, he marveled at the irony of a Jewish marriage ceremony in an SS guesthouse.

"Was there a *chuppah*?" he asked in obvious amusement, referring to the ceremonial canopy under which the marriage rite is performed.

"No *chuppah*, but they were able to use a private chamber afterwards."

"Good for the young couple, good for them. Now let's look for this Bruno fellow. It's a welcome change to hear stories of decency. There are a few. There was an SS guard who fell in love with a Jewish woman and rescued her sister as she was near one of the gas chambers. She's alive here in Israel somewhere. Helena Citrónová was her name, from Czechoslovakia. So many stories, Danny, so many fascinating stories— mostly dreadful ones, but occasionally there are truly wondrous ones too."

There was no luck with Bruno either. Ofer explained that most of the entries for SS personnel were linked to criminal acts and that SS guards, evil or helpful, had no interest in placing their names in the system. We searched for Adrian Nowak but I already knew he hadn't placed his name into the system.

Ofer, anticipating my next request, asked the name of Misha's bride. Adrian had no clear recollection of her last name but thought it was Fried or Friedman or Freeman from Berlin. We only knew she arrived at Auschwitz in early 1943 and was transferred to a sub-camp a few months later. So with such limited information we were hardly very hopeful, nor were we surprised when we again came up with nothing. "There were," Ofer said, "so many people swallowed up in the night."

I imagined people herded into cattle cars and I saw one or two pry open the wooden slats on the side, jump off, and flee into the woods. I imagined Bruno too. I saw him returning to Germany, changing his name, and becoming a school teacher, perhaps at an orphanage.

"Sorry, Danny, I guess we aren't having much luck here. We can check every week or so. More names come in, either from the survivors themselves or from their families. Any other names come to mind?"

"Let's see if we can find Misha's parents. Maybe through them we'll find him. His father's name was Moshe. His mother's name was Sara, last name Coen, of course."

Ofer entered the terms and his forehead wrinkled. He ran few advanced searches that accessed databases in the US and Europe that might not have updated into the museum's system yet that day, but with no results.

"Sorry, nothing comes up . . . ."

My mind was still imagining the lives of survivors and some of the names Adrian had mentioned. There was "Big Joe" but that was only a nickname. Then I remembered the Sephardic brothers, the boys who'd been adopted by a Polish Rabbi. Their names eluded me. I remembered the story of being hit by a car near the main gate. David . . . David and . . . Nisim . . . *Abadi!* "Yes, can we look for Nisim Abadi? He was one of a pair of brothers who came from Spain but who lived in Krakow."

Ofer entered the data and we waited, *im*patiently, for the results.

"Nisim Abadi—arrived Israel by ship in 1948—aged sixteen."

"That's our boy!" I exclaimed. "He was in the same block with Misha and Adrian. He was sent off to a sub-camp shortly before the block was killed off. Ofer, this is like finding an old friend after many decades! What else is there on Nisim? Do you have an address? Can I talk to him?"

"Danny! You're so excited. Not the computer science major I knew in school. Let's open up the other fields. Looks like he settled on Kibbutz Yagur. It's near Haifa, not far from where your father lives, as I recall. He married and had two children . . . . Oh wait, he passed away three years ago . . . he's buried in the Kibbutz cemetery."

"Ah . . . we were so close to a meeting. Nonetheless, I'm cheered to know that he came here, raised a family, and lived a long life. I hope he found peace and happiness."

"I hope so too. Where does Nisim fit into this? You'll have to tell me more of this Adrian fellow's story."

"Is there a cafeteria in the building? I'll tell you everything over lunch—on me."

"Well . . . we have some privileges here, Danny. On me, okay?"

Ofer had heard and chronicled hundreds of stories over the years but never tired of learning new ones. He asked if my father would like to have his story recorded and I said I doubted it very much but thanked him just the same. We said goodbye and agreed to have dinner one evening before I returned to the US. Ofer promised to keep looking for those people we'd looked for, though I wasn't very optimistic and I simply took it as a friendly gesture.

I drove back to Netanya and my father's apartment. He had returned from the parliament meeting which I presume had solved the world's problems or at least a dozen or two of them.

"Any luck in your search?" my father asked, looking up from his newspaper. "Our tea's almost ready."

"Well, I saw that your name is in the database."

"I knew that, Danny. I put it there. What about that boy from Lodz?"

"No luck with Misha or with a few of the other people, but I'm very pleased that we were able to find a record of one of the people in the story. He made it to Israel." I opted not to mention any more.

"Good for him . . . ," he said, his heart gladdened by a story he understood well. "Maybe we served together in the army. But we have more practical things to consider, such as dinner. Let's dine out this evening—on you, my rich American son."

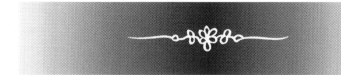

THE CEMETERY AT KIBBUTZ YAGUR

Discovering that Nisim had survived, made his way to Israel, and lived a good life gladdened my heart too. I soon felt the need to visit his grave, to somehow acknowledge understanding his ordeal and appreciating his victory. I had relatives who lived on Kibbutz Yagur, some deceased now but an aunt was still living there. I called her and asked if she knew the name Nisim Abadi but the name was unfamiliar to her.

Kibbutz Yagur was one of the early settler communes which were based on the social beliefs of many European immigrants. Initially agrarian, it industrialized with the rest of the country and was now home to a few defense industries. The kibbutz life appealed to me; I felt a sense of rootedness and openness there. Alas, semiconductor businesses are in cities and far overseas.

Only seventy-five kilometers north of my father's home in Netanya, Kibbutz Yagur called out to me and off I went.

Walking about the commune, only generally in the direction of my destination, I saw how it had changed over the years. There was a multiplex cinema and a spacious swimming pool that would be the envy of an Olympic venue. Despite the modernization, a pastoral feeling had been retained. A sign pointed to a pathway winding through a patch of woods leading to the resting places of those who'd lived on Kibbutz Yagur and wished to be laid to rest there.

I'd forgotten that the commune had been established back in 1922, twenty-six years before the country was born. Its age was clear from the grave markers showing some births in Poland, Hungary, and

Russia back in the late nineteenth century. There were also many markers of men and women who'd been killed in Israel's wars. The cemetery was larger than I'd imagined so look as I did for a marker reading "Abadi," I had no luck.

An elderly gent was watering a flower bed. I approached him.

"Excuse me, I'm looking for the grave of a man named Nisim Abadi. Any chance you could direct me to it?"

The man turned around gingerly and nodded, not so much as an affirmation, more as an assessment of me. "Are you a relative?"

"No, an acquaintance, you might say. A friend of a friend he knew long ago." I really didn't know how to describe my connection. But yes, there undoubtedly was a connection.

"Nisim Abadi. Yes, of course. Come with me."

We walked a few dozen meters in silence. There, just outside the cuff of his shirt, was a familiar tattoo. Then he said, "I'm Jacob Klein."

"A pleasure to meet you, sir. I am Danny Rittman. May I ask if you knew Nisim?"

"Oh yes. I arrived with him from Europe many years ago," Jacob explained as we continued ahead. "I was with Nisim back in Poland— in Auschwitz. A sub-camp just to the east of the main camp."

I was astonished at the coincidence.

"At a pharmaceutical plant?"

"Yes, we worked at a pharmaceutical plant until liberation. Your friend of his friend told you of that?"

"Yes, he did. The reason I'm here today . . . the connection I have to Mr. Abadi, is that a Polish man told me of knowing him in Auschwitz.

Not a sub-camp. At Auschwitz I. He last saw him at Auschwitz II, after liberation. The man who told me this story was a Polish conscript by the name of Adrian Nowak. By chance, did you know him, sir?"

Jacob stopped and thought back. Distant memories were coming forth and he handled them quite well. "I don't know the man, not by name. Nisim spoke of a few people from Auschwitz I. They all died though. One night . . . they all died. A Polish conscript . . . yes, he mentioned one—one who tried to help as best he could. A good man, a good man. The name, I'm afraid, is lost to me."

"A good man, indeed. Did Nisim ever mention a boy about the same age from Lodz? His name was Misha Coen. Perhaps five years older than Nisim. Misha and Adrian were best of friends."

"Ah . . . that name is one that I have heard, though not in a long time. Nisim spoke fondly of him in our block at Monowitz. That's the—"

"Yes, the sub-camp to the east that you were at."

"You know something of that place—and not just from a movie or television program."

"Yes, I've read a few books and this Adrian Nowak fellow spent many weeks telling me of his experiences at Treblinka and Auschwitz."

"Grim names, grim places. Well, here we are, young man. The final resting place of Nisim Abadi. I truly hope he's resting," Jacob added with a sigh.

Nisim was buried at the end of a row, only a few feet from a gentle slope which hinted at the hillocks farther away. The flowers and stones suggested that loved ones had been there in the last few days.

"Nisim . . . Nisim Abadi," I found myself whispering. "The unfortunate boy from Spain who found himself pulled into the Holocaust."

"Along with his brother," Jacob noted.

"Yes, along with his brother David."

Jacob smiled softly. "It would seem you've been well apprised of those days. Do you know of his brush with death on a work detail?"

I had to gather my thoughts as I hadn't yet written things down.

"Yes, Jacob, I believe I do. It was in the snow . . . a guard started to haul him off to his death when a dog intervened. A guard shot the dog—Max was his name—and an uprising broke out."

"The uprising that caused everyone in that block to be sent to their deaths."

"Nisim was sent to another camp right before that."

"Miracles," Jacob whispered, "miracles."

We looked at each other as though we were at a reunion and in some sense, we were. Though I was not there, I had heard incandescent stories that made those events that took place well before my birth almost parts of my life. Almost . . . almost.

Jacob leaned down and gently placed a stone on Nisim's grave. I might have seen his lips move silently.

"You know, Danny, Nisim married and raised a family and was well respected and loved here in Kibbutz Yagur, but he was never fully out of the past. I could see it . . . and he could see it in me. He spoke often of David's death, very often. He fulfilled his promise to him of having his Bar Mitzvah and I think he was proud that he'd kept faith. He remained alone, however. He was here waiting. Waiting for his time to come, waiting to leave and go on. He was never fully here. It was simply a place he was staying at . . . while he waited."

Jacob's words conjured up recollections of survivors I'd seen—teachers in school, people at Yad Vashem, old people now and then I see in shops and restaurants. They nod and say hello but their eyes are vacant. I've wondered if they look into us to determine if we'd have been a reliable friend or a cruel Kapo. Seeing so much cruelty and horror must impress into the mind the suspicion that dark potentials dwell in many if not most of us and it's just a matter of time and circumstance whether it is brought out of us.

We stood before Nisim's grave for several more minutes, each in his thoughts. I envisioned Adrian and Nisim standing in front of Krema I and hugging before Nisim went off to the group he was going away with. Perhaps the man beside me was one of them but I sensed he was tired and eager to head home. The moment to ask had flown.

"Thank you very much for sharing your memories, Jacob," I said as I extended my hand in sincere gratitude. I hope he felt that.

"You're welcome, Danny. Well, it's not that I have much to do anyway. I'm just here waiting . . . . Oh, Danny, another thing. You hold important knowledge and understanding. More than the movies and television give. You have a gift, of sorts, and you must pass it on."

Jacob walked back toward where I'd first encountered him, his gate slow but determined. Seeing Nisim's grave, oddly enough, made Adrian's story more alive. And Jacob's parting words made me see my work ahead. I placed a stone on Nisim's grave and walked back through the wooded pathway.

ANOTHER DINNER, ANOTHER IDEA

"Is it my turn to pay?" my father asked.

"Yes, dad. Your rich American son paid last night."

Off we went, by foot, into the streets of Netanya—in English, "the gift of God." And it truly is that, especially for the residents and the many people who travel there for its uncrowded beaches, salty breezes, and exquisite dining. My father and I walked along the seafront until we came to a traditional Israeli establishment that offered a little Hungarian fare as well—a delightful result of European immigration. We ordered appetizers and drinks then sat on the patio and looked out at the waves lapping against the shore. Two children were playing a game of retreating from each wave then heroically chasing it back into the sea. The sun was an orange yolk hovering just above the horizon, in no hurry to close out the day.

"You know, dad, I feel closer to the people and events in Adrian's story here. The past, as an author once said, isn't dead and it isn't even past. It's with us every day. And here, it's with us every moment.

"Faulkner. It was William Faulkner who said that."

"There are so many people still alive who have seen so much and who can tell us of those times."

I was trying to coax recollections from him.

"Or maybe such people can just pay for your dinner this lovely evening—this lovely evening that should—and shall—remain lovely."

Another skillful deflection. I saw his point though. Speaking of those events was unpleasant and, as I suspected with Adrian, had little if any therapeutic effect. Maybe recollections would simply make my father suddenly feel old, perhaps even world weary. No point pressing the matter.

"Have you and your friend had any fortune in finding information about that other fellow—Misha Coen."

"Nada." I instantly realized my father wouldn't understand that. "That's American slang for 'nothing'."

"*Bupkis* then. It's Yiddish for 'beans'."

"Yes, bupkis. We got bupkis. I've been trying to think if Misha changed his name or was not recorded correctly. In that case, we may be getting nowhere. What if someone inadvertently entered his name incorrectly, say, 'Kagan'."

"Well, computer logic is your profession, not mine. I suspect such an error has happened a few times in entering so many millions of names and dates and places. It sounds like entering all the possibilities would be a lot of work—and it might not lead anywhere in the end."

"Yes, you're right. In the end we might not find him . . . or we might just confirm what Adrian thought all along about the poor boy's fate. It's odd to refer to someone as a boy who was born well before I was."

"Many of them had no opportunity to grow into young men, adults, fathers, grandfathers, so in our minds they forever remain boys . . . and girls, of course. I can see their faces now. Those boys and girls, forever so."

We both looked out at the calm sea. A yacht lazed at anchor not far from shore and a tanker slowly churned north, probably to Haifa. Seagulls screeched their appeals to a few people snacking on the beach who gave in to them. The lights of fishing vessels flickered in the distance and I imagined the crews hauling in their nets and finding . . . bupkis. I smiled, I think imperceptibly, as I realized my search was affecting my appreciation of the evening.

"You know of these souvenirs, I'm sure," my father said as he held up his left arm showing the now-blurred blue tattoo of his Auschwitz serial number. I instantly imagined a frightened fifteen-year-old Hungarian boy being herded through a crowded building in Auschwitz I, then I had the same thought of a somewhat younger boy from Lodz.

"There were a few people from Lodz in my block. Oh, please don't ask me their names. That was too long ago. We all had our numbers tattooed onto our arms the same day so there is a chance that Misha arrived around the same time. Who knows, we might have stood in line together and looked at our arms in disgust a little while later.

I looked again at his reminder and listened intently as he continued.

"Danny, are the prisoner's numbers entered into Yad Vashem's database?"

After thinking a moment, I recalled seeing a field for that on Ofer's screen. "Yes, I'm pretty sure that information is stored. Why?"

"Why? Because it might be a new way to search for this Misha fellow. Here's what I suggest. Ask your friend to run a cross-reference of all the people who arrived from Lodz according to the numbers on their arms. You can use my number as a starting point and move up and down. See what comes of it."

"Great idea!"

Is it rude to make a call while chatting with your father? Yes. Usually. My father didn't seem to mind. He looked on with interest as I hit Ofer's cellphone on speed dial.

"Ofer? Can you get into the museum database at home? I don't mean *hack* into . . . well, can you get in somehow? Great! Here's a new search criterion, courtesy of my father."

"Courtesy of your *low-tech* father!" my father hastened to add. "All that graduate school at Yale I paid for and I have to teach you things about computer systems," he grumbled lowly.

I looked over to him and grinned. "He's in the system now and . . . ." My father obligingly raised his arm.

"Ofer, please search out B-1-4-5-3-4. Yes, B-1-4-5-3-4."

He read it back to me correctly and hit enter. I switched my cell phone to speaker mode and we waited as Ofer ran down the numerical entries. My father and I waited anxiously and silently. I imagined Ofer was looking through various databases. Would Misha be alive? In Poland? America? Israel?

"We got *something*," Ofer said, both excited and puzzled. "There's a man that fits the time and city of origin. His first name, however, is 'Michael' (מיכאל). 'Michael Kahan.' It's all that I have. Do you think it's worth—"

"Yes, of course it's worth looking into. Do you have an address or phone number?"

"That, my friend, is another search entirely and I need to get an access code. I suspect you want me to get right on it?"

"That's wonderful, Ofer. I'll be waiting to hear from you. I owe you a lunch!"

"You already do. I'll look for your friend right now. Ciao."

"I'm greatly pleased that my souvenir from the SS has been of help," my father said quirkily. "We'll see what comes of this. Meanwhile, young man, we shall savor the wondrously spiced Hungarian goulash this establishment offers. I know the proprietor and I can proudly say that he uses *Hungarian* paprika, not the tasteless stuff from Spain that grocery stores here sell."

"That sounds great. But, dad, just one thing. Can you ask your proprietor friend to use a little less paprika than you use at home? Yours, while a culinary marvel, forces me to reach for an antacid or two."

"California has made you soft, Danny. But I shall ask my friend to take your delicate constitution into consideration. Ah, here he is now. Michlosh my fellow Hungarian emigre, two goulashes—and a pitcher of water for my soft Americanized son."

Ofer called as my father and I were finishing our meal along with a second pitcher of water.

"Danny, old friend, I think I have this Misha or Michael fellow for you. This Michael Kahan is the age we're looking for and was born in the Polish town of Lodz. I have a hunch it's him. Well, there's a good chance anyway."

"Great! Where is he?"

"He's in Israel. I'm texting his address to you . . . right . . . now."

A chirp sounded and an address and phone number lit up on my phone's screen. I held it up to my father to see and he raised his arm in a toast.

"Miracles, my son, do happen," he said with greater hopefulness than I'd seen in him for many years. "Just not as often as we would like."

MISHMAR HASHARON

How to approach this Michael Kahan fellow? He might be the right person, he might not be. A phone call might be rejected as part of a con game of some sort or as an intrusion. Coming to his home presented the same privacy concern though. I discussed the matter with my father who at length said, "Well, I should go with you."

"That might be a good idea. A man his own age will be less off-putting and the potential of a common experience is there to explore his past."

"Yes, that was my point," he replied tartly. "So all that schooling at Yale has paid off."

"Okay, sorry I didn't comprehend your meaning. Do you know this place Mishmar HaSharon?"

"Sure. It's just outside of Netanya. No more than ten kilometers. Not too much traffic," he added in relief.

"Can we leave right after breakfast?"

"Fine with me. I'll drive. Not too much traffic," he repeated a little grumpily.

We arrived in Mishmar HaSharon shortly before noon and soon enough came to a smallish house, what Americans would call a cottage, surrounded by hedges and flower beds that appeared to be taken care of only occasionally.

"I'd love to settle into a place like this someday," I said softly.

"I need a city and people around me," he replied, "even if it means traffic."

The door was made from cedar and stained a light honey color. Next to it was a sign that read "Kahan." As I knocked, I prepared myself for a courteous or not-so courteous encounter followed by a glum drive back to Netanya.

"Let me handle this," my father said.

"No, no," I objected. "I know the story. Let me do the talking."

An elderly gentleman in his early seventies opened the door and regarded us rather uneasily. Gray hair, thin on top, small of height and frame, with thick bifocals drooping slightly on his nose.

"Good morning, sir. My name is Danny Rittman and this is my father Zvi Rittman. I've been doing some research at Yad Vashem about someone named Misha Coen."

The man was surprised. Was it because he never heard the name before? Because Misha Coen was a relative who passed away? He looked over to my father for a moment then nodded. I was beset by uncertainty and felt embarrassment looming.

The man smiled faintly, revealing a gentle soul—one willing to help a stranger or two.

"Misha . . . Misha Coen. Yes, I knew a boy by that name long ago." His smile widened as he added, "No one has called me by that name in many years. I became Michael Kahan when I finished medical school in 1961. Won't you come in?"

With that, he held open the door and I saw on his left arm the distinctive marks from the 1940s, blurred like my father's. Ah, I thought, that's why he nodded when he looked at my father.

Assisted by a weathered oak cane, Michael led us into a study with several hundred books untidily arranged on dusty bookshelves. Tribal rugs graced the teak floor and dozens of mementoes and bric-a-brac from Israel, Greece, and Turkey accented the desk and side table. My father and I sat on a divan and Michael slowly eased himself down on a wing chair.

"So . . . what brings you from Yad Vashem to my home? Questions . . . I presume you have questions. I've been asked many questions over the years and I've asked myself many questions. Perhaps I have answers for you. Let us see."

Michael's eyes were enlarged by the thick lenses, almost comically. Try as I did, I could not find the words to begin my story and pose my questions. I looked for signs of the world-weariness and emotional detachment I'd noted in many survivors but they weren't there, at least not then. Would the purpose of our visit cause him pain, whether or not he was the boy from Lodz that Adrian knew? I didn't want that at all, of course. For an instant I thought the visit was a mistake and that I should let bleak dormant memories remain that way.

"Allow me to speak for my suddenly speechless son—an affliction he has only rarely exhibited since birth, I assure you." My father accented his explanation with theatrical hand gestures that ably established a friendly atmosphere. "My son met an elderly Polish gentleman, a man about our age, while working in California. This elderly man had an interesting story. One might call it without any exaggeration an amazing story. One of the more amazing stories to come out of that unpleasant period Europe went through."

Michael leaned forward.

"Yes," I interjected as my affliction relented for the moment. "This man was from a town in Poland—not far from Warsaw."

Michael's nodded and his face showed interest. "I once lived near Warsaw, just to the southwest, if memory serves—and too often now it doesn't serve very well! What is this Polish town your friend came from?"

"The town of Lodz," I replied. "My friend lived there as a young boy and saw the SS take away many Jews, including his best friend."

Memories were running through Michael's mind. Anyone could see that. He was trying to make connections but not hasty ones, reckless ones—ones that would bring back old hopes only to see them dashed.

"This man," Michael said slowly, "this man who long ago was a boy in Lodz . . . what was his name?"

"His name was Adrian Nowak."

"Adrian . . . Adrian Nowak . . . ." Michael's glasses fell from his nose and he smiled gently as memories, I think mostly pleasant ones, flooded his soul. "Adrian Nowak is alive? . . . Adrian is alive and in America. Wonderful news, wonderful . . . ."

With that, Michael sat back in his chair and his head slumped to one side. My father and I raced to him and called his name. I held his wrist and found a healthy pulse. Happily, we were able to rouse him after only a few moments. I brought a glass of water from the kitchen.

"You've seen Adrian? You've talked to him?" he asked all but euphorically.

"Yes, only last week. In California. He told me of you and him, in Lodz . . . and in Auschwitz. We spoke for many hours, over many weeks."

"In California . . . that's good, that's good. Adrian was a good boy."

"Adrian and I design semiconductors, like the ones in your laptop over there," I said pointing to a PowerBook amid some piles of paper on a desk.

"Adrian was smart, always smart," Michael whispered wiping his eyes with a handkerchief. "Computers . . . he makes computers!"

"Adrian thought you perished in a gas chamber one night in 1944. I searched out your name at the museum and after considerable effort, we thankfully found you." I said, hoping for answers.

"I *should* have perished that night—along with the others. Miraculous are the ways of the Lord. Truly miraculous. And the agents of his miracles can be very strange ones."

I thought of my father's encounter with the Angel of Death. I suspect my father did as well.

"How," I found myself saying, to my father's annoyance as he thought I was intruding. I was intruding. There was no doubt I was intruding. Nonetheless, I felt I had the right to know a crucial part of a story I'd been obsessed with—a story whose final chapter I thought I knew until this morning.

Michael recognized my father's concern and motioned with his hand that my question was not entirely out of bounds.

"I was near the Krema, praying aloud, as were many others. An unexpected blow to my head sent me to the ground. I looked up in the dark night and saw the silhouette of a towering SS corporal. He hit me across the face and kicked me in the stomach, shouting hatefully, 'I'll take this one! By God, I'll take care of this one myself! Out of my way! Kommandant Liebehenschel's orders! Out of my way or by God you will answer to him in the morning!' The other guards were paralyzed by the man's wrath and invocation of the dreaded camp commander's name. He dragged me away to a clump of trees, slapping and kicking me all the way. Only when he hurled me down behind a tree did I recognize him. It was—"

"Bruno . . . Bruno Müller," I whispered.

"Yes, it was. How . . . . Oh yes, Adrian has told you of him then. He'd heard at the SS mess hall of the block's liquidation and raced to find me. His slaps and kicks and angry words successfully hid his intentions from his less merciful colleagues that night. He took me out of the main entrance of Birkenau and into the forest. He gave me bread and his canteen and told me to walk north for several hours until I came across partisans he knew to operate there. He then fired his pistol in the air to feign shooting me in case we'd been seen leaving the camp. I thanked him as much as circumstances allowed, then off I scurried. The next day, a partisan group found me sleeping in the brush.

"I went back to Auschwitz a few weeks after liberation and was told that the Russians had killed all the guards and Kapos. Some were still hanging from trees or sprawled on the snowy ground but none resembled Adrian or Bruno. Nonetheless, I had to assume that they had met their fate at the end of a rope or from a bullet."

"I searched for Bruno in the archive also but without success. Perhaps he too is alive somewhere," I added hopefully.

"I hope so. I hope so." Michael's voice was stronger than before. "Gentlemen," he said clapping his hands and standing on his own despite our outreached arms, "it is not every day that I receive such astounding news. We must celebrate with a toast. I have a bottle of Calvados—a delightful but highly potent apple brandy from a French village a neighbor liberated in 1944 while with the American army."

Michael went to a cabinet with the help of his cane and took out a bottle of Calvados and three crystal snifters.

"L'chaim!" he exclaimed. My father and I repeated the toast to the gift of life.

Calvados is quite strong and though my father and Michael downed theirs unflinchingly, I had to take a seat.

"I've prayed for Adrian," Michael announced as he poured another round. "Every morning, I prayed for this."

"Michael," I said, "Would you like me to arrange a reunion with Adrian?"

Well, I suppose I've asked stupider questions, just not recently. The three of us smiled warmly and tossed back another round. This one went down a little easier.

TOGETHER AGAIN

A hurried trans-Atlantic call and a conversation with a skeptical retiree ensued. A *very* skeptical retiree. But at length I convinced him that this Michael Kahan of Mishmar HaSharon was indeed Misha Coen of Lodz—and Auschwitz.

"A doctor? Misha's a doctor?" Adrian kept exclaiming. "He was always a smart boy. A doctor . . . that's wonderful. Absolutely wonderful."

"Would you like me to arrange a reunion with Misha?"

Yes. Another stupid question.

I thanked Ofer for his invaluable assistance, especially for finding museum funds to fly Adrian over and put him up for a few days at the David Citadel Hotel. That was most welcome as Adrian and Michael were retired and I was between positions as they say. No intrusive cameras and reporters, just a little help defraying the expenses. I told Ofer I'd ask the old friends for a photo of their reunion, if not for a spot in the museum then for his office or home as a personal memento. I know I wanted a copy of the photo, though an older memento was not far from mind.

I drove down to Ben Gurion and picked up Adrian at the baggage carousel, while my father took Michael to the Jerusalem hotel where a modestly appointed suite overlooking the ancient city and the Western Wall had been provided courtesy of Yad Vashem. Adrian was subdued during the trip south, probably from the long flight. I asked if he wanted to delay things until tomorrow but he wouldn't hear of it. "Of course not, of course not."

We drove silently past the charred tank hulks I'd seen a few days earlier on my drive to Jerusalem.

"History is always with us," he murmured. "Always."

Arriving at the room rather early, Adrian and I looked out from the balcony upon the ancient city, the Tower of David standing out along the skyline.

"It was a fortress city, you know," Adrian said. "The Temple itself was a fortified position with its own underground water supply. A refuge in time of war."

"We'll all tour the city tomorrow, if you like, Adrian. The four of us." I replied, noting that he'd evidently done a little historical preparation for the visit. "History indeed is always with us."

"Yes, with Misha," he answered. "Misha will be with us."

There was a knock on the door. Adrian and I looked at each other, like children awaiting a beloved relative's return home after a long absence. The door opened and Misha walked in, cane in hand. My father remained behind him in the doorway. A social instinct told me to make introductions but I caught myself before I engaged in such unnecessary etiquette. The two boys from Lodz walked toward each other as quickly as their aging legs would allow. They stood not more than a meter apart and looked at each other, amazement and joy slowly building, until each put his hands on the other's shoulders and laughed and cried and moved their legs about as though in dance.

It was as moving a moment as I can ever hope to see. I too laughed and cried, though less profusely than the two old friends. My father entered the room and nodded his head, perhaps with a trace of a smile.

"I knew we would see one another again someday, Adrian. However, I assumed it would be in the next world, not this one—let alone in Jerusalem, the capital of a Jewish state."

"It is a miracle, my friend," Adrian said in quavering voice. "More than we could have hoped for."

"Yes, and we hoped for so many things, Adrian, so many things. Many did not come to pass, though we are blessed that at least a few did."

"This one foremost among them, Misha my friend."

The two men stood there for a while without knowing what to do with their abundant joy. Then a self-reproving look came across Adrian's face, as though he'd almost made an error of some kind.

"Misha . . . Misha, I've brought something for you. Something that is yours, something I've been keeping for you."

Misha was puzzled. I was not.

Adrian reached into his valise and carefully removed a worn leather pouch with the faded Hebrew letter "Shin." Misha's recognition came only slowly. He was unprepared to see the gift his father had presented him in Lodz before the world changed so swiftly and terribly.

"Adrian . . . my Tefillin . . . all these years, all these many years! How wondrous!"

"It was your Tefillin that gave us hope through that time. The two of us . . . and Big Joe, Nisim and David, Bruno, and Naomi."

"Yes, and Naomi . . . ."

Misha gazed upon his prized, sacred object then to our puzzlement, he shook his head.

"No . . . no. I cannot accept this. Adrian, I want you to keep the Tefillin. I love you and cherish you, and from time to time we can pray with it together. I gave my Tefillin to you one night long ago and so it shall remain yours. Please, I want my Tefillin to stay with you."

Adrian took the pouch in his hand, albeit reluctantly. It was not the time for debate and Misha's sincerity and determination were clear. I wondered if Misha's graciousness implied foreknowledge of impending decline.

"Thank you, Misha. I have treasured the Tefillin since that night and I will continue to do so. I shall consider it not mine, but ours. Misha old friend, have you prayed yet this day?"

"I have prayed *for* this day though not *on* this day! Come, let us pray together once again. Let us pray for our friends from those days. Let us pray for all of them and let us give thanks for this day as well."

My father and I looked on wordlessly. I think each of us imagined, more vividly than we thought possible, the two old men before us as young boys, praying in a dark concentration camp block as scores of men walked by, some beyond hope, others given hope.

My father had a connection to these men and to their past. I could see that on his face, more soulful than I can recall ever seeing before. I had a far more meager connection. I was the repository of an astounding story, the ending of which neither the narrator nor the scribe knew until that morning in Jerusalem.

The two friends stood next to a side table near the window overlooking Jerusalem. Misha reverently wrapped the leather straps around his arm then placed the headpiece to his forehead. They bowed their heads and began to recite an ancient prayer.